"You've got t
thanking me,

Kane told Jennifer. "I haven't done anything yet."

"No, but you will, Kane." She had never been more certain of anything in her life. Somehow, she *knew* he'd be the hero she was holding out for. The man to return her child to her. "You will."

There she went again, placing a burden squarely on his shoulders, a burden so heavy, he could hardly stand beneath it. Didn't she understand that? Or did she? Was that innocent, vulnerable look in her eyes there by devious design? He'd spent so much time with people who deceived, who lived by their wits and would lie their way out of anything, that he had trouble believing that she was as straight and sweet as she seemed.

No, that wasn't fair, he thought. She was exactly what she seemed. Trouble.

Dear Reader:

We at Silhouette are very excited to bring you this reading Sensation. Look out for the four books which appear in our Silhouette Sensation series every month. These stories will have the high quality you have come to expect from Silhouette, and their varied and provocative plots will encourage you to explore the wonder of falling in love – again and again!

Emotions run high in these drama-filled novels. Greater sensual detail and an extra edge of realism intensify the hero and heroine's relationship so that you cannot help but be caught up in their every change of mood.

We hope you enjoy this Sensation – and will go on to enjoy many more.

We would love to hear your comments and encourage you to write to us:

Jane Nicholls
Silhouette Books
PO Box 236
Thornton Road
Croydon
Surrey
CR9 3RU

Holding Out
For a Hero

MARIE FERRARELLA

SILHOUETTE

Sensation

First published in Great Britain in 1994
by Silhouette Books, Eton House, 18-24 Paradise Road,
Richmond, Surrey TW9 1SR

© Marie Rydzynski-Ferrarella 1993

Silhouette, Silhouette Sensation and Colophon are
Trade Marks of Harlequin Enterprises B.V.

ISBN 0 373 59326 0

18-9410

Made and printed in Great Britain

Other novels by Marie Ferrarella

Silhouette Special Edition

It Happened One Night
A Girl's Best Friend
Blessing in Disguise
Someone To Talk To
World's Greatest Dad

Books by Marie Ferrarella writing as Marie Nicole

Silhouette Desire

Tried and True
Buyer Beware
Through Laughter and Tears
Grand Theft: Heart
A Woman of Integrity
Country Blue
Last Year's Hunk
Foxy Lady
Chocolate Dreams
No Laughing Matter

To Leslie Wainger
and
impossible dreams coming true

Chapter 1

"You are the world's most beautiful baby."

Jennifer Sinclair murmured the words to her three-day-old daughter as she cradled the infant against her. Jennifer was always amazed that something so precious felt so light in her arms.

The baby stirred slightly. Her eyes were opened wide as if she actually understood her mother's words.

Jennifer smiled and cuddled Katie to her, savoring the contentment that flooded through her like life-giving water in the desert. She had been warned by a well-meaning friend that bonding would take time and not to be disappointed if it wasn't instantaneous. Her friend, she thought, might as well have saved her breath. Bonding had been immediate. As soon as the nurse had placed her newborn daughter in her arms, Jennifer had felt that strong, maternal pull spring up within her. It had wound all through her like the strong scent of honeysuckle in the spring, wafting through the still air, filling every corner of her heart, mind and soul. It had been there despite the fact that she had been dry and couldn't nurse her baby. Just holding Katie was enough.

Now, three days later, Jennifer felt as if she had always loved this tiny human being in her arms.

Jennifer looked down at the lips that seemed to form a perfect rosebud. "I know mothers tend to be prejudiced about their own babies, but trust me on this, I know you're the best baby in the world. Even Mommy's doctor said so." As she spoke, Jennifer gently stroked Katie's hand. Besides her head, it was the only part of the infant that was exposed. She was tightly bound in a cotton blanket that the nurse assured Jennifer provided the baby with a sense of well-being and security. "And she's in a position to know. Dr. Reynolds has delivered hundreds of babies."

Very carefully, Jennifer placed Katie into her bassinet. Though Julia would be here soon to take them home, Jennifer allowed herself a few more moments just to look at Katie. "Dr. Reynolds said that in all her twenty years of delivering babies, she's never seen one as pretty as you." Jennifer nudged her finger into Katie's tight fist. The delicate fingers opened, then shut again, like a rare cactus flower that bloomed only for a few minutes at night. "What do you think of that?"

Katie yawned, her small mouth opening wide to show tiny pink, toothless gums as her eyes fluttered shut. Jennifer laughed. "Hey, this is all supposed to be new to you. You're not supposed to be the bored little princess until you've heard it a couple dozen times."

With a reluctant sigh, Jennifer tucked the small cloth blanket over Katie. It was time to get ready.

"I can't seem to get enough of holding you, honey. But if I don't get dressed, we're not getting out of here and Mommy's insurance company won't like that."

Leaning over the bassinet, Jennifer lightly kissed the baby's forehead. Katie was her own miracle, Jennifer thought. Her very own special miracle. Her throat tightened as she stroked the satiny cheek where a tiny dimple flashed when Katie smiled. There was so much she wanted to give Katie, so much she wanted to do for her. But the little girl's life would be missing one very important ingredient.

"I'm so sorry you won't have a daddy like the other little children. But you do have an Aunt Julie and an Uncle Nik," she whispered, emotions stealing the volume from her voice. "And we'll all love you so much that you won't ever feel deprived, I promise."

Katie's only answer was to try and kick out of the snugly wrapped blanket.

It was going to be all right, Jennifer promised herself. And best of all, they weren't going to have to make a go of it alone. She had her family there for her.

Shaking off the encroaching somber mood, Jennifer opened the small locker in her room that served as a closet and took out her dress. Three days ago, it had clung tightly to her swollen abdomen. Now it looked like a shapeless pink army tent. She'd been lucky in her pregnancy, she mused, laying the dress out on the bed. She'd only gained the traditional twenty-five pounds and most of that in the last few months. Katie had been a large, healthy baby, weighing in at just one ounce shy of ten pounds. The rest of Jennifer's weight seemed to leave her within the next forty-eight hours. When the nurse weighed her this morning, she was almost down to normal. The delivery had been practically painless and though she still ached a little, Jennifer felt wonderful. She'd kept in shape during the pregnancy and she'd always healed fast.

Lucky, she thought again, picking up her hair brush. She pulled it carefully through her long, straight, black hair. She was only lucky if she didn't think about Brad. Even her delivery had been relatively simple, up until the last minute. She had woken up that morning not feeling quite right. She'd attributed the sensation to the extra weight she was carrying and the fact that she was almost due.

But by the time she had begun peeling her customary orange for breakfast, she knew it was showtime. Her water had broken during her drive to the hospital. She only had time to call her brother and sister from the information desk in the hospital lobby. She had no sooner hung up than an orderly was whisking her to the maternity floor in a wheelchair.

Katie had stubbornly clung to life in the womb but five hours after Jennifer had entered Harris Memorial Hospital, she was holding her daughter in her arms. The baby had immediately begun rooting about like a hungry newborn blue jay, demanding to be fed by its mother.

She had discovered then that she hadn't produced any milk. A nurse had quickly come to both their rescues with a bottle of formula, telling Jennifer that these things happened sometimes. Mother's milk wasn't the most important ingredient for a baby, she had assured Jennifer. Mother's love was.

Everything surrounding Katie had turned out well. It helped to make up, Jennifer thought as she placed her things into her suitcase, for the fact that she had been completely abandoned by Katie's father.

At the thought of Brad, a bitter pang shot through her like a poison-tipped arrow. Jennifer pushed the feeling aside. She had her daughter and that was all she wanted. She hadn't been looking for money or even a wedding band when she had told Brad that she was pregnant with their child. Happiness had been the only thing that she had been hoping for—happiness because she was about to bear a child conceived in love.

A child conceived in deception was what it had turned out to be. Jennifer stiffened, stopping the shiver that threatened to slither up her spine as she remembered the expression on Brad's face when she told him. Looking shocked and angry, acting as if she had somehow betrayed him, Brad had informed Jennifer that he was married. In the same breath, he had ordered her to have an abortion.

Hurt and dazed, Jennifer had firmly refused. It was the last time she had seen or heard from Brad. He had, in essence, disappeared from the face of the earth. Certainly out of her life.

"Good riddance," were the first words out of Julia's mouth when Jennifer had told her the story. Embracing her, Julia had never displayed even a moment's disappointment or hesitation regarding the matter. "We'll stick it out together, Jen. And it'll be okay."

Julia had held her and let her cry herself out. And then, when the tears on her face were drying, her sister added, "We're a family and we love you. As I see it, we only have one problem to face."

Jennifer had rubbed away the last traces of her tears with the heel of her hand. "What?"

The smile on Julia's face mingled with a hint of malicious anticipation. "How do we keep Nik from going out and killing Brad?"

It had been all right after that.

And now, Jennifer thought as she slipped on her dress, the pink material draping around her loosely, she had the perfect daughter. At least Brad had been good for something.

She entered the closet-size bathroom and splashed water on her face, then patted it dry with a white hand towel. She had met Bradley Kingsley over a year ago, while helping Julie and Nik cater a party in Laguna Niguel. It had been a theme party and Brad had attended dressed as a Spanish grandee from old California. Dark, handsome and dashing in his custom-tailored costume, Brad had gone out of his way to pay attention to her, insisting that she dance with him even when she protested that she was merely helping to cater the party, not to participate in it.

By the end of the evening, Brad had gotten her telephone number. As he'd pocketed it, he promised to call the next day. He hadn't. Instead, he'd sent roses and then turned up at her door. Jennifer had been flattered and smitten almost instantly.

He had wined and dined her, leaving her very little time to think clearly. His overwhelming personality had taken up all the available corners of her life. There were gaps, absences, but he was part owner of a pharmaceutical company, which necessitated his being on the road a great deal. It was what he told her and she had never thought to question him. She was in love.

She hadn't had a clue until the end.

Jennifer sighed as she measured out the clear blue gel onto her toothbrush. There was no sense in dwelling on the past. She had a radiant future to look forward to.

A noise in her room caught her attention. Curious, toothbrush in hand, Jennifer peered out of the bathroom. The first thing she saw was that the bassinet was empty. Heart pounding, she hurried from the bathroom. A gray-haired nurse was just about to leave the room. One hand on the doorknob, the woman held Katie comfortably in the other.

Jennifer crossed quickly to the woman. "Excuse me, is something wrong?" she asked, surprised.

The nurse swung around, obviously startled to find someone in the room. And then a genial smile spread over her relatively smooth face. Short, heavyset, with wispy hair that surrounded her round face like thin gray smoke, the woman resembled a drawing of Mrs. Claus come to life. Her eyes were almost as bright a shade of blue as Katie's and her smile was warm and gentle.

"Nothing to concern yourself about, my dear." Her words were softly wrapped in just the lightest hint of a lilting Irish brogue. "It seems that the good doctors forgot to do a PKU test on the little darling." Katie made a noise that sounded a bit like gurgling. The nurse smiled down and cooed to the infant. "Can't let you go without that, now can we, my pretty? My, but she is a beautiful one." The woman placed a hand over Jennifer's and patted it reassuringly. "It'll only take a moment."

Jennifer didn't recognize the woman. The last three days had contained a bevy of faces, between the hospital staff and her friends, marching in and out of her single care unit. Out of habit, Jennifer looked at the woman's name tag. Claire Orbach, it read. "But I'm checking out today, Claire."

The nurse glanced at the toothbrush in Jennifer's hand. She jiggled what sounded like coins in her right hand as she shifted the baby more comfortably against the crook of her arm. "I'll have this wee one back to you before you can finish brushing your teeth, don't you worry."

Well, if they had to do a test, they had to do a test. But it was cutting it awfully close, Jennifer thought. "All right, but please hurry. I'm supposed to be out of here by twelve."

Crepe shoes squeaked against the newly mopped floor as the nurse shuffled toward the door again. "Won't take but a minute." She stopped at the door. "Besides, if you do happen to be delayed because of this, it's what's known as a late discharge due to doctor's orders. The blackguards at your insurance company have no choice but to pay when it's put that way."

Reassured, Jennifer nodded and returned to the minuscule bathroom.

She was dressed and ready by the time Julia arrived. Up since three o'clock in the morning, Julia rushed into the room the way she rushed through life, doing double time. Their brother had said more than once that Julia was living proof that a body in motion tended to stay in motion.

"Hi, Jen."

Julia gave Jennifer a quick kiss on the cheek, then looked around. She frowned at the empty bassinet and drummed her nails against the side of the thick glass. She was oblivious to the clinking sound they made.

"So, where's my niece? I have an hour and a half before the diPauli party gets underway." She combed her coral-tipped fingernails through her auburn hair. It fell into unruly, thick waves around her shoulders. On Julia, the effect was always breathtaking.

"Nik is up to his armpits in veal scalopphine and kitchen disasters." Julia blew out a breath, but appeared to take none in. "Rachel didn't show up again." She shook her head. "Another fight with her boyfriend, probably."

Too softhearted to fire the girl, Julia hoped that the problem could be bullied away. She looked out the window and watched sailboats calmly bob in the bay. It looked inviting. Maybe someday...

She swung around to look at Jennifer. "We're going to have to have a long talk with that girl."

By Jennifer's observation, Julia had crossed the room twice and she hadn't even been here more than two minutes. "Slow down, Julia."

Julia gave a short laugh. "If I slow down, I'll remember that I'm exhausted and then I'll drop in my tracks. Nik'll have to find someone else to help with the serving and he won't like that." She looked around again, as if she had somehow missed something in the nine-by-twelve room. "Really, is Katie ready? I don't have that much time to get you home and settled before I have to rush back. I wish you had let me hire a nurse to help you." She placed her hands on her sister's shoulders. "God, I can't wait until you come back to work. This catering business on top of running the restaurant full-time is killing me."

Jennifer laughed. "And you love every minute of it."

Caught, Julia shrugged, dropping her hands to her sides. "That's the trouble with going into business with your relatives. They know all your bad habits ahead of time. There's no room for drama or sympathy." Julia slowed her pace by an iota as emotions tugged at her. She smiled as she took hold of Jennifer's hands. They had played together and wept together and, along with Nik, been each other's rock of support when the times called for it. Still, this was a giant step in their collective lives. "Hard to believe my baby sister's a mom."

At times, Jennifer found it difficult to believe it herself, despite the very strong flutter of life she had felt within her womb for the last four months.

"There's only a year's difference between us," she reminded Julia. At times, it seemed like more. Julia had always been the one to forge ahead, while she had slowly brought up the rear. Of the two of them, Julia had always led.

Julia shrugged. "You were the baby of the family, that qualifies you as my baby sister." She released Jennifer's hands and glanced impatiently toward the door. "Now, where *is* that gorgeous child who looks exactly the way I did when I was her age?"

Jennifer glanced at her watch. It was close to half an hour since the nurse had taken Katie. "I don't know. The nurse said it would only be a minute." Julia's brows rose in question. "They had to run a test on Katie before they released her."

At the last minute. It figured. "What for?" Julia grinned at her sister. "We already know that Katie's the world's smartest, prettiest baby."

This was going to be one spoiled little girl if she let Julie and Nik have their way, Jennifer thought. She reached for the buzzer to summon the nurse. "Maybe the doctors want to be reassured of that for themselves."

Julia took the buzzer from Jennifer's hand. "No need. I'll go get the nurse and see what the delay is myself. It'll be faster."

Jennifer sat down on the bed next to her closed suitcase. "Jul, sometimes I think that if you moved any faster, you'd be vibrating backwards."

Julia stopped at the door. "Interesting theory. We'll test it out this summer. We've already got bookings for twenty banquets and it's only April." She let out a dramatic sigh. "It's shaping up to be a very busy three months."

Julia pulled the door open and almost collided with the nurse who was entering. Moving quickly, Julia avoided bumping her shins against the wheelchair the woman was pushing in front of her.

"All ready to go?" the tall nurse asked Jennifer cheerfully.

"Yes, except for the baby." Jennifer gestured toward the empty bassinet. Her eyes met the nurse's only to see a question in them that mirrored her own. "Where's my daughter?"

The blond woman frowned, confused. "She should be here with you."

Jennifer exchanged glances with Julia, a flash of concern washing over both of them at the same moment. Instinctively, Julia moved toward Jennifer, closing ranks.

"A nurse took Katie for a test over half an hour ago." Jennifer struggled to remember what the older woman had said. "She called it a TK—no, a PKU test. She said it would only take a minute."

The nurse closed the wheelchair and moved it to the side. "No, I'm afraid that's impossible. We do that immediately when the baby is born."

Julia heard Jennifer's sharp intake of breath and placed a calming hand on her sister's shoulder, even as her own pulse began to drum.

"Maybe there's been some mix-up," she suggested, though a small, gnawing feeling told her that there wasn't. "Are you sure?" Julia asked the nurse.

The nurse's expression grew concerned as possibilities began to present themselves. Her voice lost its cheerful cadence. "I've been on the maternity floor for twelve years. I'm sure."

Jennifer looked from the nurse to her sister. "But then, where is she?" A thin web of fear began spinning within Jennifer, ensnaring more and more of her with each turn.

The woman shook her head. "I don't know."

"You can't just lose a baby," Julia insisted. "Find the nurse."

"That's right, the nurse." Jennifer attempted to conjure up the woman in her mind, focusing on the name tag. "Her name was, um, Claire." It came back to her. "Claire Orbach, that's it." Jennifer looked at the nurse, hoping for a sign of recognition.

There was none. Pressing her lips together, the woman shook her head. "There's no one on the floor by that name. I know, I'm the head nurse."

Panic shot through Jennifer, like the quills of a porcupine at an encroaching enemy. She grabbed the woman's wrist, as if that could make her recant her words and remember the nurse who had walked off with her baby.

"Are you absolutely certain?" Jennifer struggled not to let her voice crack. "She was about your height, a little heavyset. In her fifties or so. She had a round face, a kind face." It seemed ironic now. "As if she could fit into a Christmas pageant."

There was pity and alarm in the nurse's eyes. "There are six nurses on the floor today. All of them are in their twenties and thirties. I've never heard of anyone named Claire Orbach."

Jennifer vaguely felt Julia's arm slip around her shoulders. She suddenly felt as if her knees had gone out from under her and sank down on the bed with a jolt.

"She said the baby was beautiful," Jennifer murmured under her breath. Struggling to keep from shaking, she covered her mouth with her hands, afraid to think of what this meant. She looked up at her sister. "Jul?"

"It's going to be all right," Julia said firmly. She turned to the nurse. "Call security. Give them her description. Maybe she hasn't left the building yet." Crossing to the small nightstand, Julia picked up the telephone and dialed out.

She wasn't going to faint, she wasn't. There could still be an explanation for all this. Jennifer clung to slender threads of hope as she looked at her sister. "What are you doing?"

Julia's finger covered the first number on the telephone pad. "I'm calling the police."

The nurse hesitated, appalled at the repercussions this would have for the hospital. "But—"

The look Julia gave the woman evaporated any protest that was forming. "My niece has been taken by someone you don't recognize for a test that you say isn't done at this stage. I want the police."

With a nod, the nurse hurried into the hall to summon security. Julia's voice barely registered in the back of Jennifer's mind as she fought the wave of nausea that threatened to overtake her.

The late morning sun shone into the room, slicing through the clear sides of the bassinet. The rays broke up into a rainbow of lights.

Kane Madigan stepped out of the unmarked gray sedan and reached into his shirt pocket, then swallowed an oath. It was empty. He knew it was empty. After four weeks of successful abstinence, he was still reaching for the cigarette pack that had perpetually occupied his breast pocket for the last fifteen years. Annoyed, he wondered when he would get over that habit of reaching for a cigarette whenever tension arose. He doubted the craving would ever leave.

The police sergeant next to him hurried to keep up as they strode toward the electronic hospital doors. "The elevators are that way, sir." The man pointed toward the rear of the building. When Kane raised a disinterested brow in response, the sergeant was quick to elaborate. "My son was here last fall for a tonsillectomy."

Kane nodded absently. They walked down a long, narrow hall. Closed doors marked the way, except for the bright gift shop on the left. Kane noted everything and filed it away. Funny how things worked. If the call had come into the precinct twenty-four hours later, he would have been on vacation. Instead, it looked as if his vacation was going to have to be temporarily postponed. No big loss for him. He hadn't had plans. Just a week at the beach to recharge. Nothing that couldn't be rescheduled at a later time. There was no one else involved, which was the way he liked it.

Jabbing at the up button, Kane thought about the call that had come in a few minutes ago. Unless he missed his guess, it had happened again.

Someone was stealing babies. And he intended to catch them, no matter what it took.

This made eleven. Eleven infant abductions in as many months from as many hospitals. Eight in southern California, one in Nevada, two in Arizona. It left a horrid taste in his mouth that the smoke from a cigarette couldn't begin to camouflage. The cases were all the same. Newborns vanished from their bassinets. No one saw anything. No one knew anything. Perhaps this newest abduction would help shed some light on the case, but more than likely not.

Kane walked into the elevator ahead of the sergeant. It was empty except for an orderly. Flashing a wide grin, the short, thin man moved his mop and pail to the corner, out of the way.

"Maybe somebody saw something this time," the sergeant suggested hopefully, cracking the heavy silence.

"Maybe," Kane echoed.

But he doubted it. Hope was something completely foreign to Kane. It had never had a place in his life, not since his mother had walked out on him and his father over twenty-two years ago. Hope was for other people to try to grasp and hold on to. Facts were all he had to work with, all he believed in. There were times when that wasn't enough, but it would have to do.

When the elevator doors opened on the fifth floor, all three of them got off. The orderly went off to begin his work as Kane and Henderson, the sergeant, stopped at the nurses' station. Showing identification, they were quickly brought to Jennifer's room.

As Kane walked into the noisy room, his attention was immediately drawn to the tall, pale woman sitting beside a closed suitcase on the bed. Her hands were clenched together in her lap as if that was all that was holding her together. She looked to be somewhere in her mid to late twenties. She would have been pretty, with her straight, black hair framing her face, if she didn't look so dazed and disoriented. She reminded him of soldiers he had seen right after a mine had gone off near them.

She had to be the mother, he thought, feeling as much compassion for her as he was able.

Kane looked around the room and saw no one who would qualify as the father. A woman he took to be the hospital administrator was animatedly speaking to a very vibrant-looking woman. The latter bore a slight resemblance to the woman sitting on the bed. He wondered who she was and how she fit in.

The door shut behind him with a small creak. It was enough to draw all eyes in his direction. Kane fished into his pocket as he stepped farther into the room. Taking out his wallet, he flipped it open.

"I'm Detective Madigan." Rather than show his identification to the officious woman who reached for it, he addressed the woman sitting on the bed. He let her examine the shield before he replaced it in his navy windbreaker.

Dazed, dark blue eyes looked up into his face and he felt something twist inside his gut, though he had long ago schooled himself that pity had no place in his work. It only served to interfere. But the blatant anguish in the woman's eyes was almost impossible to ignore.

She couldn't go to pieces, Jennifer told herself. She wasn't going to do Katie any good that way. With superhuman effort, she got herself under control and placed her hand in his.

"I'm Jennifer Sinclair." Aware that Julia had sat beside her and had placed hands on her shoulders in a gesture of support, she automatically introduced her sister. Then Jennifer licked her lips and said the hardest words she had ever managed to utter. "I think my baby's been kidnapped."

Her voice was raspy, he thought, as if she had been crying. Or trying not to. He nodded in response to her words.

"That's why we're here, ma'am." Kane indicated the balding, uniformed man behind him. "This is Sergeant Henderson. He took your call."

She looked frail, he thought. Too frail to bear something like this. He wondered where the woman's husband was. He found himself wanting to say something that might make her feel better, though the cold, hard truth of the matter was that as it stood, there wasn't anything that would.

"There's an entire task force devoted to tracking down your baby's whereabouts."

Jennifer looked at Kane in surprise. Julia put their thoughts into words. "Isn't that a little fast?"

He turned slightly to look at her. "No, ma'am, this isn't the first kidnapping of its kind." He addressed Jennifer. "Your baby is the eleventh infant stolen in the last year from hospitals in the Southwest region. The ring has hit several times in southern California."

"Ring?" Jennifer echoed. An iciness spread like a thousand tiny sharp needles at the implication of the detective's words.

"We have reason to believe that it's the work of some sort of a ring or organization," Kane told her. His voice was neither kind nor unkind, merely detached.

It matched the way Jennifer felt. Detached. Lost. Jennifer didn't know whether what the detective told her made the situation better or worse. If a ring was involved, then it meant that her baby hadn't been stolen by some crazed woman attempting to replace her own child with Katie. A professional organization had to have contacts. If there were contacts, they might leave clues.

Even so, the thought of someone selling her baby brought tears to Jennifer's eyes. She blinked, trying to banish them. They shimmered in her lashes like unshed jewels.

Julia pulled out a tissue from the box by the bed and silently pressed it into Jennifer's hand. Jennifer wiped the tears from her lashes. A few slid down her cheeks.

Kane hated tears. He never knew how to handle them. They made him uncomfortable and reminded him of the ones he had once shed as a child.

"Mrs. Sinclair—" he began, wanting to get this over with.

"Miss," Jennifer corrected automatically. Her throat felt constricted as she forced the words out. "Jennifer."

Kane nodded, though it wasn't his practice to use first names. Surnames were much more antiseptic, giving him the distance he preferred to maintain. "Jennifer," he repeated. "If you could tell me everything that happened, it would be a great help." He saw the doubtful look enter her eyes. "Slowly, as you remember it." He turned to the sergeant. "Henderson, I want you to ask around the floor to see if anyone saw or heard anything out of the ordinary in the last twenty-four hours."

The sergeant nodded and began with the administrator. Kane turned his attention to Jennifer.

"There's not much to tell." She felt so helpless, so lost, as if she had just tumbled into a long, black tunnel that had no end to it.

"You'd be surprised at what 'not much' might yield." He took out a tape recorder and placed it on the bed between them. "Now, nice and slow," he coaxed. "Just speak into the microphone."

She looked at the tape recorder as if it were some dark stranger intruding on her grief. "Is that really necessary?"

"Sometimes it helps to jar my memory. There might be something I overlook while taking notes." He flipped open a small notepad.

Though it had been a long time since he had experienced anything similar to the feeling that was pervading him at this moment, something within Kane reached out to this woman in her agony.

His voice softened slightly as he awkwardly covered her hand with his and said, "I'm here to help."

Chapter 2

The soft whirr of the small, black tape recorder on the table next to Jennifer's bed was the only other sound in the hospital room as Jennifer answered Kane's questions and recounted the events that were so fresh they still had not completely woven themselves into the tapestry of her life.

It was almost physically painful for her to speak. Guilt rose like a dark specter, surrounding her, growing with each word. Why hadn't she known something was wrong? Why had she surrendered her baby so easily, without a second thought?

Jennifer cleared her throat, fighting back tears. "I heard a noise and when I came out of the bathroom to see what it was, she was just leaving the room."

Kane looked up sharply, his fingers tightening on his pen. "She?"

"The nurse—the woman," Jennifer amended, "who took my baby."

Kane stared at Jennifer, hesitant to grab at the nugget she offered. "You actually *saw* her?"

Henderson abruptly stopped questioning the administrator in midsentence and turned toward Kane. The two men exchanged looks. A break?

Jennifer's eyes never left Kane's. Was there hope after all? "Yes."

In the other ten cases, no one had seen the person, or persons, involved in the abductions. This could be the break they had been waiting for. Kane cautioned himself not to get carried away. It could turn out to be nothing. In his experience, witnesses were usually not very reliable. Five people saw five different things. "Can you describe her?"

"Yes." Her answer rushed out in a wave of mounting enthusiasm.

The woman said the single word so emphatically, it made Kane think that perhaps she would be accurate, at least to a degree. Right now, beyond questioning other people on the floor to see if they noticed anything or anyone unusual, they didn't have much else to work with. "Are you sure?"

Jennifer could see the woman as if she were standing right in front of her. "I'm positive."

"Henderson—" Kane looked over his shoulder. "—get me Noah. Tell him to come down here. Now." He reached toward his pocket. With a stifled huff, he dropped his hand. God, he wanted a cigarette badly.

"Who's Noah?" Julia wanted to know.

Kane had almost forgotten that Jennifer's sister was in the room. Looking at the two women, he saw definite traces of family resemblance. The one appeared vibrant, fiery, the other subdued, almost regal. But the shape of the mouths, the slight slant of the eyes, the oval faces branded them as family.

"The police artist," Kane answered Julia after a beat.

He watched Henderson tap out the numbers to the squad room and attempted to curb his impatience. They'd gone so long without a single real lead and now, perhaps, they were being handed their first break.

All it took, he thought, was one.

He saw a smidgen of hope flash in Jennifer's eyes. He didn't want to lead her on, yet it seemed only humane to give her something to hang on to.

"If we can get a reasonably accurate drawing of the woman and circulate it via the news media, we might be able to find someone who knows her." Kane made a mental note to tell the captain to put a few more men on the phones. They'd be ringing off the hook by evening. "There'll be a lot of kooks who'll call in, but sometimes we get lucky."

Jennifer was afraid to hope, afraid not to. "You don't have to wait for Noah," Jennifer told him. She turned toward her sister. "Julia?"

Before she could put her request into words, Julia was digging out a pad and pencil from her purse. At times, they had the ability to practically read one another's minds. As soon as the police detective had said the word artist, they had both thought of the same thing.

Julia handed Jennifer the pad. "Here, Jen."

Kane looked at the two sisters, silently waiting for an explanation. He had discovered that at times, the less specific his questions, the more he found out. Sometimes, all it took was a look.

"Jenny was a commercial artist before she came to work for the family," Julia explained.

Being a commercial artist didn't immediately enable her to be able to create realistic-looking drawings of people. "Do you think you can sketch the woman?"

"I know I can." If she lived to be a hundred, Jennifer knew she would never forget that face. It had deceived her, lulled her into complacency. The woman's face was forever tattooed on the membrane of her mind.

While Kane watched, Jennifer picked up the pencil. Her hand shook as she brought the point to the pad. Her nerves had been stretched to the limit.

Kane still intended to have the police artist work with Jennifer, but it might be an added help if she attempted to conceptualize the suspect's image herself while they waited for Noah to arrive.

"Take your time," Kane encouraged.

There was something in his voice, a strength that seemed to reach out to her, that enabled Jennifer to calm down and focus her attention on the blank page. Slowly, she envisioned the woman's face. The way it had appeared, deceptively benevolent, as she had spoken to her, holding Katie in her arms.

Jennifer squeezed back the tears that formed and threatened to fall. She began to draw.

Her strokes took on a boldness as she continued until finally, a face emerged complete with minute details. Jennifer let out a breath, as if in doing so she could purge all traces of the woman from herself. It was impossible.

"This is her." She handed the page to Kane.

Kane scanned the drawing methodically. It was good, he thought. As good as anything Noah could produce. They had a winner. "Sergeant, call backup. We're going to need them."

Julia moved forward. Time was growing short. She felt guilty, thinking about the business in light of what had transpired. But Nik did need her.

Nik.

Julia suddenly realized that their brother had no idea what was happening. It was going to be awful, telling him. But she was going to have to be the one to do it. Jennifer had been through enough.

"Can she go, now?" Julia asked Kane. Maybe she'd bring Jennifer with her to the restaurant. She could lie down on the old leather sofa in the back office. Julia didn't want her sister to be alone right now.

Kane shook his head. He pocketed the tape recorder in his jacket. He noted that it was beginning to tear the lining.

"Not yet. If you don't mind, I'd rather wait until the police artist gets here." He turned to Jennifer. "Just in case he could add something to your drawing that might trigger something for you, a detail you might have forgotten or missed."

He was doing all he could, she thought. Would it be enough? "Of course." Jennifer mustered a smile from somewhere as she gave her sister's hand a squeeze. "Go ahead, Julie. I'll be all right. You can't leave Nik in a lurch."

Julia wrapped her fingers tightly around Jennifer's hand. "I can't leave you in one, either," Julia returned stubbornly.

Jennifer appreciated her sister's dilemma. But there was nothing she could really do for her. There was nothing anyone could do, except for, hopefully, the detective.

"Not even you can be in two places at once. I'll call a cab when I'm through here," Jennifer assured her.

Having to look after herself would force her to do something, however minor. She couldn't just sit here like a lump, letting Julia care for her. She had to start putting one foot in front of the other or else she was going to go crazy.

Momentarily conferring with the sergeant, Kane looked up at Jennifer's statement. "I'll have someone take you home when we're through questioning you, Miss Sinclair—Jennifer," he amended when she began to open her mouth to correct him.

Julia bit her lower lip, torn. But there wasn't really any tangible good she could do here, while she could be a help to Nik. He was working too hard these days as it was.

Though it was difficult, Julia made her decision. She embraced Jennifer. "I'll call you as soon as we're finished," she promised.

Giving Jennifer one last doubtful look over her shoulder as she opened the door, Julia swept out of the room.

The artist arrived a few minutes later. By then, everyone except for the head nurse had been cleared from the room. The sergeant and two additional uniformed patrolmen were busy questioning other people. The artist, an older man with just the slightest fringe of faded brown hair surrounding a slightly misshapen dome, glanced at Jennifer's drawing.

Taking it into his hands, he studied it and seemed impressed with the detail he saw there. He looked up at Jennifer.

"Hey, you're good. It isn't often we get witnesses who are so accurate. You might think about getting a job on the

force when this is over.'' Noah spread out his sketch pad and
box of charcoals on the raised table next to Jennifer's bed.

She knew the man was only trying to keep her mind off
the tragedy that was enshrouding her. She smiled weakly in
response, grateful for his effort, even though it failed. ''I
have enough work waiting for me once I get back on my
feet.''

Placing the drawing Jennifer had made on the table where
he could see it, Noah made himself comfortable and began
sketching. His strokes were quick and sure.

''Oh, what is it that you do?'' he queried in the same
voice he used when he asked his grandson what he wanted
to be when he grew up. There was an abundance of patience in the gentle tone.

Jennifer attempted to focus on the positive things in her
life. She knew she was luckier than most people. It was just
hard to remember that at the moment. ''My brother, sister
and I own a restaurant and catering business in Newport.
Sinclair's.''

Someday, Noah mused, he would love to be able to sketch
the woman sitting opposite him. She had good, clean lines.
Aristocratic lines. The kind one envisioned belonging to
princesses in fairy tales.

He realized that she had stopped talking. ''The food
good?''

''Nik thinks so.'' Jennifer remembered how excited he had
been when they had received their first review in a local
newspaper. The words had been positively glowing. Nik
walked on air for weeks. ''He's my brother and the chef.''
She thought of the booming business they now had. ''A lot
of other people seem to like it, too.''

''I'll have to remember to get down there sometime and
have lunch.'' He glanced into her eyes and saw the pure agony that well-intended words could not begin to erase. Poor
kid. He stopped sketching and leaned over to pat her hand.
''It's going to be all right, wait and see. Kane's the best.
He'll get your little girl back.''

Jennifer looked at him blankly. ''Kane?''

"Detective Madigan," Noah nodded toward the rear of the room. Kane was reviewing some data another policeman had brought him. "He doesn't talk much, unlike me—" he smiled at her, a network of tiny lines forming about his mouth as his cheeks spread "—but he gets results."

A fresh wave of despair threatened to overwhelm her, as she thought of her baby being carried off. "That's all I care about. Results."

"Speaking of results—" he placed his pencil down on the table next to his box of charcoals "—how's this?" Noah turned his pad around for her inspection. He had made a full-size exact copy of the sketch that she had drawn.

Jennifer looked at the recreated sketch as if seeing it for the first time. She had drawn the woman who had abducted her baby without the slightest bit of malice to be found in her face. There hadn't been any to warn her, Jennifer thought ruefully. *Why* hadn't there been any? Why hadn't there been a telltale nervousness to alert her? Something? Anything?

She swallowed her pain. "It looks just like her."

"All right." Making himself comfortable again, Noah rested the sketch pad on his lap. "Now, let's give the lady some color." With an array of charcoals before him, he looked up at Jennifer. "Hair?"

"Gray."

"Light or dark?"

She pointed to a stick that most closely resembled the color. "Like steel wool."

"Steel wool it is." Taking the slender stick of color into his hand, Noah made several passes over the drawing, then returned the charcoal to the box. "Next, eyes?" He looked at her, waiting.

"Blue. Light blue," she embellished, selecting the charcoal for him. "She looked like the picture of everyone's grandmother."

"That's what makes her so dangerous," Noah mused out loud. Carefully, he shaded in the eyes. "No one stops to think that someone's grandmother could be up to no good."

Finished, he replaced the wand of color in the exact place he
had taken it from. "All right, what about her complexion?" When Jennifer made no answer, he supplied words to
choose from. "Clear, blotchy, ruddy?"

"Except for the fine lines, here and here—" Jennifer
pointed the areas out on his sketch "—she looked like an ad
for face cream."

Peaches and cream, Noah thought. He made the necessary additions. "Hey, Kane," he called out, "she's got a
good eye." Noah finished with a flourish, then turned the
drawing around for both their perusals. "How's this?"

Jennifer's heart jumped, lodging in her throat like a huge
peach pit. The colors had transformed a memory into
someone vivid. "That's her. That's the woman who stole my
baby."

Kane took the sketch from Noah and looked it over carefully. Yes, this should jar a few memories. And probably
have the weirdos calling to turn in their grandmothers. It
was up to the task force to sift through the chaff to get to the
grain.

"All right, you know what to do." Kane handed the
sketch back to Noah.

Kane looked toward the door. He had people fanned out
all over the floor, asking questions. The story of the latest
abduction had spread like a fire consuming dried prairie
grass. He knew it was a matter of time, perhaps even minutes, before the news media would descend upon them. A
few would go for the lesser human interest elements or accost the hospital administrator with their microphones. But
most of the news hawks would come after Jennifer. It had
happened before.

And while publicity was what he both needed and wanted
at this point, what he *didn't* want was to subject Jennifer to
the probing, heartless questions that was part of the territory. He didn't know why, but if that happened, he would
feel responsible for any additional anguish she would be put
through.

Henderson entered the room to inform Kane that everything was proceeding according to instructions. So far, no one seemed to recall the woman Jennifer had described. Security hadn't seen her and only one of the orderlies thought he might have, but wasn't sure. And the man, according to the head nurse, had a rampant need for attention. Temporarily, they were still at square one.

"We're done here for now," Kane told Henderson quietly. Noah was already packing up his equipment. Kane directed his attention to Jennifer. "I'll take you home, Jennifer, if you're ready to go."

Jennifer nodded, rising to her feet. She couldn't wait to get away from here, away from the empty bassinet that stood in the corner, a constant reminder of the tragedy that had entered her life.

Henderson took a step toward the door. "Want me to get one of the uniforms to take her home?" he asked Kane.

"No, I'll do it. You get a ride with one of the men." He ignored the surprised look Henderson gave him. Instead, he nodded at Jennifer's suitcase. "This yours?"

"Yes."

Kane took it from the bed. He looked around. "Anything else?"

Yes, my baby. She wanted to scream the words out. "No," Jennifer answered dully. "Nothing else."

Because she suddenly looked unsteady, Kane took her elbow. The head nurse moved to block his exit.

"We have to discharge her in a wheelchair." She pointed toward it. The wheelchair was still leaning against the wall where she had left it.

Kane felt Jennifer stiffen ever so slightly as the nurse started to open the wheelchair for her. He looked at Jennifer. "Do you want to sit in it?"

Jennifer shook her head. Somehow, being wheeled down the hall in the chair would just serve to intensify the lack of control she was experiencing.

"No," she told him, her voice filled with emotion, "I just want to be out of here."

Kane dismissed the chair with a wave of his hand. "We won't be needing that."

The nurse looked flustered. "But the rules clearly state that she has to leave in a wheelchair," she insisted. "It's hospital policy. Our insurance clause—" the woman rambled on.

Holding the door open with his elbow, Kane reached for Jennifer's arm. "I'll take full responsibility for this," Kane told the woman as he escorted Jennifer from the room. There was no arguing with the authority in his voice.

Neither one of them said a word as they waited for the elevator. When it arrived, Jennifer got on ahead of Kane and sagged against one worn, gun-metal gray wall. It took effort not to slide down to her knees and stay there. "Thank you."

Kane studied her. She looked pale, far paler than he thought she probably was under normal circumstances. "Maybe I should have taken that nurse up on the wheelchair."

Jennifer shook her head, making an effort to straighten. "No. I need to walk, to move." The doors opened and she got out quickly, as if trying to reassure herself that she was still able, that nothing else had changed.

It didn't take Kane more than two steps to catch up. Though she was tall, he was taller by a good six inches. They wove their way through the halls, following the signs that pointed toward visitor parking. The exit doors yawned open and Jennifer waited for Kane to take the lead.

"The car's parked over there. Its a gray sedan." He pointed toward the left. She had all but jogged out of the building. She kept the stride up as they walked through the lot.

"Is that advisable for a woman in your condition?" He indicated the way she was moving. "I mean, a woman who just *was* in your condition? Shouldn't you be going a little slower?"

Jennifer shook her head. She wanted to be tired, so tired that she couldn't think. She wanted to move so quickly that her thoughts couldn't catch up to her. It was foolish, but she felt desperation clawing at her. She had to do something to keep it from tearing her apart.

"I've had three days to recover." She had always been in excellent condition, excellent health. "I come from very strong peasant stock. My great-grandmother supposedly gave birth in the field and went on working."

Kane's lips twitched slightly in what appeared to be a smile. He made her think of a gunfighter in the old west, one who wasn't necessarily on the side of right, or of wrong. Just on his own side. "She's the one they're always referring to."

"She's the one." Jennifer's false buoyancy faltered. By nature, she had always been one to take any bad event and turn it every which way until some good could be seen in it. It just wasn't possible with the situation she found herself in.

As they approached his car, she finally allowed herself to voice the question that had been plaguing her. "What do you think my chances are of getting Katie back?" Her eyes held his, warning him to be straightforward. "Don't lie to me."

He unlocked the passenger side and held the door open for her. "I make it a habit never to lie, Jennifer. It only delays arriving at the truth and getting caught could be very unpleasant."

Closing her door, Kane came around the front of the car to the driver's side. He slid in and slammed the door shut. Automatically, like an artificial intelligence programmed to serve, the seat belt moved forward and tightened around his waist and shoulder.

"Hate these things," Kane muttered, sticking his key into the ignition.

He started the engine and looked at Jennifer. "To answer your question, I think you've increased everyone's chances of finding their babies." One hand on the back of the seat, he guided the steering wheel lightly and backed out of his parking space. Another car waited a few feet away to refill it.

"I don't understand."

Kane pulled out of the lot, onto a winding road that led into the main drag. "So far, you're the only one who's seen

the suspect. We're going to show the sketch around at the
other hospitals where the abductions took place. Maybe
even stir up a few memories. We're definitely better off than
we were before.''

She stared straight ahead as the road merged into traffic.
He was taking the freeway to her small town house. ''Maybe
you are, but I'm not.'' She whispered the words so quietly,
he had to strain to hear them.

Kane cursed mentally. He hadn't thought when he spoke.
That was unusual for him. Normally, every word was eco-
nomically metered out. Guilt nipped at him like the tiny bite
from a flea. Small, insignificant and annoyingly itchy.

The silence hung like a dark cloud above them until he
broke it. ''I'm sorry, I didn't mean that the way it sounded.''

She knew he didn't. She had just allowed herself to slip
into self-pity. ''It's all right. I'm afraid I'm not myself.'' She
drew in a shaky breath. It didn't help to steady her. Nothing was going to help for a while.

''It might help to talk a little.'' It never helped him. But
it seemed to work for other people. Maybe it'd work for her.
Anything was better than the uncomfortable silence wrapping its steel tendrils about the car.

She laced her fingers together in her lap, forcing herself
to stave off the hysteria she felt rising in every corner of her
being.

''This is something that happens to other people. Something I see on the eleven o'clock news. I never thought—''
Hearing her voice rise, Jennifer bit off the sentence. ''I
should have stopped her.''

Traffic was light as they entered the ramp. He glanced in
her direction. ''You had no way of knowing anything was
wrong.''

She dragged a hand through her hair impatiently, restlessly. No, she had had no way of knowing. But she should
have. Somehow, she should have. Where was that world-
famous mother's intuition when she had needed it? ''That
still doesn't change anything.''

''No,'' he agreed. ''It doesn't. But raking yourself over
the coals won't, either.''

It wasn't said to make her feel better, she realized. The detective was stating the facts as he saw them. And he was right. She turned slightly in her seat and looked at the man for perhaps the first time. The illusion he cast of strength was more than that. It was real. She could almost feel it. There was a determined set to the square jaw that told her he didn't just pay lip service to his job. He lived it. She felt a little better.

"You're right. Thanks." Jennifer thought of what the police artist had told her about Kane. "He was wrong."

Kane frowned as a white minivan almost swerved into their car. "Who?"

"Your artist. Noah." Kane glanced at her, waiting for an explanation. "He said you don't talk much."

He let out a short sound that was a cross between a laugh and a hiss. "I don't." The green overhead sign told him he had three more miles to go before the turnoff. She lived in a secluded section of Bedford. "Usually."

Jennifer offered him a thin smile of gratitude. It barely creased her lips, but it was all she could manage. "Thanks for breaking your rule."

Her gratitude made him uncomfortable. Anything but the most distant of human contact made him uncomfortable. The reason he was good at what he did was because of the distance he could maintain from his cases and the victims involved. Feelings, emotions, friendships—they only served to get in the way and obscure things.

"It's not a rule. It's just…the way I am." The way he had been all his adult life and longer. It worked for him and it didn't leave him open, the way he once had been. But that was because he had been a boy at the time, not a man.

He paused, reflecting on the case again. That was all it was for him, a case, a puzzle. He couldn't let it be more. Worse, he had forgotten how.

"On an outside chance—"

She turned toward him eagerly. Had he thought of something? "Yes?"

"Would the baby's father have tried to have her abducted?"

Jennifer sank down into her seat again and laughed. It was a short, mirthless sound. Kane thought he detected a note of suppressed pain in it.

"Not if the color he turned when I told him I was pregnant is any indication of his feelings." Jennifer realized she was saying more than she had intended to. She stared straight ahead at the road again. They were approaching her exit. "I haven't heard from him in seven months."

"Were you married to him?" When he had previously asked Jennifer her marital status, she had replied single. He had taken it to mean divorced. Now he wasn't certain.

Jennifer shook her head. "No, thankfully I didn't make that mistake." And that's what it would have been, a mistake. Brad's true colors had all come out that afternoon, in that one awful hour when she had told him about the baby.

The bitterness in her voice was hard to miss. "Is that your opinion about marriage in general or just the baby's father in particular?" It wasn't a professional question, but he found himself wondering.

She realized what she must sound like. All things considered, she decided she had the right. At least for a few moments.

"The latter. My parents had a wonderful marriage. Someday, I hope to have one just like theirs. Katie's father unfortunately wasn't the right person for that happily-ever-after ending, that's all." She turned slightly in her seat as they came to a stop before a red light. "To answer your question, I know he wouldn't have wanted to kidnap Katie. I'm sure as far as he's concerned, he'd be much happier if we had both been abducted and then dropped off the face of the earth for good measure."

Kane nodded, taking his foot off the brake as the light changed. She was probably right. This had all the earmarks of the kidnapping organization. Still, it might be a lead to check out. There were precious few rocks available without leaving one intentionally unturned.

Kane made a mental note to find out the man's name and address after he brought Jennifer safely home.

Chapter 3

Kane pulled the gray sedan into Jennifer's driveway. It looked the same, she thought. The light gray stucco walls, the white and yellow daisies along the walk that she and Julia had planted. The stone pine, its candles raised in homage, majestically guarding the corner. Everything was just the way it had been when she drove off to the hospital three days ago.

But things weren't the same. They were different. The world had turned on a dime in the space of a few minutes and now nothing would ever be the same for her again.

Kane turned off the engine and waited for Jennifer to make the first move. He wanted to give her a moment to pull herself together before going into the house.

Nerves jumped around her body like beads of water on a hot skillet. Jennifer turned to him. "Would you like to come in?" Suddenly, she didn't want to walk through that door alone.

Kane saw the need in her eyes without quite understanding it. There was work to do, but for some reason, he couldn't refuse her.

"Just for a minute. I'd like the name and address of your—" He stopped. What was he going to call the man? Her lover? Somehow, that seemed too cruel a term to throw up at her given the present situation. "The baby's natural father," he finally said.

Jennifer shrugged. "I think it's a waste of time, but I'll give it to you."

And wouldn't Brad just love that? Having the police call on him because of a careless affair he had indulged in? Jennifer didn't want revenge or to make any waves. She just wanted Katie back. And as hateful as Brad had turned out to be that last day, she knew he wasn't responsible for the baby's abduction.

She placed a hand on Kane's wrist, as if that would bind him to his word. "But you have to promise that I won't have to have any contact with him." He was part of her past and she intended to keep him that way.

Kane looked down at her hand. It wasn't hard to read between the lines. "Did he hurt you that much?" It wasn't a question he would have normally asked, but somehow, it needed answering.

Jennifer straightened, releasing her grip on his wrist. "Yes. At the time." It had hurt very, very much. He had turned his back on her. Abandoned her. Abruptly she was forced to come face-to-face with the fact that everything she had believed in was just fashioned out of papier-mâché. But she had gotten over it. And she had no intention of reliving any of it. "Now I just don't think he's worth any of my time."

Kane came around the front of the car and took her hand to help her out as she opened the passenger door. She gripped it as she rose, still somewhat unaccustomed to the ease with which she could maneuver now that her extra weight was gone.

She let go of his hand and smiled. "I'm not that frail, Kane." He looked a little surprised that she was using his first name. "Is it all right if I call you Kane? I feel that if we're on a first name basis, it's like we're friends." She bit her lower lip when it began to quiver. She didn't want to break down in front of him. "And friends do what they can to help each other."

He slammed the car door a little harder than he should have. He felt frustrated. Frustrated because after eleven months, he still hadn't gotten any closer to solving the case.

"Miss Sinclair—Jennifer. It doesn't matter what I call you or what you call me, I'm still going to do my job to the best of my ability."

She was being silly, but she couldn't seem to help herself. She *needed* some sort of talisman to hang on to, some sort of pretense.

"I know. Maybe I'm just being a little desperate, that's all." Turning her back to him, she took out her key and unlocked the front door.

Jennifer took one step inside the house before the scene in front of her actually registered. She stopped dead. The living room was decorated with pink and white balloons. Streamers were everywhere, hanging down like colorful weeping willows. A huge banner declaring Welcome Home, Jennifer and Katie, Love, Irene and Martha, took up part of the rear wall.

"Oh, God." Jennifer covered her mouth with her hands, trying to block the sob that suddenly throbbed in her throat at the sight of the banner her neighbors had made. This wasn't the way she had envisioned coming home. With her arms empty and her heart aching. She felt so dreadfully overwhelmed, so dreadfully lost.

Jennifer turned her face from the banner, a strangled cry on her lips. Swinging around, she bumped against Kane's chest. His hands went up to steady her. And then he left them there as he awkwardly held her against him. And let her cry.

Jennifer tried to pull herself together. She couldn't seem to manage it. The tears refused to stop flowing. "I'm sorry, it's just that—" Her voice broke and the rest of her words were choked off, muffled against his chest.

He felt the warmth of her breath as it penetrated his shirt. Something stirred within him and he held her closer.

"It's all right," he told her, his voice soothing. "You've been through hell. Nobody's going to blame you if you cry."

It felt strange, standing there, holding her. It had been a long time since he had held anyone, a long time since he had tried to comfort anyone. She was struggling so hard to be brave as she clutched at his shirt and sobbed against his chest. He could face down an armed suspect easier than he could offer any measure of solace. He knew how to handle himself in a life-and-death situation. He had no idea what to do when faced with heart-wrenching sorrow.

Slowly, some faraway instinct had him tightening his arms around her. It was the only thing he could think of doing. He offered her what little physical comfort he could. God knew there were no promises he could make. He didn't believe in saying anything unless he knew he could make good on it.

Jennifer felt embarrassed, coming unglued this way. Yet she couldn't untangle herself from the strength she felt emanating from him. It felt as if she had metamorphosed into a leaden statue. She needed to be held, even by a stranger. To be told lies that she could cling to and pretend were true. She needed to be told that her baby was safe and would be returned to her.

It wasn't fair to him, she thought, putting Kane on the spot this way. Drawing in air, she took a step away from him.

"I'm sorry." Her voice was husky with tears that were still unshed. She took the handkerchief he handed her and wiped her cheeks. "I don't usually fall apart like this." She returned it to him.

He pocketed the handkerchief. "You've got plenty of reason to fall apart."

Kane looked around the room. Years on the force had trained him to take in everything, no matter what the situation. It was a small, comfortably furnished house from what he could see. Nothing wild or outlandish. Just nice. The word fit her like a glove. Nice. Bad things always seemed to happen to nice people, he thought. There was no justice to it.

He gestured toward the sofa. "Do you want to sit down? Can I get you anything?"

She shook her head. "No." She hesitated a moment. "But if it's not breaking any rules, could you just stay and talk to me for a little while? I don't think I can be alone just yet. I thought I could, but I can't." Stepping back, she looked at his shirt and flushed. "I got your shirt all wet."

He glanced down. There was a jagged damp spot on his shirt just over his heart. It looked a little like a misshapen storm cloud. "It'll dry."

His skin tingled slightly beneath the wet material, as if she had touched it with more than just her tears. He supposed she had, in a way. Her plight had him reacting in something more than just a professional, detached manner. And that wasn't good. The first rule for a police officer was never to get involved. It had been Kane's own personal credo long before he had become a policeman. He had to remind himself of that now. There was something about her, about the way she looked at him, that made him forget.

Kane touched her arm. She gave the appearance of someone who could be knocked over by less air than it took to blow out a single birthday candle. "You look shaky."

Her eyes darted toward the decorations. Her knees felt as if they were made out of the consistency of water. "Maybe I will sit down."

Without asking, he began taking down the decorations. She didn't need this kind of a reminder, he thought angrily. She had been through enough and, like the other families who had had their babies stolen from the hospitals, would continue to go through hell until and unless he could find her baby.

If it wasn't already too late.

Jennifer watched Kane pull down the banner and crumple it up with his large hands, grateful that he was doing what she couldn't bring herself to ask him to do. He gave the impression of being disinterested. But he wasn't. "You're very kind."

Her words, whispered so quietly, had Kane pausing for a
moment without turning around. Then he tossed aside the
banner and began pulling down the streamers.

"Now there's a word I don't hear very often, at least, not
applied to me," he commented.

Holding on to the balloon strings, his arms full of party
paraphernalia, Kane turned to her. "Where do you want
these?" He expected her to say the trash.

The contrast of such a solemn-looking man surrounded
by an assortment of gaiety was enough to make her wonder
about him. Was he always this somber? Was there a wife
somewhere who knew how to make him smile? Or did he
face life alone?

Jennifer rose. "In the baby's room."

She led the way down the hall. Steeling herself, she opened
the door. It was a bright yellow room with colorful murals
comprised of characters from popular nursery rhymes. She
had painted them all herself, during the last months of her
pregnancy. This was a room where love resided. A room that
was empty. "I'll take them out when we get her back."

He made no comment as he placed the decorations in the
room, leaving the banner and streamers on the changing table. The streamers hung down the sides like multicolored
seaweed, waiting only for a child's imagination to trans-
form them into something special. Something magical.

Jennifer firmly closed the door behind her, then turned to
Kane in the hall. She placed her hand on his arm in suppli-
cation. "Kane, what can I do?"

He wished she wouldn't touch him. He didn't like the way
that felt. No, he amended. He didn't *want* to like the way
that felt. He had no business liking it.

His voice was gruff and impersonal as he answered.
"Well, you can start by giving me that name and address."

Jennifer shook her head. That wasn't what she meant and
she had a feeling that he knew it. "No, I mean besides that."

Kane shrugged, at a loss as to what to tell her. "Pray, if
it helps you any." He had long since forgotten how to form
the words or even the reason why anyone would pray. But
he knew that others seemed to find solace in offering up

words to a deity who, if there, paid less than no attention to mere mortals.

They walked back into the living room. The dim hall seemed somehow too intimate for either of them.

"That's not enough. I want to do something." She searched his face and saw that he understood. "Anything."

He knew what she was going through, but there was nothing he could do for her, other than his job. "We'll be handing out flyers with the woman's face on it. Like I said, maybe we'll get lucky." It was all he could offer her.

She had to keep busy. There had to be *something*. "But—"

Kane took hold of her arms. It amazed him that they could feel so sturdy when she appeared to look so delicate. "Look, there isn't anything you can do except to go on hoping." He uttered a word that was almost foreign to him. "I'll do all I can to find her."

She knew he would without being told. But she needed to be kept informed, needed to *know*. "Will you call me if you get a lead?"

That wasn't playing by the rules. He began to tell her that, but the look in her eyes stopped him.

"Please?"

Kane blew out a breath, angry, though he wasn't completely sure why. "Yeah. I'll keep you posted. Want to write down that name and address for me now?"

Getting a pad and pencil from the desk in the hall, Jennifer scribbled down Brad's name and his phone number at work. He had never given her the one to his home. That should have been her first clue, she thought ruefully. But she had been far too in love, far too trusting, to think in terms of deception. Jennifer had grown up a lot in nine months.

She handed the paper to him. Kane folded it in half and creased it slowly, his eyes on her face, before tucking it into his pocket. He'd send someone to talk to Brad. Kane moved toward the door. And then, he did something that was completely out of character for him. He made her a promise.

"If there's a way to find your daughter, I'll find her for you."

She leaned her hand against the doorknob and nodded. Motivated by the gratitude she felt for the words he offered and by the need to make contact, she brushed a kiss on his cheek.

He looked at her, startled. Though it was just the slightest of touches, it was etched into his skin. His expression would have been no different if she had taken a hot poker and jabbed him with it. "What the—?"

A small, sad smile barely lifted the corners of her mouth. "I just wanted to say thank you."

"I haven't done anything yet."

He was wrong, there. He had brought her home and taken down the painful decorations without being asked. He had held her while she cried. And he had made her a promise.

"But you will. I know you'll find my baby."

"Yeah." He nodded curtly, then pulled the door shut behind him.

Kane felt at his shirt pocket before angrily shoving his hands deep into his pants pockets. *No pressure, right?* He could still feel where her lips had touched him. It was as if she had isolated that small segment of skin. He shook his head as he got into his car.

The lady knew how to lay a guilt trip on a man, he thought. Too bad for her that he was beyond guilt and the entire tangled world of feelings. Otherwise, it might have worked.

Kane gunned the car as he peeled out of her driveway. He had things to do and cages to rattle. There was no more time to waste. He tried not to think about the fact that without meaning to, she had managed to rattle him.

Jennifer couldn't take it any longer. It had been two weeks, two long, horrible weeks and she hadn't heard a word from Kane, not a single word.

Julia had set up camp at her house when Jennifer had refused to move into her apartment. Both Julia and Nik had all but abandoned the restaurant to be there with her when the reporters had descended, seeking their headlines. Jennifer had seen herself on news broadcasts on all the major channels and read about the account in two different newspapers. The sketch of the so-called nurse that she and Noah had worked on was shown over and over again with instructions to call either the news station or the police if anyone had any information about the woman. Nik had even put up a reward for any information leading to Katie's recovery.

The offer had brought the vampires out in force, Julia said. Jennifer's phone number was in the book and the telephone rang incessantly. People who dreamed they saw her baby called with regularity. Julia refused to let Jennifer answer the telephone after the first call. She took all the calls herself, or let Nik handle it when he was around.

No one let her do anything. Out of love, they were treating her like an invalid, both physically and emotionally.

Jennifer felt like a chloroformed butterfly, wrapped in cotton, already more than half-dead. But she wasn't dead. She was alive. And she wanted to find her baby. If she didn't do something soon, she was going to snap.

She eyed the telephone accusingly. For once, it was silent. Why hadn't he called?

By his estimation, Kane had had perhaps five hours' sleep spread over the past three days. Two weeks had passed much too fast. When his eyes refused to stay open any longer, he'd napped in the captain's office on a sofa confiscated from a drug king's house during a bust. It felt as if the crime lord was getting his final revenge. Kane shaved in the precinct bathroom and had worn the same suit of clothes for the past three days.

Stretching at his desk, Kane looked down at his shirt. He was going to have to go home and change soon, he thought. He was beginning to smell a little gamey. And for what? All the effort had yielded nothing so far. He rifled through the stacks of paperwork on his desk. All the leads they thought they'd had had gone nowhere.

And every hour made the trail that much colder, that much harder to follow.

Kane sighed impatiently. The look in her eyes as he left her house haunted him. There had been despair mirrored there, despair mingled with hope and such faith that it had temporarily undone him. Damn her, who was she to prey on his mind like this? He was doing the best job he could. What the hell made her think that he could find her baby just like that? He wasn't God, he was only a man.

He was letting this get to him, he thought, dropping the papers on his desk. They fluttered down, separating and drifting to opposite sides of the desk as they fell. Behind him was a map with a pushpin for every location where a baby had been stolen. A different color for each state. Jennifer's was blue. He hated pushpins, he thought.

Raking a hand through his dark blond hair, Kane decided that it was time to go to the two-room apartment he called home and catch a few hours of sleep in a real bed. There was nothing to be gained by staying here, sifting through the same useless data over and over again. He'd had enough of dead ends to last him a lifetime.

As he turned in his swivel chair, Henderson hurried into the conference room that Kane had taken over for the task force. Light brown waves were sloshing dangerously up the sides of his cup as he crossed to Kane's desk. He was waving a sheet of paper in his other hand.

"Hey, Madigan, I think we've got something here."

Kane eyed the sheet of paper in Henderson's hand. "Another kook calling in to say he saw the woman being whisked aboard a spaceship by aliens?"

Henderson shoved the sheet in front of Kane. "No, this one sounds legit." Letting Kane take the page, Henderson straightened and wrinkled his nose. "Hey, when did you last shower?"

Kane rubbed the back of his neck. There were knots there the size of cat's-eye marbles. The captain's couch was not made for sleeping, but private interrogations, he thought.

"I don't know. What century is it?" He picked up the page and scanned it. "Okay, what've you got?"

Henderson took a deep swallow of his coffee.

"Woman on Figueroa Street thinks she recognizes the woman in Noah's sketch." Henderson tapped the page for emphasis. "Says she's a neighbor." He leaned his ample bulk against Kane's desk. "Or was."

Kane raised a brow. "Was?" He didn't care for the past tense being used. That meant the woman was gone.

Henderson nodded. "According to our caller, the woman hasn't been seen for a little over a week." He pitched the empty cup into Kane's wastepaper basket and straightened up. He reached for the sheet. "Want me to give it to Valdez to check out?"

Kane rose, still holding the paper. "No, I'll do it myself."

"Think it might be the one?"

Kane glanced at the sheet. They were due for a break, but he wasn't going to pin his hopes on this one yet. "Right now, I'd trade my soul for a lead."

The laugh was a cross between a blue jay's and a witch's cackle. "You ain't got one, remember? The police department requisitioned it when you signed up."

He was too tired to offer the obligatory smile. "Oh yeah, I forgot."

"I'll be in the squad room if you need me," Henderson told Kane as he left the room.

Kane began to follow the sergeant out, then glanced over his shoulder at the phone. Just the receiver peered out from beneath the stack of papers he had scattered there. He hesitated, wavering. It was against procedure to keep a victim abreast of police activity, but he could see Jennifer, sitting by the telephone. Waiting. He tried not to let that bother him, but it seemed to be a losing battle.

He supposed she deserved to know that he was at least working on it, even if he hadn't really had a break in the case yet. Muttering to himself that he was getting soft in his old age, Kane dug her phone number out of his wallet and tapped the numbers out on the black telephone pad.

When the shrilled ring suddenly cracked the throbbing silence in the room, Jennifer jumped. Julia was in the shower, getting ready to go to the restaurant. She had told

Jennifer to let the answering machine handle any calls that came in.

Jennifer hesitated for a split second before picking up the receiver. She held it in both hands, as if it was a lifeline to her baby. "Hello?"

There was an incredible amount of hope packed into that one word. "Jennifer?" He said her name needlessly. Kane knew it was her.

Finally, she thought, clutching the phone even tighter. "Did you find her, Kane?"

It transformed from a case to his own personal mission with that one sentence. Kane found himself wishing that he had some good news to give her, then damning himself for making the call in the first place.

"No." He could almost see her wilt as he said the word. Kane rubbed his brow, tired. He had to get some sleep before he started really hallucinating. "But we think we might have a lead. A woman called in from Los Angeles She thinks she recognizes the woman in your sketch as a neighbor. I'm on my way to check it out now."

Jennifer snapped to attention. "Can I come along? I'm going crazy, waiting. I can't—"

He blocked out the eagerness in her voice. "Civilians aren't allowed to come along."

She felt like screaming at him. Didn't he understand? "I'm not a civilian, I'm her mother."

The anguish in her voice came across the wires. He thought of just hanging up, but that was the coward's way out. Instead, he attempted to distance himself. "I'm sorry. I'll let you know as soon as I come in."

She nodded, though he couldn't see her. Her voice was dull when she answered. "I understand."

No, no she didn't understand. She didn't understand why she had to be going through this. But it wasn't his fault. She couldn't take this frustration clawing at her out on him.

"I'm sorry," Jennifer began. "It's just that—"

"You don't have to apologize." He moved to hang up the phone, then felt almost compelled to add, "I'll give you a call later."

"Later," she whispered. She hung up the receiver and stared at it, willing time to go by quickly.

There was no answer at the apartment. With Mrs. Meadows, the woman who had placed the call to the precinct standing behind him, Kane knocked on the door several times.

"I know she was there last week," Mrs. Meadows swore. "I talked to her." In her hand she clutched the sketch she had clipped out from the newspaper. "This is her. This is Rosalind Ward. You going to break down the door?" she asked hopefully.

The woman watched too many television shows. "No, I'm going to get the landlord."

"There's Thelma. She collects the rent and acts like a landlady," Mrs. Meadows told him. "Wait, I'll go get her," she volunteered. Her mules slapped sharply along the dank linoleum floor as she scurried off.

Within a few minutes, she was dragging a disgruntled looking woman in her wake. "I tell you, he's a policeman. Here about that woman." Mrs. Meadows turned to Kane. "Tell her."

Kane succinctly informed the other woman why he was here. She studied him skeptically until he showed her his shield. Confronted with authority, Thelma immediately produced her passkey and opened the door.

The stale air within the apartment was oppressive. Thelma moved to open a window as Kane looked around the single-room dwelling. It was a furnished apartment with furniture that barely deserved the title. It was worn and chipped and literally on its last legs. The coffee table was propped up on one end with telephone books. Someone had spilled coffee over the pages. A faded brown line spread out to the floor, pooling on a faded rug beneath it.

"Can't see anyone wanting to live like this," Mrs. Meadows pronounced, crossing her arms before her wide bosom. The words immediately launched her into a heated discussion with Thelma.

Kane tuned them both out as he prowled carefully about the room. Except for the mess, there was no sign of anything personal within the room. He opened the single closet and found it empty.

The woman was gone.

He found a trash can under the small sink in the corner and poked through it gingerly. The women had stopped arguing to watch him. He found several soiled disposable diapers stuffed into it.

Bingo.

He looked toward the women. They had moved from the doorway and were now bracketing him on either side. "Did anyone hear a baby cry in the last couple of days?"

Thelma shook her head, her faded blond hair bouncing about her shoulders.

"Last week I did," Mrs. Meadows announced smugly, as if she had just guessed the winning numbers on the lottery ticket. "At first I thought it was a kitten or some kind of small animal."

She leaned forward toward Kane, as if disclosing a guarded secret. "Animals aren't allowed here." She gave Thelma a sidelong glance that told Kane what Mrs. Meadows thought of that rule. "So I knocked on her door, thinking maybe she didn't know that. I was only being neighborly," she protested as if out of habit.

Probably brought on by a lifetime of being called nosey, Kane thought.

"The noise stopped and then she comes to the door, nice as you please. When I said we couldn't keep pets, she tells me that what I heard was coming from the TV." Mrs. Meadows pulled herself up importantly. "I didn't believe her for a minute." Her eyes narrowed as she looked expectantly at Kane, waiting for praise. "It was the baby I heard, wasn't it?"

When he said nothing, she continued to press. "The one you're looking for?"

"Possibly." Kane slanted a look toward the landlady, who had grown visibly incensed and uncomfortable. "Let's go to your office, ma'am. I need all the information you have on the woman who rented this apartment. Credit check, references, anything.''

The look on the woman's face said that she was resigned to this intrusion. ''Come on, then.'' Thelma turned to lead the way to her office.

Mrs. Meadows trudged right behind them, obviously afraid to relinquish her tiny bit of glory.

Chapter 4

It wasn't in his nature to be hopeful. Hope was something that had long since been effectively siphoned from his life, cut off completely at the source when reality had burst upon him with its sharp, jagged edges at the age of eight.

Eight had been a tender age at which to grow up, but he had. Not instantly. It had been as if a starting gun had gone off, propelling him into a competition he didn't want to take part in. Yet he was forced to run. And he ran well. He ran hard. He won.

That dreary day in May had been the genesis of the man he now was. At eight he'd become a small, abandoned boy, no longer anyone's son. The mother he had adored but who had not adored him had run off, unable to deal with the terminal despair of being married to an abusive husband and of living in a coal-mining town whose horizon was perpetually dark with the dust from the mines. His father, when he was aware of Kane at all, only referred to him as "hey you," or "boy." Never "son," never his name.

Kane had insulated himself to keep from hurting. He had weaned himself from the desire to make contact. To matter to someone. Eventually, all shreds of hope had dissipated with it. He viewed hope as something constructed of spun sugar. It was an elusive substance shimmering on the horizon, without depth, without breadth.

He placed no trust in the word.

But the information he had found in the apartment on Figueroa Street did open up definite possibilities. Now he had something to go on. Finally, after over eleven months of chasing false leads, he had a name and a face. Perhaps soon, he would have more than that. Sometimes, he thought as he walked into the precinct, patience was rewarded. He was going to have Valdez check a few things out for him and then finally go home and see to a few personal needs of his own.

Putting his leaden state temporarily on hold, Kane walked quickly into the room designated as the task force headquarters. And stopped dead.

There was a woman standing by the window. Jennifer. She was looking out, her hands clasped behind her, obviously marking time. Her profile still looked pale, but color seemed to be returning. The straight mint green dress she wore gave no clue to the fact that she had given birth less than three weeks ago.

The overhead lighting was harsh, institutional, filling the room with yellowish white spikes that offset the dreariness of the day. She didn't look as if she belonged in such an austere setting.

Kane cleared his throat as he moved forward. "What are you doing here?"

She turned, startled at the sound of his voice. She tried to smile. "Waiting for you. The captain told me it would be all right."

The captain had one eye on publicity, the other eye on a seat in the legislature. He would agree to anything that would ingratiate him to a possible constituent. Kane draped his jacket over the back of the chair closest to him.

"I thought I told you I'd call when I got back."

She tried not to let the harsh tone he used affect her. It was just his way. "I thought I'd save you the trouble of dialing."

That, and because she was going to go mad if she had to sit by the telephone another hour. She wanted to be at the precinct and hear what he had to say the moment he walked in.

Jennifer looked at his face. Excitement rippled through her like surf rising into a wave. "You found something." It wasn't a question. She could sense it.

He never counted chickens ahead of time, even if their shells were cracking open from within. "It might be nothing," Kane began. He didn't want to raise her expectations falsely.

In the heat of the moment, Jennifer wrapped her fingers around his forearm, as if that would coax the answer from him. "Tell me," she implored.

He motioned her to a seat, but she remained standing next to him. She needed the closeness. When he looked down at his arm, she finally released her hold. Kane looked around the room. They were alone. The others had to be at lunch, he guessed.

"Do you want any coffee?"

He was stalling. Why? Didn't he think she had a right to know what was happening? She wasn't asking to be privy to secrets. This was about her daughter.

"I don't want coffee," she said impatiently. Jennifer pressed her fingers against her lips and took a breath, regaining control. "Did you find her? Did you find the woman?"

He thought of the airless, stale apartment and the type of person who could live that way. The woman had to be eccentric. But to what degree? And where was she now? "Maybe."

Wouldn't he allow himself to be pinned down on anything? "What does that mean?"

"It means that we had a positive identification from both a neighbor and the landlady."

"Had." She heard the unspoken word in his voice. Something was wrong. "But?"

He shrugged. It felt like such a helpless gesture. Kane wasn't accustomed to feeling helpless. At least not anymore. "She's gone."

Gone. With her baby. The frustration within her threatened to boil over like a pot left on too long. Jennifer sagged visibly in front of him.

Afraid that she was going to faint, Kane grabbed her, jerking Jennifer against him to keep her from falling. The contact had been completely unexpected, as was the quick flash of a powerful undercurrent that sliced through him with the suddenness of an electric shock.

Dazed, Jennifer slowly shook her head. "No, I'm all right, really." The words dripped from her lips as she looked up at him.

Kane released her, a little shaken by what had just transpired. For him, it defied immediate identification.

Drawing a breath, Jennifer steadied herself. "What are you going to do now?"

Kane wasn't accustomed to being questioned. Even his superiors had learned how to phrase inquiries so that they seemed more like casual conversation. Kane resisted the temptation to remain closemouthed. He was better at doing that than at talking. But she was entitled to something, however slim.

"I've got a name and some past addresses which may or may not be genuine." Kane saw the spark of hope flare in her eyes. It coaxed more words from him, against his better judgment. "I'm going to run her name through the police computers and the Department of Motor Vehicles in Sacramento, see if we get a match." It was probably an alias, but it was all he had at the moment. Sometimes people got sloppy or too confident. Maybe this was one of those times. "If we're lucky, she has priors, or at least parking violations."

Kane stepped out of his office. The squad room was just beyond his door. A handful of men were scattered about, some booking suspects, others on the phone.

"Valdez." A young man, with dark hair pulled back in a snub of a ponytail, rose in answer to his name. Kane waved him over and handed him the paper with Rosalind's name on it. "Run this through for me, will you? See if any of the other states have anything on her. And I mean *anything*."

The tall man flashed a quick grin as he allowed his eyes to slowly slide down the length of Jennifer's body. "Sure thing. How fast do you want it?"

"Yesterday."

Valdez gave him a two-fingered salute. "I'll see what I can do."

Kane turned from the doorway to see Jennifer looking at him. She had that damn hopeful look in her eyes. "There's something else."

His expression, his voice, his body language, nothing about him gave her a clue whether it was something good or bad. Unconsciously, she held her breath. "Yes?"

"The woman who called the precinct swears she heard a baby crying last week." He saw the expression on Jennifer's face freeze and something twisted inside him, hurting with her. Except that wasn't possible for him, he thought abruptly. "And I found diapers in the garbage, along with this." He fished the crumpled page from the pocket of his windbreaker. It had fallen behind the trash basket and he had only seen it after he looked through the apartment again.

He smoothed the page out on the desk. It was a single sheet from a Las Vegas newspaper, dated over a month ago. It was obvious that something had been wrapped in it. What, he had no idea. Maybe the lab would come up with something.

Jennifer glanced at the map on the wall with its single pushpin in Nevada. "She might have been there when the other baby was kidnapped."

Kane lifted a shoulder and let it drop. He didn't want to assign too great an importance to the discovery just yet. "Or it might not mean anything at all. Maybe someone wrapped something in it and mailed it to her."

She knew he was right in proceeding cautiously, but it irritated her. She couldn't curb her own desire to run with any scrap they found. "Are you always this cautious?"

He had learned the hard way. "It doesn't pay to jump the gun."

She looked behind her at the map again. Tiny pins for tiny souls that were lost. Would her tiny soul ever be found? Oh God, she had to be. "A little bit of hope is better than nothing."

The sun had finally come out. Without realizing it, Kane watched as a ray seeped into the room. It seemed to outline her body as Jennifer stood near the window. "All depends on your point of view."

His comment made her turn around and look at him for the first time as someone other than just the police detective assigned to her case. Forcing herself to set aside her own anguish for a moment, Jennifer looked into his eyes. They were blue, like her baby's. They were also flat, unfathomable. Distant. Had he always been like that? Or was it something that had happened to him because of the nature of his work? She found herself suddenly wanting to know.

"What other view is there?" she asked.

The thin smile on his lips did not reach his eyes. It was almost self-mocking as he remembered all too clearly.

"Hope can tease you and then torture you when it turns up empty." He had hoped for a full year that his mother would return. He'd hoped longer than that that he could somehow win his father's respect. His father's love. Neither had happened.

To her, hope represented life. She shook her head at his words. "Anything is better than feeling this way. Hopeless. Dead from the inside out, like a shell." The sensation was totally foreign to anything she had ever felt. She took a step toward him, her eyes locking with his. "I've got to believe we're going to find her."

He could almost feel the emotion pulsating within her. Hope. They were as different as the south sea summer breeze was from the Arctic winter wind. He raised and lowered his shoulders indifferently. To each his own. He didn't believe in shams.

"Whatever sees you through the night."

She couldn't believe he was as distant, as disinterested as he seemed. He wouldn't have taken down the decorations in her living room without being asked, if he had no heart.

She looked around. "Can I wait?"

He wasn't certain if he understood her question. "You mean here?"

She nodded. "Yes." The conference room was austere and there was something almost chilling about the map on the wall, but being here was preferable to sitting in her nice, comfortable home, slowly going crazy.

"Wait for what?"

She gestured toward the door, where Valdez had disappeared. "For whatever results your computer search has."

The precinct had a high density of criminal traffic. It wasn't the place for a distraught woman. "We're really not set up for—" The silent plea in her eyes stopped him. He started to reach toward his breast pocket, and stopped. Curling his fingers, he shoved his hand into his jeans. "All right, I guess it can't do any harm."

A noise from behind him made Kane turn around. Back from lunch, Henderson peered into the room. "Hey, I thought you were going to go home and shower." The fleshy face dissolved into a smile as he recognized Jennifer.

Kane glanced over his shoulder toward Jennifer. "Something came up."

The smile became wider as Henderson crossed to Jennifer. "So I see."

Kane merely grunted a response as he pulled out a worn notebook from his back pocket.

Jennifer responded to the warmth in the man's expression. "Hello, Sergeant."

Henderson took her hand and coated it with both his own. "How are you doing?"

She slanted a look at Kane. "That all depends on what Kane finds out."

Henderson lifted one eyebrow speculatively as he released her hand. "You know, Detective, I forgot you had a first name."

Kane was jotting down thoughts in a notebook already crammed with notes. He glanced up in Henderson's direction. "Yeah. It's 'sir.'"

Henderson did an elaborate bow before turning his attention to Jennifer again. "He get you some coffee yet?" He indicated Kane with a nod.

She shook her head. "No." The sergeant took a step toward the doorway. She saw the frown crease Kane's lips. She didn't want to do anything that might make him ask her to leave. It was important to her to be here, close to the hub. "No, really, I don't want any. I don't want to be any trouble."

"No trouble. Be back in a minute. The coffee's not much, but it keeps us going." He hurried out.

She laced her fingers together before her. She felt awkward standing in the room, as unwanted as a stick in the path of a lawn mower, but she couldn't go home. "I didn't know you had a sense of humor."

Kane raised his eyes to her as he finished writing his notes. "I don't."

She blew out a breath. So much for that. "Is he your partner? The sergeant, I mean," she added when Kane made no answer.

"No." He slipped the notebook into his back pocket again. "Just one of the men assigned to the case with me."

There were five in all, counting himself. He never put himself above the other men, nor with them. Just apart, even though the captain had placed him in charge.

There was a great deal that went unspoken in his response. No, he wouldn't have partners, she thought, studying him. He was a loner, someone who didn't share his thoughts unless forced to do so and who metered out his words sparingly. A partner would have intruded on his self-communion. She wondered if he ever got lonely and what it had to be like to be so self-contained. She had always been part of a family, her life entangled indelibly with theirs for as long as she could remember. She would have hated to have had it any other way.

He was aware that she was studying him. She had crept up out of the corners of his mind more than once in the last two weeks. And she was partially to blame for his dogged approach to the case. It was her eyes. When he closed his own, her eyes haunted him. It was the faith he saw there more than the despair that did it. The woman didn't know better than to trust him, he thought.

He in turn trusted no one. No one ever measured up to the faith placed in them anyway. But the fact that she had placed hers in him brought with it obligations. Even if he didn't want them, he had to try to live up to them as best he knew how. It was his way.

Kane knew Jennifer was only trying to make conversation to take the edge off the fact that they were both waiting for Valdez to return with some sort of positive word. Kane wasn't very good at making conversation. He saw it as a waste of time. Still, something compelled him to make the effort.

"So, how have you been holding up?"

He had seen her on the eleven o'clock news the first night after the abduction. She had looked pale and worn. There was a little color in her cheeks now. He wondered if it was real or due to the wizardry of cosmetics. For a moment, he was tempted to brush his thumb along the curve of her cheek, just to see if the color came off. And to see if her skin felt as delicate as it looked.

Jennifer felt warmed by his question. Silence made her uneasy. "Well enough, I guess, now that I'm here."

He looked around. There wasn't anything to offer comfort as far as he could see. "What does being here have to do with it?"

She gestured about the room. "At home I feel too isolated. There's nothing to do but think. And worry. Julia and Nik won't let me do anything. Not that I probably could if I tried. Being here makes me feel that somehow, something'll happen to end this." Her nerves felt like a wire stretched as far as it could go across the bridge of a violin. Any further and she would snap.

He didn't want her harboring any false hopes. Valdez could return at any moment and tell him they had come up empty. "This is a police precinct, Jennifer, not a television studio."

"Are you telling me that there's no hope?" They had a name, a lead, how could he think that way?

Kane realized he was steeling himself off against the time that he might have to tell Jennifer that they couldn't locate her baby. Despite all the safeguards he was taking, he knew that saying it would hurt him almost as much as it would her.

"No, I'm telling you that there are no guarantees. I don't wrap this up in fifty-nine minutes, minus commercials." His frustration mounted. "We've got more unsolved crimes than solved ones in our files—"

Kane passed a hand over his face, attempting to pull himself together. She didn't deserve to have him taking out his frustration on her.

"Look, I've had next to no sleep these past two weeks, lived on that motor oil that passes for coffee in this place and I'm a little fuzzy around the edges. I didn't mean to say what I just said."

His apology had her tucking away her own frayed temper. "You're only being honest."

Her response made him feel worse. Was she always this forgiving? he wondered. "I'm being a horse's rear," he snapped. Kane blew out a cleansing breath. "Lack of sleep tends to do that to me."

She leaned against the scarred conference table. "Maybe you should go home and I should stay."

Kane laughed, a little of his self-imposed tension abating. "After we get some word from Valdez, we'll both go home. Deal?"

She didn't want to go home. She wanted to go with him, to follow up any lead, talk to anyone who might be able to shed some light. But she put off saying anything for the time being.

"Deal." Jennifer placed her hand in his. As her fingers slid against his, the warmth of flesh touching flesh generated something between them. A feeling neither quite understood.

He had the impression, just for the briefest of moments, of really making contact. Of coming home.

It was absurd, he thought.

His lack of sleep was apparently getting to him more than he had anticipated. He'd be lucky not to crash into anything while driving to his apartment.

There had been something there, just for a second, something she couldn't identify. A sensation. A feeling that told her she was safe. That everything was somehow going to be all right.

They looked at one another for a long moment, their hands joined.

Valdez hurried into the room, bringing an air of charged enthusiasm with him. Kane and Jennifer moved apart, dropping their hands self-consciously to their sides. If Valdez noticed, he made no sign.

"Detective, look at what just came in on the fax." He waved a sheaf of papers in the air, then placed them on the table. He smoothed out the first sheet, beaming as if he had written it up himself.

"What is it?" Jennifer asked before Kane could say anything.

"A list of priors," Valdez explained to her importantly. "From Phoenix." He verbally handed her the first salvo and watched her face. "Rosalind Ward was arrested for kidnapping ten years ago."

Jennifer exchanged glances with Kane. This was it.

"She was never convicted," Kane read from the paper before him. Removing the first sheet, he looked down at the facsimile that had come in with the report. A ten-year-old mug shot.

"That's her," Jennifer cried out. Excitement filled her throat so that she could barely speak. "That's the nurse who was in my room."

"And we have a winner," Kane murmured under his breath. "Good work, Valdez."

The younger man looked surprised at the careless praise sent his way. On a roll, he pointed to the next sheet.

"Our suspect doesn't drive all that hot, either. I checked with the DMV like you said and Sacramento sent us a copy of her registration. She drives an '82 Corolla. Here's the license number." He pointed it out for Jennifer's benefit. "And here's the printout of her traffic violations. All unpaid." He handed the sheet to Kane. The list was extensive, dating back over two years. The last year was the time frame they needed. "Kind of takes your breath away, doesn't it?"

"Do we have a set of prints yet?" Kane wanted to know.

"Ask and ye shall receive." Valdez shuffled through the papers and produced the final sheet. "Courtesy of the Phoenix Police Department."

"Just like Christmas," Kane muttered, scanning all the pages again. He stacked them together and placed them into a brown folder. "See if you can get Arizona or Nevada to come up with any traffic violations. It might help give us more of an idea as to her whereabouts." He turned to look at the map. "I'm betting that she was in Nevada six weeks ago." Jennifer looked at him quizzically. He tapped a yellow pin. "That's when the Sanchez baby disappeared from County General."

Jennifer looked at the pins scattered so colorfully on the map, each representing a tragedy. "You think one woman's responsible for all those abductions?" It seemed almost incredible.

He looked at her. She wouldn't begin to know about the seamier side of life. Her kind was too trusting to understand what motivated people like this. "It's highly possible that's how they operate."

Jennifer stared at the pins. "But how?"

And what would make a person do something so horrendous? How could people live with themselves knowing they had generated so much grief, so much heartache?

"Apparently easily. She does what she's good at. She's undoubtedly connected to an organization. They sell the infants to couples so desperate, they don't care where their baby comes from. Or, maybe it's even some unsuspecting couple who think they're just conducting a private adoption. 'Fees' cross hands, probably cash. No paper trail is generated for us to follow.''

He was doing it again, she thought, stealing her slender threads of hope from her, cutting them free of the parachute that could land her safely to the ground. "But then how—?''

Something forced him to hand her a lifeline back to the nebulous world of expectations. "The 'how' is what they pay me for.''

She knew she should be satisfied with that and just let it go. But she was greedy. "What's your next move?''

She was crowding him. He reacted before he thought. "I'm going to have some food that doesn't come in a disposable container, get a shower before they move my desk into the parking lot.'' He thought of the leather sofa in the captain's office. "And get maybe two or three hours' sleep on a flat surface I don't stick to.''

He looked worn. She realized that she was pushing too hard. He was, after all, human. He just didn't act that way. "I can take care of the food part.''

He checked the folder. He'd take it with him and look things over when he was more alert. Maybe there was something else that he could work with. "That's all right, I tend to my own needs.''

She knew he'd say that. But she wanted to make amends. "Please? You can eat at our restaurant.'' Her eyes indicated the folder in his hand. "Maybe I can help you with that.''

He had already let her intrude as far as he was going to. "You're not on the payroll.''

His stern voice didn't put her off. She raised her chin stubbornly. "My stakes are higher than a paycheck, remember?''

He supposed it wouldn't hurt him to have a decent meal. He remembered his refrigerator was almost empty except for a few vegetables that were probably on their way to becoming penicillin. "Where is this restaurant?''

"On Pacific Coast Highway. Not too far from here," she added quickly when she saw the beginnings of a demur on his lips.

It was a small world, he mused. "I live on Balboa Island."

"Then it's on the way." She wanted to crack his exterior wall. To get to the point where he would share things with her immediately. Somehow, she didn't know just how yet, she wanted to be included in this investigation. She couldn't remain on the sidelines any longer just watching her fingernails grow.

He let out a breath, debating the wisdom of his decision. He was violating his own rule about not getting any closer to a victim than learning their name, rank and serial number, but maybe it would be all right, this one time. After all, it was only food.

"Okay." He picked up his windbreaker from the back of the chair and shrugged into it. The navy material covered his shoulder holster. "Give me the address."

Jennifer recited it for him.

Kane motioned her out the door. "You lead," he instructed. "I'll follow in my car." He picked up the folder from the table and walked to the door. Henderson was just entering with Jennifer's coffee. In rapid fire, Kane gave him a list of things he wanted taken care of. "I'll be back at five," he told him.

"What about the coffee?" Henderson lifted the cup slightly in the air.

"Drink it," Kane answered.

Henderson only grinned as he watched Kane and Jennifer leave the building.

Chapter 5

Kane drove up behind Jennifer's blue Volvo and then parked next to it in the lot surrounding the restaurant. He got out and looked at the restaurant's stone-and-wood exterior. Sinclair's resembled a medieval cottage, lifted intact from the Irish countryside. It was nestled between two huge Ficus benjamina trees that stood like sentries on either side of it, their shaggy green heads held up proudly. Located on a corner lot, it was strategically positioned so that it caught the eye of everyone turning either right or left onto Pacific Coast Highway.

Jennifer joined him as he stood appraising the quaint building. Kane had no doubt that the restaurant did a fair amount of business. It wasn't noon yet and the lot was half-filled. He glanced at the make and models of the cars parked around his. They made his own look like a poor relation. The restaurant apparently attracted a moneyed clientele.

"You've done well for yourself," he observed.

Kane didn't seem inclined to enter the restaurant immediately, so Jennifer remained where she was. "It's not just mine. It belongs to all three of us. I was brought in full-time last year when the catering business began to really take off. Up until then, I just helped out when things got hectic.''

And that was how, she thought, she had met Brad. But she refrained from saying it aloud.

There was a tinge of pride in her voice that she didn't bother to disguise as she continued. ''Nik supervises the cooking. Julia acts as hostess and keeps the books.''

Kane turned to look at her. ''And what do you do?''

''A little of all three.'' She smiled a bit ruefully. ''I'm a jack-of-all-trades, I guess.'' She was neither an artiste in the kitchen, the way Nik was, nor a whiz at accounts, like Julia. But she tried her best and she did enjoy being in business with her family.

For a moment, Kane watched, distracted, as the breeze flirted with the ends of her hair, rippling through them, stirring them. Stirring him.

He wondered if lack of sleep had him hallucinating. He saw no other reason for his reaction. Catching his thoughts before they wandered too far off course, he looked down at his rumpled clothing. He definitely wasn't dressed for anything fancier than a drive through.

Kane glanced at his car. ''Maybe I'd better not—''

Jennifer second guessed the remainder of his statement. She wanted him to stay. Needed him to stay right now. She wanted a chance to talk to him away from the precinct, to find an opening to plead her case.

Jennifer threaded her arm through his. ''The lighting's dim inside. No one'll notice,'' she promised.

Against his better judgment, he allowed her to draw him through the heavy green door.

She was right. It was dim inside. Dim and somehow intimate, despite the fact that he could see other patrons scattered about the dining room. It was a place to bring someone you cared about. Someone you wanted to spend hours talking to. This wasn't the kind of place for a dead-tired police detective to grab a bite to eat before collapsing in his bed.

Kane looked doubtfully at Jennifer, but Julia was already hurrying across the highly buffed hardwood floor, her heels beating out a rhythmic tattoo like well-coated mallets across the slates of a wooden marimba.

Julia's alert eyes darted from one face to the other, attempting to fathom expressions. They settled on Jennifer.

"Jen, is anything wrong?" It seemed like a ridiculous thing to ask, in light of the last two weeks. "I mean—" Julia turned to Kane, her countenance a masterpiece of suspended hope "—have you found her?"

Kane merely shook his head.

He didn't belong here. He was used to a dimly lit bar where he could quietly nurse a drink and listen to a jukebox loaded with scratchy forty-fives play bluesy music throughout the evening. No one spoke. No one cared. Here, the dim setting evoked another set of emotions. It wasn't impersonal, the way the dimness in the bar was. It asked too much of him. It asked for intimacy and he instinctively retreated.

"No," Jennifer said. "But Kane's found the apartment where the woman was staying. Someone said they heard a baby crying there last week." Jennifer's voice rose with hope that was bursting to be set free. Hope mixed with gratitude. "He has the woman's name and—"

"Wait." Julia held up her hand to stop any further flow of information. "Nik's going to want to hear this." She grabbed Jennifer's hand, then turned and looked over her shoulder to see if Kane was following. He hadn't moved. "You too, Detective. Follow me."

It was either that, or take root on the Oriental rug spread out before the front door.

"She always pushy like this?" he asked Jennifer, nodding toward Julia as he caught up.

There had been a time when Julia's manner had grated on her. But that was far in the past. Now Jennifer just accepted it as Julia being Julia. "It's never been any other way."

"You have my sympathy," he muttered.

Julia ignored the comment as she led them through the dining room. The soft buzz of voices mingled with the clink of glasses and the sound of cutlery moving across fine china plates. Palm out, Julia pushed the swinging door that divided the kitchen from the outer room. The noise and heat immediately increased twofold.

Julia looked around. Then, like a magnet in search of an iron filing, she honed in on the tall, brawny man in the center of the busy kitchen. "Nik."

Nikolas Sinclair was intent on delicately filleting salmon for the elaborate meal requested by table seven. He looked up at the sound of Julia's voice. Concentration broke, giving way to surprise and concern when he saw that Julia was accompanied by Jennifer and a somber, hard-looking man. He abandoned his work on the huge butcher-block table and crossed to Julia and the others.

His deep green eyes swept from Jennifer toward Kane and rested there with an unspoken question.

When her parents had died within seven months of each other, Jennifer had been fifteen and Julia sixteen. Nik had just barely turned twenty-one. He had taken over the job of being both mother and father as well as provider for his two younger sisters. Years of putting his own life on hold gave him the right to critically appraise anyone who entered his sisters' lives.

"Nik—" Jennifer placed a hand on her brother's arm "—this is Detective Kane Madigan."

At the mention of Kane's name, recognition set in. Nik flashed a welcoming smile that transformed his expression from one of austerity to one invitingly warm and friendly. Nik wiped a damp hand on the half apron that was loosely cinched about his waist and grasped Kane's hand before the latter had a chance to extend it.

Nik pumped the detective's hand, his eyes searching Kane's face. "Is there any news?"

Kane met the probing gaze with his own. When Nik didn't look away, Kane decided that, for the moment, he liked what he saw. He always reserved final judgment for later, when more chips were played. "Some."

Nik turned to Jennifer, waiting for her to elaborate on the singularly noncommunicative response.

"Kane thinks they know the woman who kidnapped Katie." Her voice overflowed with excitement.

"Wonderful." Nik, still holding Kane's hand firmly in his own, pumped it again in congratulations. "Have you arrested her?"

Kane extricated himself before his fingers went numb. "No."

"No?" Nik echoed incredulously. "Why not?" The demand was impatient.

By now, they had drawn a crowd from the kitchen crew and Kane looked toward the swinging door, contemplating his exit. He didn't care to be the center of attention.

There was a sudden lump in Jennifer's throat. She had thought that she had cried all the tears that she could. But she was wrong. She swallowed, determined not to cry in front of these people who knew her.

"Detective Madigan said the woman fled. With Katie," she added.

Nik draped a protective arm around Jennifer's shoulders, hugging her to him. The reward he had offered was obviously not doing the trick. Maybe he'd hire a detective of his own, he thought.

He looked pointedly at Kane. "Don't worry, Jenny, they'll find her." The words were almost a mandate.

A murmur of agreement from the people around them echoed Nik's sentiment.

It seemed to Kane that everyone had a hell of a lot more faith in his abilities than he had at this moment. He wanted to tell all of them to wake up to the reality of the situation. But somehow, it would have been tantamount to telling an orphanage full of six-year-olds that no one would ever adopt them. He just couldn't make himself do it.

So he went along with it, for the moment. Maybe things would work themselves out.

"Possibilities are stronger now than they were before," was all he would commit himself to.

Even that was more than he was really willing to say. More than he would have said if Jennifer hadn't looked up at him like that, her unshed tears shining in her eyes like dew drops on the petals of a wildflower.

He didn't look like the type who socialized easily, Nik thought, studying the expression on Kane's face. He wondered if the man looked uncomfortable for any other reason. "So, what brings you here, Detective Madigan?"

"He hasn't eaten in three days," Jennifer answered for him, grateful for the shift in topic. She needed a moment to regain control of her overwrought emotions. These were the people she knew and worked with. She didn't want to go to pieces in front of them.

Now they were in his home territory. Nik grinned. "Well, then by all means, we'll feed you," Nik said enthusiastically.

She made him sound like a stray she had brought in out of the rain, Kane thought, annoyed. He would have been better off grabbing a sandwich from the local convenience store in his neighborhood.

Nik produced a large, green-covered menu and presented it to Kane. "Anything you want. It's on the house. Back to work, everyone. There are people going hungry out there." He turned to Julia. "Julia, seat them in the booth in the back. It's private."

Julia was already leading them out. "I know my job, Nik," she answered sweetly, an exaggerated smile lifting the corners of her generous mouth.

"Then do it." Nik gestured toward the swinging door. "And get out of my kitchen."

"*Our* kitchen," Julia tossed over her shoulder as she pushed open the door.

"Right." Nik picked up his knife and returned to delicately separating the salmon from a myriad of minute bones. "If I let you cook, the fire department would be here for the first course."

Julia muttered something unintelligible under her breath as she continued walking.

"Maybe you people should forget about serving dinner and just charge admission for the floor show," Kane said to Jennifer as they returned to the dining room.

Jennifer was used to this. She knew there was nothing but affection beneath the peppery words her brother and sister exchanged with regularity. "Don't mind Nik, he tends to get a little testy on Fridays."

Julia stopped by the curved booth and waited for them to be seated. "Not to mention Mondays, Tuesdays, Wednesdays, and all the other days of the week," Julia added cheerfully. About to take their order, the intrusion of a shaft of sunlight suddenly streaking across the floor had her looking toward the front entrance. A couple was just entering the restaurant. "I'll be back in a minute to get your order."

"That's okay," Jennifer told her. "I can have Patrice or one of the other waitresses take it." Jennifer turned to Kane and noticed he was fumbling with his breast pocket, before dropping his hand. A frown creased his face like a dark flash of lightning across the sky. "Something wrong?"

Something was wrong, all right. He felt nerves tightening like a wet leather thong left out in the sun. "Yeah, I quit smoking." Right about now, he would kill for a cigarette.

Sinclair's had a no smoking policy, but she wasn't about to mention that. She had a feeling that, policeman or not, Kane Madigan was a maverick who didn't always stick to the rules. "It's not a good habit."

He shrugged. "Everybody's got to have a vice." And at the moment, he sorely wished he still had his.

Being here, with her family and on her home ground, made him feel restive somehow, as if he were supposed to juggle a dozen eggs before an audience and he didn't know how to juggle. He didn't belong in quiet, nice places like this. He belonged in squad rooms, on stakeouts, dealing with the misfits of society and clearing them away for the likes of people such as Jennifer and her family. That was what he was good at. Making busts, being a detective, not making small talk in a dimly lit restaurant, sitting across from a woman who looked as if only good, clean things should be happening to her for the rest of her days.

"Maybe you're right," she agreed. He looked suddenly so uncomfortable, she tried to think of something that might put him at ease. He was at his best talking about work, and after all, that was what was keeping them together. "What was on that paper?"

He was trying to make out the words over the coat of arms that hung on the rear wall. Her question caught him unprepared. "What paper?"

"The one the policeman handed you just before we left the precinct." She tried to remember the man's name. "Valdez, I think you called him."

"Oh, that."

He hadn't forgotten. He had stuffed it into his pocket, intending to look it over when he was by himself. He was about to say as much, but she was looking at him with those eyes of hers, waiting for him to divulge another piece of the puzzle. With a sigh, Kane shifted in the booth and pulled out the folded sheet from the pocket in his jeans.

Jennifer moved closer to him in the booth in order to read it with him. The chunky, mint green candle flickered in its glass bowl. Her hair, streaming down her shoulders like liquid black gold, brushed against his arm. The barest flash of an urge zipped through him, reminding him that he wasn't a machine, but a man, with a man's urges, however ignored they tended to be.

He moved his arm away and looked down at the paper on the table. Clearing his throat, he tried to focus his mind on the case.

"This is a printout of traffic violations in other states," he read and them smiled to himself. He was on target again. It felt good. "Looks like we were right. Our suspect's traveling between states." He pointed to the top of the page. "This has her in Arizona over two months ago." He shifted to the middle of the sheet. "And in Nevada six weeks ago." He carefully folded the paper in fourths. "Both violations occurred around the same time the abductions took place."

Jennifer clapped her hands together as if to contain the spiraling excitement she felt coursing through her. "Looks like your theory about Rosalind stealing those babies was right."

It looked that way, but he had learned that puzzle pieces could be deceiving. Sometimes they could fit together in two entirely different ways.

"Working theory," Kane reminded her, slipping the sheet into his pocket.

He was being cautious again and she didn't want to be. She wanted to run with something, to make it finally happen. To hold her baby again in her arms.

"Don't you ever have an urge to commit to anything?" she asked impatiently as she looked at him.

"Sometimes." The word had dripped from his lips unintentionally, propelled by a fragment of a memory from his past, when longings had still been alive and fresh. He didn't have longings anymore. He just existed. But that was enough for him. At least that's what he had gotten himself to believe. "But I don't pay attention to it."

She shifted in her seat, realizing that she was sitting closer to him than she had intended. The contact made her a little uneasy, as if she were in the presence of an animal that hadn't quite been domesticated yet.

"Why?" She would have thought that a policeman had to commit to things, concepts like honor and truth, and simple things like plans of action. She didn't understand what he was saying to her, only that it went deeper than what they were talking about.

"It might be wrong." He drew a breath, consciously separating himself from the situation. He was best when he looked at things from a distance. And he wanted to keep his distance from her. "The theory might be wrong," he explained more easily. "Never pays to put all your eggs in a single basket unless you're looking for an omelet."

Maybe it was the restaurant, she thought. "Now you sound like Nik."

He looked past her shoulder toward the swinging door that hid the kitchen. The only men he knew who cooked for a living were short-order cooks in fast-food places. Nik Sinclair didn't remind Kane of any of them. "Food the only thing he talks about?"

She toyed with her water glass, watching the way the light from the candle danced across the ice. "The only thing he talks about passionately."

Was she trying to equate them? "I didn't know I was being passionate."

She tilted her head slightly as she reflected on the conversation. "You weren't. Exactly," she added with a smile. "You were being passionate about not being passionate."

He choked off a laugh. "That kind of double-talk could qualify you to be a public defender."

She laughed then. It was the first time he had heard the sound. It surprised them both. She'd been so wrapped up in the depth of her tragedy, she had forgotten she could laugh. It felt good, even for the briefest of moments.

Kane was taken by the musical cadence the sound of her laughter possessed. It was like listening to distant church bells in West Virginia, ringing on Christmas morning.

Jennifer refocused on the topic. "So, if your 'working theory' looks good, how do you 'work' on it?"

Her constant digging annoyed him, but the relentless tenacity she displayed won his grudging respect at the same time. He leaned back, stretching his long legs out beneath him. He was careful not to touch her.

"We've already placed an all points bulletin out on her." He thought of the sheet in his pocket. "Since she seems to have such a rotten driving record, it shouldn't be too long before we catch up to her."

Oh God, she hoped so. "But will she still have my baby?"

For just an instant, he almost lied and said probably. But he couldn't bring himself to go against a lifetime of training. "I don't know. If it's soon, the possibility might exist that—"

The shadow falling over the table had Kane looking up. Julia had returned. Saved by the hostess, he thought.

"Sorry that took so long," she apologized. She looked at Kane. "So, what can I get you?"

An escape route, Kane thought. He handed the menu to her. He hadn't even bothered to open it. "A club sandwich."

Julia smiled and shook her head as she accepted the menu. She could just hear what Nik would have to say about that. "There isn't one on the menu, but I'll see what we can turn up in the kitchen." She looked at her sister. "Jen?"

Jennifer shook her head. "Just a cup of coffee."

Since Jennifer had returned from the hospital, she hadn't consumed enough to keep a parakeet thriving. Julia was getting seriously concerned, though she attempted to mask it.

"Jen, you have to eat." Julia saw the expression on Jennifer's face and retreated. Jennifer wasn't in the mood to be bullied, even for her own good. Julia let out a dramatic breath. "You two are going to give Nik a complex. Don't blame me if he sends out something entirely different to your table."

Kane glanced at Jennifer. Agreeing to come here with her had not been one of his better ideas. It generated other ideas that had absolutely no place in his life, certainly not in this case. "Make that to go, will you?"

His request had Julia stopping in her tracks and slowly turning around. "To go?" she echoed. People didn't get food to go at Sinclair's. They sat and enjoyed their meal and the quiet ambience. That was what the family prided itself on.

Julia watched as he took out his wallet. "To go it is, but I'm not responsible for the words that'll be flooding out of the kitchen." She waved a dismissive hand at his wallet. "Put that away, Detective." She saw the suspicious look enter his eyes. This was not a man who trusted easily, she thought. "Your money isn't any good here."

He tossed a five-dollar bill on the table. "I always pay my own way."

Julia looked about as she cocked her head. "Don't look now, but I think I hear the 'Dragnet' theme in the background." Her voice softened. "No one's going to accuse you of accepting a bribe." She folded the bill and handed it back to him. There was no arguing with her. "No one'll ever know. Certainly Nik isn't going to admit he actually made you a sandwich.'' She looked at both of them. ''Want a bit of advice?''

''No,'' Jennifer answered before Kane had a chance to say the word.

''Well, you're getting it anyway. Eat something so that you have the strength to go on with this investigation. The two of you look as if you're going to keel over any second.''

Five minutes later, they were both back in the parking lot. Kane deposited an incredibly thick sandwich wrapped in foil on the passenger side of his car. It reminded him of something a cartoon character would fix for himself. Kane wondered if his mouth could open wide enough to accommodate it if he tried to take a bite of it intact.

He looked at Jennifer over the roof of her car while she unlocked her door. ''Your sister made it sound as if she thinks you're part of the ongoing investigation.''

Here it came. Jennifer drew herself up, braced. ''I am.''

His eyes turned dark and flat. ''Jennifer, get this straight. I'm the detective and you, unfortunately, are the victim. I 'detect.'''

The definition wasn't enough for her. ''I don't 'victim' very well.'' She came around the hood of her car to face him. ''Kane, I *need* to be part of this. I need to know everything you know, when you know it. I need to help.''

Well, she had a right to talk all she wanted about it. But he didn't have to listen, or be talked into anything. He slid behind the wheel. ''I'll get back to you.'' He started the car, one hand on the sandwich to keep it from landing on the floor.

''Yes,'' Jennifer promised softly as she watched the car pull out of the lot. ''You will.''

With a sigh, she got into her own car and turned on the ignition. She was going to return home to take care of a couple of things. She had absolutely no intention of remaining on the sidelines and sitting this out, no matter what the rules said.

Somehow, she swore to herself, she was going to make him understand that.

* * *

When Kane returned to the police station four hours later, he was not anywhere as rested as he had hoped to be. He'd fallen asleep the minute he'd lain down, but dreams kept haunting him. Bits and pieces of his own childhood somehow dovetailed with the case and he'd woken up more tired than when he had gone to sleep.

The shower had been sufficiently cold to bring him around enough to get back to work. Kane had left a score of instructions in his wake when he had walked out of the precinct. As soon as he returned, he began assembling the information that had come in during his absence.

"Jones and O'Riley got lucky," Henderson told Kane as he stepped into the conference room. "They showed the suspect's photo around Queen of Angels Hospital. One of the orderlies recognized her."

Kane wasn't jumping for joy yet. "It's an old photo. Is he sure?"

Henderson nodded his head. It reminded Kane of an apple bobbing in a tub of water.

"He's sure." The look on Henderson's face was one of confidence, like a man holding all the winning cards in his hand. "Said he remembered her because she had this funny nervous habit. She kept shaking her hand as if there was something in it." He made a move imitating a mobster he had seen in an old gangster movie during a late stakeout. "You know, like a marble or coins. Guy thought it was kind of weird."

Kane wondered if it was a nervous habit, or if the orderly had gotten confused. "Can he pin down the date he saw her to something? The day the—" Kane looked at the chart on the wall, locating Queen of Angels Hospital "—Wells baby was stolen?"

Some of the luster left Henderson's smile. "He's not sure. But it was a positive ID."

"Close enough." Kane made a note to cross-check dates against the various DMV violations.

"Hey Madigan, we're in business!" Valdez yelled to him before he had a chance to enter the room. "A black-and-white just saw our suspect on I5. They chased her, but she lost them." He placed the report into Kane's hands. "They're pretty steamed."

That made twice she had barely eluded them. He hoped it wasn't going to become a habit. "That makes three of us. Which way was she heading?"

Valdez pointed to the bottom of the sheet. "East. Bailey said he did some background on her like you requested. The Ward woman grew up in Arizona. Could be she's heading for home."

Kane nodded. "It's a definite possibility." It was time to go into action. "Get me on the first flight to Phoenix out of John Wayne Airport and tell the Phoenix PD why I'm coming. I'm going to need help. We might be getting hot."

"Madigan." Henderson tapped him on the shoulder. When Kane looked at him, the older man jerked a thumb toward the doorway. "You've got company."

Annoyance drummed angry little fingers through him. He didn't have time to talk to anyone who wasn't directly involved in the baby-nappings. Biting off an oath, Kane turned toward the doorway.

"Tell them that I'm—"

Kane's sentence trailed off. Jennifer was standing in the doorway.

Chapter 6

How long had she been standing there?

He could see by the expression on her face that Jennifer had overheard at least part of the conversation. Kane suppressed an annoyed sigh. He supposed that having her here now saved him the trouble of calling her to let her know what was going on before he left for Phoenix.

But he had a feeling it wasn't going to end with her merely being informed. Not after what she had said to him in the restaurant. As far as he was concerned, though, his obligation to her went no further than letting her know what his next course of action was.

And somehow, miraculously, finding her baby.

Jennifer was only marginally aware of the other people in the room. Her eyes were on Kane as she crossed to him.

"You're going to Phoenix?" Excitement hitched in her throat, the way it did when the first car of a roller coaster tottered on the brink of a eight-story drop.

Kane heard Henderson murmur something to Valdez behind him. The other man laughed in response. Kane cast an annoyed look over his shoulder and the two men sobered, but only for a moment.

Giving up, Kane turned his attention to Jennifer. "As soon as I can get a flight out, yes."

Her hand tightened about the thin chain that anchored her purse to her shoulder. "I'm going with you."

The hell you are. Kane opened his mouth, then looked around at the three other men in the room. They were all watching Jennifer and him as if they had secured free front row seat tickets to a heavyweight championship boxing match. This made twice in one day that he found himself in the center of things.

"I'd like a minute alone with Miss Sinclair." It wasn't a request.

Valdez, Henderson and O'Riley left, taking no pains to contain their amusement. Kane pushed the door closed with the flat of his hand and then leaned against it for a moment, gathering his words before he trusted himself to speak to her.

He turned and saw that she was watching him with large doe eyes. But there was no fear in them. What he saw instead was stubbornness.

Terrific.

Kane crossed to her until he was almost toe-to-toe with Jennifer, hoping to use his size if nothing else to intimidate her. She stood firm. He had a hunch she would. "You're not coming with me."

If he thought his manner and his tone left no room for argument, he underestimated her.

"Yes I am," she replied quietly. "I have to."

There was no "have to" about it. He struggled to refrain from blowing up at her.

"Lady, can't you get it through your head that this isn't some television program where a smartly dressed woman—" his eyes swept over the black-and-white suit she wore almost contemptuously "—armed with only her tongue, can win out over the bad guys?"

He was shouting. Kane took in a breath and then continued, his tone only slightly lower.

"Things might get ugly. Very ugly." He thought of the people he could be dealing with. People who would not take being discovered well. "Guns might go off. You could get hurt. Killed." To his exasperation, she didn't even flinch. Wasn't any of this registering with her? "I can't be responsible for you."

Far from being intimidated, Jennifer seemed to rally at his words, growing angry herself. She wasn't going to be frightened away. Didn't he understand that she had more at stake than he did?

"And can't you get it through your head that I'm not asking you to be responsible for me? I can take care of myself." She purposely ignored the smirk that rose to his lips. "And as for things getting ugly, in case you haven't noticed, they already have."

She splayed her hand across her chest, as if trying to contain a spreading wound. A wound to her heart. "That's *my* baby she stole. *My* baby you're attempting to recover. I don't intend to sit around, waiting for the telephone to ring in order to find out what's happened to her." As she made her plea, her voice rose, almost mirroring the pitch he had used. "I can't live like that. Right now, my whole life is on hold."

Her eyes searched his face for a sign that he comprehended her feelings. It was impossible to see anything there.

The vulnerability that was evident beneath the heated words affected Kane. He realized that he was reacting to the woman, to her plight. This was a first. And it wasn't good. Not for him. This was something entirely out of the ordinary for Kane. He couldn't begin to explain to himself how he felt. Simply addressing the knowledge that he felt at all was alien to him. He dealt in facts, in reality. Feelings weren't part of that.

He tried appealing to her common sense. "Look, I admire courage." His lips twisted in a slight smile. "Even foolish courage. But I've got my rules. I work alone," he said firmly.

Kane didn't interface well with people on any sort of a personal basis. Having Jennifer along would not only get in the way of the investigation, but would also make him decidedly uncomfortable. It might even interfere with the quality of his work, he rationalized. He was already more aware of her than he wanted to be. In a sense, with Jennifer there, it would be too much like having a relationship with someone. He wasn't into relationships. They were too much trouble and they were painful. He was better off alone.

"I won't get in your way, I promise." Jennifer raised her hand as if she was taking a solemn oath. "And I'll follow all of your instructions to the letter."

She dropped her hand as she took a step toward him. Suddenly, the room changed on him, shrinking like an old comfortable sweater that had been washed in hot water. It was too tight. She was crowding every corner of it. Crowding him.

"I need to be right there with you, knowing I'm doing everything I can."

Kane moved to the other side of the desk, on the pretext of picking up a stack of data printout. It wasn't like him to retreat. But it also wasn't in his nature to react to someone.

"Stay home. I'll call you every day and let you know what's happening."

It was a lie, Kane thought. He'd never remember to call her every day. But she didn't have to know.

She shook her head. The dark strands brushed against her shoulders, resurrecting his image of candlelight playing in it. He shook himself free of the illusion.

"Not good enough," she told him.

Kane hid behind a disinterested tone as he shrugged carelessly. "Sorry, it's the best deal I can offer. You can't come with me." He said it as if it was an unwritten commandment.

Jennifer squared her shoulders, part of the Light Brigade about to charge into the Valley of Death. She raised her chin. "It's a free country. I can go anywhere I want to." Her eyes narrowed. "If I choose to go to Phoenix at the same time you do, I will. I'll just follow you."

He doubted if he could shake some sense into her, but he really had to curb the urge to try. He curled his fingers into his palms and carefully kept them against him. "You would, wouldn't you?"

Had it worked? Was he relenting? she wondered hopefully. "Yes."

He folded his arms across his chest, amused at this display of bravado despite himself. How far would she go? "I could have you placed under arrest."

"For what? Assaulting an officer?" And then a small smile flickered on her lips as she purposely looked him up and down. She was tall, but he was taller. And far more powerful looking. "I don't think they'd believe you."

No, not for assaulting an officer. For driving me crazy, he thought, dragging a hand through his hair.

Kane paced around the room, mainly to place some distance between them. He stopped before the map and tapped it with his finger, then turned to look at her. "This could really get dangerous." He was repeating himself, he thought in disgust.

He was wavering. She could feel it.

Jennifer stepped toward him, placing her hand on his arm, as if he could somehow experience her feelings, her emotions symbiotically.

"I only held that child in my arms for what feels like a blink of an eye now, but I love her with all my heart. And I will do anything, *anything* to get her back. It's worth any risk to me."

Kane looked down into her face, almost mesmerized by what he saw there, by the passion in her words. His eyes probed hers, looking for the lie. And coming up empty. "Even at the cost of your own life?"

There wasn't even a moment's hesitation. "Even at the cost of my own life."

A mother's love was something he had never really experienced firsthand. He knew that now. Had known it for a long time. It was something, as he grew older, that he was only vaguely aware of as existing. Existing totally apart from his own world. It was nothing that had anything to do with him. But once, when he was very, very young, he had wished it had.

For a split second, before he could successfully bank down the sensation, he was envious. "Wish someone had loved me that much," he muttered under his breath.

Though she was standing as close to him as she dared, Jennifer wasn't sure she had heard him clearly. When she replayed the words in her head, they didn't seem as if they could have come from him.

"Excuse me?"

Annoyed with himself for slipping, Kane impatiently waved away his words. "Just muttering to myself," he snapped. Having her here, hovering like this, was getting him on edge. "It gets to be an occupational hazard."

There was nothing else she could do in her situation, except to push. "If I'm around, you won't have to mutter to yourself." She smiled encouragingly at him. "You'd have someone to talk to."

As if he wanted that, he thought. He valued his privacy, not conversation. And he didn't want conversation with a woman who seemed to look prettier every time he saw her.

Kane blew out an angry breath. She was giving him no choice. He didn't like not having a choice. He didn't like having his back against the wall.

He gave her a black look as he hooked his thumbs through the loops of his jeans. "Let me get this straight. Short of my finding a way to place you in irons, you're going to be dogging my trail?"

Any second now, he was going to start shouting at her. She could feel it coming. His voice was too low, too controlled. She was becoming familiar with his behavior. She braced herself for the storm. "Yes."

He eyed her, his respect growing grudgingly. "There's no way to reason with you?"

She pressed her lips together. "No."

He laughed shortly as he shook his head, mystified in the face of such stubbornness. "And to think I actually felt sorry for you because I thought your sister was bossing you around. She's got nothing on you when it comes to being pushy."

It wasn't much of a laugh, but it was a laugh. And he was smiling. Sort of. "Then you'll let me come?"

"I don't think the word *let* has any real meaning in this sentence." She was practically threatening him. "If I don't allow you to come along, I'll have to keep looking over my shoulder, constantly watching my back, making sure you don't get hurt or foul things up for me not knowing where you are half the time. If you're going to be that much trouble, I might as well keep you in my sight. It'll give me less to worry about in the long run."

Relieved, Jennifer threw her arms around his neck and hugged him in an impetuous display of gratitude. "You won't regret this."

There was no way for Kane to avoid her eyes. "I already am."

All he meant to do was remove her arms from his neck as quickly as he could. The first rule he came up with for this uneasy partnership was that there was to be no physical contact, no contact whatsoever.

Somehow Kane never completed the maneuver. His hands didn't move to hers, didn't remove them from his neck. They slipped around her back instead.

Rather than freeing himself, he was pulling her to him. Until the day he died, Kane would never be able to testify honestly who made the first move. Whether it was he who kissed her or she who kissed him. But suddenly, there they were, kissing one another. If he could analyze it, he would have said that her kiss was begun in gratitude, his in anger.

That was all he felt, he told himself. Anger. Nothing more. Anger at being cornered. Anger at being trapped.

And above all, anger at being made to feel something.

Over the long, hard, solitary years, he had carefully evolved into a man with an impenetrable shell. Nothing could get out, nothing could get in. He kept the world with its pain out and himself intact within.

She, with her warm, giving mouth, with her liquid blue eyes, had placed all that in jeopardy.

There was no mistaking the fact that it was an angry kiss, meant to frighten her, meant to make her back off and leave him in peace. It was a silent warning that went beyond telling her not to interfere with police business. It was a warning meant to make her stop interfering with his business, with his life. She was getting to him, he thought, the way no one else had ever been allowed to before.

Allowed had nothing to do with it. He wasn't allowing anything. She just seemed to keep coming despite all the safeguards he constructed and Kane knew that if she went with him to Phoenix, it would somehow open doors within him that had been nailed shut.

There was absolutely no trace of affection in his kiss. There was hunger and need, threats and passion. But no tenderness, no affection.

What surprised him was that the tables were completely, cleverly, unsuspectingly turned on him. He was the one issuing a warning. He wasn't suppose to be receiving one himself. But he was. They were warnings that threatened to undo him. He didn't expect to find hot needs within her kiss that made his own almost pale in comparison.

He meant to bring her to her knees. It had never been in his plan to fall to his own. Yet he did. Dear God, he wanted her.

His body seemed to seal against hers as electricity all but crackled throughout the small, humid room. She scared the hell out of him.

And yet he didn't want to end the kiss, not just this second. It would be the last time he would ever experience anything even close to this. So he let the kiss, the sensation continue for just a moment longer, his mouth plundering the sweetest taste he had ever experienced, his hands sweeping along the slender, strong planes of her back, completely, frighteningly captivated.

Seeking to imprison, he was taken prisoner.

Jennifer's hands tightened around Kane's neck as she molded her body urgently against his, the sizzling heat of his body soothing hers. Agitating hers. She hadn't meant for this to happen, but somehow it had. It almost felt as if something unseen were moving her toward this man by some plan that she couldn't fathom.

There were things within his kiss that made her want to cry, not for herself, but for him. It was as if he were empty and she were striving to fill that void. While he unearthed passions within her from a place she had thought completely abandoned, he aroused her tender heart as well. He was needy, far needier than she.

And she longed to help him.

Passion rose within her, a raging river threatening to overflow the banks. No one was more surprised by it than Jennifer was.

Cold air assaulted her face as Kane pulled abruptly, painfully away. Jennifer stood, dazed and shaken, her hands still woven around his neck. Now it was a matter of support rather than affection.

With his eyes on hers, Kane slowly removed her arms from around him.

Hands at her sides, Jennifer took a deep breath before she attempted to speak. When she did, it was as if she was tasting every word before releasing it. "If you did that to frighten me off—"

It didn't frighten you half as much as it frightened me. "Yes?"

She wasn't embarrassed to place a hand on the table, to brace herself. "You almost succeeded."

Damn, he wanted to do it again. He wanted to kiss her until this torment within him dissolved. Not trusting himself, Kane moved so that the table was between them. "But you're still coming?"

She nodded slowly. "I said I would risk anything." And she had a feeling that before all this was over, she would be, in more ways than one. Her tongue flickered over her lips. She could still taste him. Tart and tangy, and male. "When are we leaving?"

We. He didn't like the sound of the word. It asked things of him he couldn't give, didn't know how to give.

"As soon as I can arrange for a flight." Maybe there was still a way out. He looked at the outfit she was wearing. "You don't exactly look ready for travel."

She couldn't help the look of triumph that slipped over her face. "I have an overnight case in my car. It's packed."

He raised a brow quizzically. "How did you know?"

"I didn't," she confessed. "But I listen." The brow rose higher on his forehead. "You mentioned Arizona and Nevada at the restaurant," she reminded him. "And I like being prepared."

Maybe she wouldn't be a total hindrance after all, he thought in mild admiration. At least, not as far as the investigation went. As to the other matter, he already had his answer to that.

Giving in, Kane ran a hand over his face, then opened the door leading out to the squad room again. "Valdez," he called. "Get in here."

Kane had no sooner stepped back into the room than the young plainclothesman was at his side, following him in. While he spoke to Kane, his dark eyes were appreciatively gliding over Jennifer. "I got you that flight. You're scheduled to leave John Wayne Airport in a little less than two hours."

Kane glanced over his shoulder at Jennifer and all but growled his next instructions to Valdez.

"It seems I need another ticket to Phoenix." He sighed, knowing he was undoubtedly making a mistake, but for the moment, he felt as if his hands were tied. "I'll pay for the new ticket myself." His laugh was dry. "I can just hear accounting if they saw two tickets to Phoenix on my expense report."

Valdez shrugged. "Phoenix isn't exactly mentioned in the same breath as Hawaii. You could just say you needed her with you to identify the suspect."

Jennifer smiled at the younger man. It was nice having someone in her corner for a change.

The last thing he needed was someone encouraging this woman, Kane thought. "Just call the airline and change the reservation for two."

He turned, shoving his hands into his back pockets as Valdez left the room again. Kane studied Jennifer for a long moment, calculating the risks involved in taking her along.

They went off the scale. How had he gotten himself so tangled up? "I want you to follow my every order, is that clear?"

She nodded emphatically, relieved he wasn't still attempting to argue her out of it. "Clear. Every one."

Like hell she would. There was an independent streak in her he'd missed the first couple of go-arounds. "I say duck—" He waited.

She spread her hands wide, the soul of cooperation. "I duck."

He pressed on, his eyes probing so intently, Jennifer could almost feel them holding her in place. "I say stay—?"

Oh no, he didn't. If she followed along this path he was laying out for her, she knew exactly where she would wind up. Sitting next to her phone. "And I decide whether or not to stay."

He frowned. He thought as much. "You're not playing this right."

"I'll play it your way, Kane," she answered, her voice rising. As she spoke, she circled the desk to stand before him. It was as if she were attempting to wipe out any barriers between them. "But I won't be tricked into something. I want you to remember that. To you it's a case, a job. To me it's the most important part of my life. Right now, she *is* my life."

She forced herself to relax. Tension made her feel as if she could snap as easily as a brittle icicle. Jennifer ran her hand along her neck, trying to iron out the knots there.

"And I'll pay you for the ticket and anything else that we need. Money doesn't matter to me. Only Katie does." She smiled as she resisted the temptation to take another step closer to him. Instead, she only looked at him. But it was enough. All her feelings were in her eyes. "I know you'll get her back for me. I just want to be there to hold her when you do."

When she handed her faith to him as if it were a precious jewel with which she was ransoming her daughter, it only made him more restive.

No pressure, right? "You've got a hell of a lot of faith in me, lady, considering that two and a half weeks ago, you didn't know me from Adam."

She wondered if he kept everyone at arm's length with that temper of his. It had almost worked with her. If he hadn't kissed her.

"You're wrong, there, Detective. I would have *always* known you from Adam." She started to walk out, then turned, hesitating in the doorway. "If I go out to my car to get my bag, will you still be here when I return?" She wouldn't put it past him to sneak off. But she knew if she made him give her his word, he would stick by it, no matter how much he chafed against it.

"Yeah." Kane gave her the promise grudgingly, his fingers impotently strumming against his empty breast pocket. "I'll still be here." Even though he didn't want to be.

She watched his fingers curl in frustration. Did she make him nervous, she wondered. It seemed almost impossible to believe, but there were signs there not to be ignored lightly.

"They're not there," she told him.

"What's not there?" What the hell was she talking about now?

"Your cigarettes." With that, she hurried off to the parking lot.

He scowled, unaware that he had been reaching for them again. He thought about the last remaining cigarette machine in the precinct. It was located just outside the locker room. He slid his hand into his jeans and felt for change. There were several coins in his pocket.

Kane was halfway to the door, when he cursed and retraced his steps. Smoking wasn't going to solve anything. The faster he got on with the case and pulled all the pieces together, the faster his life would return to normal. And the faster she'd be out of it.

"Phoenix PD is all set," Henderson announced as he walked into the room.

Kane looked down the hall in the direction Jennifer had taken. He muttered a curse and hooked his thumbs in his jeans. "I wish to hell I was."

Henderson didn't bother to hide the grin that wreathed most of his jovial face. "You want me to tell the Captain she's going along?" He jerked a thumb in Jennifer's direction.

"No," Kane snapped, then got himself under control. "We'll talk to the captain if and when I get results." Kane didn't have to tell the man that he was issuing a warning. "And not before."

"You sold me." Henderson's face was the picture of innocence.

Not trusting himself to comment, Kane gathered together the various data they had on the infant-nappings and walked to his desk in the squad room. He stuffed the pages into a battered briefcase that had doubled as an overnight bag more than once.

Yanking the bottom drawer of his desk a little more firmly than he had intended, Kane rummaged through the chaos there until he located what he needed. Living from moment to moment, he always kept a few essentials there that would see him through several days. A clean shirt, underwear, a razor and a toothbrush. He tossed them into the briefcase, then snapped it shut. He didn't need much.

He glanced toward the hall again as if to reaffirm his silent declaration.

No, he never needed much. And he wasn't going to start now, either.

Chapter 7

The airline terminal at John Wayne Airport was the last word in sleek design.

Jennifer couldn't find a comfortable spot in it.

She paced along the length of the waiting area like a panther seeking an opening in its cage through which to leap. Henderson had driven them to the terminal in plenty of time to make the flight. More than enough time, it turned out. A last-minute glitch in the maintenance check had delayed takeoff an hour and three minutes by Jennifer's watch.

More time, Jennifer thought restlessly, than it took to fly to Phoenix. Where was her daughter now? she wondered. Was she hungry? Was anyone seeing to her needs? She knew that newborn infants had no capacity for fear, so there was no way, mercifully, that Katie could be frightened. But Jennifer had enough fear for both of them.

Kane watched in silence as Jennifer's long legs divided the length of the waiting area in so many equal strides. She had shapely, graceful legs. Legs that belonged to a dancer or a runner. Legs to make a man dream.

But not him, he reminded himself. He didn't believe in dreams, or feelings. Or trust. Not in anyone. Not even in himself. That had been made abundantly clear to him by his lack of control in the conference room.

He had had no business kissing her. And no business wanting to do it again.

She passed in front of his seat once more, every fiber of her body tense, waiting. She was going to wear herself out from the inside out, he mused. He was in no mood to play nursemaid to her.

"Pacing like that isn't going to make the plane ready any faster," Kane told her.

She looked at him ruefully and dragged a hand through her hair. "No, you're right." Exhausted from the tension that was playing along her body like an unseen hand along a string instrument, she sank down in the white bucket seat next to him. "It's just that we could have already been there by now."

He dug into his pocket and took out a roll of mints. He had to do something to keep from surrendering to the craving for a cigarette that was eating away at him. He stared, fixedly, at the cigarette machine at the end of the long terminal. Popping a mint from the roll with his thumb, he offered her the rest.

"Valdez faxed ahead photos of all the missing babies as well as the mug shots taken of Ward during her arrest, although they could just pull up one of their own if they wanted to. If there's anything to be done, the Phoenix P.D. won't be waiting on us to do it."

He knew that although California had eight kidnappings to their two, the Arizona police were just as anxious to solve this case as he was.

Jennifer accepted the mint and returned the roll to him. "How can you stay so calm?" She held her hand out and realized that there was a slight tremor going through it.

Kane reached over and steadied it, covering her hand with his own. Jennifer dropped her hand self-consciously in her lap. The passing contact reminded them both of what had happened just hours before. It was something neither felt up to dealing with yet.

"Practice," Kane told her, his voice deceptively even. "Getting ahead of yourself only wears you out." He looked at her face for a moment. It was a study in barely suppressed anticipation. He wondered how long it would be before she snapped and what he would do if she did. "You could still go home."

He never gave up, she thought. She hoped he conducted his investigation in the same dogged fashion. Somehow, she felt he did. She doubted if he knew another way.

"No, I can't." An announcement over the loudspeaker drowned out her next words. Their flight was finally ready for boarding. Jennifer smiled brightly at him, a part of her tension being placed in abeyance for the moment. "See?"

He saw all right. He saw a woman who was unbelievably stubborn. Unfolding his long legs, he rose, picking up his briefcase. With his free hand, he took the corner of her elbow.

"Let's get going, then, before they find something else wrong with the plane."

He ushered her along ahead of him as they crossed the long ramp to the side door of the small passenger plane. Up close, the plane did not inspire confidence.

"Are they sure this thing checked out?" she murmured, strapping in.

They began taxiing down the runway and she could have sworn that the plane was playing its own musical accompaniment as it shuddered and shook along.

Kane looked at her, amused. "I thought you were so anxious to get going."

She pried her clenched hands from the armrests. "I'm even more anxious to reach there."

She was beginning to look a little green to him. She wasn't going to faint, was she? He glanced around for the flight attendant just in case. "Never flown in a small plane?"

"Never flown at all," she answered.

He stopped searching for the attendant and looked at her. "You're kidding."

She shook her head. "There was never any place to go." She forced the tension from her as she thought of her fam-

ily. "I've had everything I wanted or needed right here in
Southern California."

"You sound like a vacation ad."

She couldn't tell by his expression if he was being cynical
or sincere. "It's true, though."

A small smile, completely without mirth, played on his
lips. "Then you also sound lucky."

She could tell, without asking, that he had never had the
kind of life she had. How different were they? she wondered. And where was all the passion she had felt in his kiss?
There was none evident in the man sitting next to her. Kane
Madigan was a total mystery to her. With his dark hooded
eyes and his probing gaze, it was as if he could see right into
her mind, almost second-guess what she was thinking. She
had no such window into his soul. His eyes were flat, barring her entrance.

Yet she needed a hero right now, a hero who could ride in
and make things right. Kane was the only one she had.

They barely had time to settle in and brace themselves for
the bumpy ride before they were deplaning again at Phoenix Sky Harbor International Airport. Kane led the way into
the terminal. Jennifer had to hurry to keep up. He had
probably forgotten she was with him, she thought. They
hardly exchanged any words during the flight. He seemed
to be deep in thought and she felt it best to leave him at it.

"Is someone supposed to meet us here?" she asked. She
noticed someone holding up a placard that read Welcome
Home, Dan, but no one was holding any sign for them.

Kane looked around. "Supposed to," he answered.

She remembered that the police artist had said that Kane
didn't talk much. Maybe he was reverting back to type.
Well, she hadn't come for conversation, she had come to
help, to place the horrid torture of waiting beside the telephone at home as far from her as she could.

"How will we find them?" The faces in the crowd all
mingled together as people met one another, embracing.

"They'll probably find us."

Just as he said the words, he saw a swarthy-skinned man in jeans and a colorful turquoise shirt approaching. There was a surety to his gait, an air of authority present that set him apart from the others. This was their man, Kane thought.

"Detective Madigan?" the man asked. His jet black hair was slicked back and his eyes looked as if they had seen centuries pass by instead of just four decades. Kane nodded in response. The man produced a shield that identified him as part of the Phoenix police force, then pocketed it. "The captain sent me to bring you back. Detective Graham Redhawk." He extended his hand to Kane, then lifted one solemn brow in Jennifer's direction.

"This is Jennifer Sinclair." Kane inclined his head in her direction. "Hers was the last baby stolen. We feel that she got a good look at the suspect before the woman disappeared."

The words Kane was saying to Redhawk were all very cut-and-dried, all very matter-of-fact. He had no way of knowing that each sliced through her heart like a stiletto, cutting out large chunks. The words had images attached to them, images of Katie in that woman's arms, images that were far too painful for Jennifer to deal with directly at this time. The only way she was able to survive was to tell herself that somehow, they were going to find her daughter.

The solemn detective looked genuinely sorry to learn about her loss. "We're doing everything we can to help out here," Redhawk said more to Jennifer than to Kane. "My car's just outside." He pointed toward the exit.

Without asking, he took Jennifer's small case and escorted her out. Kane followed behind.

"We've got the woman's rap sheet, of course," Redhawk continued. "We started showing copies of her photograph around as soon as we discovered her possible connection. We're going over all the data you people faxed. You have no jurisdiction out here, but there's to be full co-operation between the two departments. Captain says if we find her, you can be there when we make the arrest."

Whether or not official permission was granted, Kane was coming along. He had had no intention of flying out merely to rubber-stamp anything that had already been decided upon. As far as he was concerned, this was his case. He had spent the last eleven months poring over leads, enduring the frustration of coming up against dead ends, agonizing each time the kidnapper struck again, despite the fact that security at all hospitals in the region had been either beefed up or at least alerted to be on the lookout. He doubted that Ward worked alone in these kidnappings. He felt she was a link to the organization and right now, the best lead he had.

Redhawk held the rear car door open for Jennifer and waited until she slid in. "It's kind of late, but the captain's still waiting at the precinct. There isn't much to be done at this time of night, but he did want you to check in with him when you arrived."

The man got in behind the wheel. Kane took the seat next to him rather than riding in the back with Jennifer. Redhawk turned toward Jennifer before starting the car. "I could drop you off at a hotel first, before going to the precinct."

No, she wasn't about to be tucked away in a hotel. One room was as bad as another if she was to remain by herself, useless. She shook her head. "No, thank you. I'm coming along."

Kane made himself comfortable against the worn vinyl upholstery. Though they had left behind a moderate seventy-degree evening in California, here it was over ninety in the shade. The heat was dry, but still oppressive. He wondered how the people who lived here could stand it.

"Don't waste your breath trying to convince her to stay out of it," he advised Redhawk. "I've already gone all through that. Ms. Sinclair is in for the duration."

"I can understand that." Redhawk nodded. "Taking care of your own. It's important." He carefully pulled his automobile out from between two smaller cars. He stopped and held his breath as he eased the shell pink fins past obstacles. He drove a vintage '59 Cadillac and it was obvious that he was enamored with it.

Kane finally had to ask. "Isn't this a little conspicuous for an unmarked car?"

"Who says I want to be inconspicuous? Keeps the bad guys on their toes. Besides, I only drive it once in a while. This is my baby." Redhawk patted the dashboard with a wide, sun-darkened hand.

Kane couldn't see developing an attachment to a possession, but it obviously seemed to make the other detective happy. He wondered what it would be like, to find joy in something like that. To find joy in anything.

He glanced behind him at Jennifer, then buried any thoughts that were struggling to emerge.

Captain Hernandez greeted them warmly when they arrived at the precinct. "About given up on you. It's almost eight-thirty."

"Plane got delayed," Kane explained. "Detective Redhawk says you're already circulating Ward's picture."

Hernandez nodded. "Newspapers, newscasts. A couple of the men are contacting our regular informers, seeing what we can come up with. What makes you think she's heading out here? The last kidnapping was in L.A., right?"

The last kidnapping. A statistic, Jennifer thought. Katie was just a statistic, a description. Something people looked up from their dinner to glance at on the evening news. She dug her nails into her palms and realized she was getting hysterical. She had to get a grip on herself. If she broke down now, Kane would send her home on the next plane out and she would only have herself to blame.

"Newport Beach," she corrected.

The Captain's dark eyes swept over Jennifer with more than a hint of an appreciative glint. "And you are?"

"Jennifer Sinclair." She placed her hand in the man's and steeled herself off as she said the next words. "Mine was the last baby Ward stole. Almost three weeks ago."

Hernandez looked as if he would have willingly bitten off his tongue. "Oh, ma'am, my deepest apologies. I didn't realize. If I had known you were the mother, I would not have spoken so bluntly."

Jennifer offered a tight smile. "That's all right, I understand."

The best way around the discomfort he saw evident in her face was to change the direction of the conversation back to details, Kane thought.

"We're playing a hunch," he told Hernandez honestly. "One of our black-and-whites spotted her car on I5. It was on the outskirts of the city, heading east." He knew it was a long shot, but success was built on long shots that paid off. "She might have been going any one of a number of places," he granted, "but she's originally from Phoenix. We thought she might be coming home for some reason."

He pulled out his folder. A toothbrush accompanied it, tumbling down to the floor. Jennifer grabbed it and returned it to him. Kane gave her a rueful look as he stuffed it into the briefcase. He was going to have to get a larger briefcase, or find some other way to transport his personal belongings.

"We've got a DMV traffic violation that puts her in the vicinity when the Alvarez baby was abducted."

Hernandez looked at the collection of photographs Kane had with him.

The captain shook his head. "Takes a cold-blooded woman to do something like that." He fingered the faxed picture of Ward that his office had received earlier that day. "Looks like someone's sweet *abuela*. Grandmother," he corrected.

"Well, she might be, but we're hoping that she's going to be receiving her next Mother's Day cards in the state prison." Kane tucked the photographs into his manila folder.

"One of our informants has come up with an old address here in Phoenix. I'm sending a man to check it out in the morning to see if there're any relatives still living in the area and if they've heard from her."

Kane nodded. It was all they could do. Just thread together separate beads and hope that they could come up with a single necklace in the end.

Hernandez took his cue from Kane and began to edge toward the door. "Well, if you don't mind . . . I have a school play I'm already late for. My wife takes a dim view of my missing what she insists on calling the golden moments of my kids' lives."

Would she ever get that kind of a chance with Katie? Jennifer wondered. Would she ever be able to sit in a school auditorium, watching Katie stumble over lines while searching for her face in the audience? Hot tears threatened to spill out again.

Kane caught the glint in her eyes and without thinking, placed his hand on her shoulder. The small gesture communicated more than he could ever hope to say and just possibly more than he wanted to say. Jennifer let out a breath and smiled at him. It was going to be all right, she told herself over and over again. Kane wouldn't let her down.

Hernandez gestured toward the other detective as he left. "I'll have Detective Redhawk leave a car at your disposal."

"Not the pink Cadillac," Kane said a little too vehemently.

Jet black eyebrows furrowed. "Hey, that's my pride and joy. I don't let a Californian touch that," Redhawk said with a touch of indignation. "She needs a gentle hand. We've got an '87 Ford in the back."

"Sold," Kane told him.

Redhawk opened the drawer of the captain's desk and took out a set of keys, then tossed them to Kane. "C'mon, I'll show you."

Kane and Jennifer followed Redhawk to the rear of the stucco-walled building. The Ford was parked several feet from the Cadillac, maintaining a respectful distance like a peasant in the presence of a king.

"Where's the closest hotel?" Kane asked.

Redhawk pointed to the street that ran behind the parking lot. "Two miles straight down Chickasaw. It's not very big, but it's clean and the rates are reasonable."

"The accounting department will love it." Kane unlocked the passenger side of the car for Jennifer, then came around the hood to the driver's side.

"It's called the Happy Inn," Redhawk told him. "Usually, it is." He leaned against his beloved automobile, careful not to get any smudges on it.

"What do you do if the car gets dirty?" Kane couldn't resist asking.

"Shoot the guy who did it."

Kane laughed and shook his head as he pulled away.

"They seem nice," Jennifer commented. "The policemen, I mean."

Kane nodded, absorbing the area as he drove through it. "Yeah, they seem okay. A little weird for my taste."

It seemed like an odd thing to say. She looked at the hard ridges of his profile. "Because they hurry off to see their kids in a play and love their cars? That's not weird, that's normal."

He shrugged. "Maybe for some people."

She was hardly aware of forming the words before they were out. "What's normal for you?"

What was normal for him? He didn't really know. He only knew the pattern his life had fallen into. Working on cases, eating and sleeping. There wasn't anything else. There wasn't room for anything else. He saw to that.

Kane summed it up in one sentence as he slowed for a traffic light that shimmered like a red ruby before him. "Being a good cop."

"That's all?" Didn't he want anything else? *Do* anything else?

He thought of the heavy caseloads he carried. "That's enough."

He placed demands on himself that were heavy to carry, she thought. No wonder he hardly smiled. "Don't you do anything for fun?"

"Yeah." Kane stepped on the gas again. "I solve cases."

She had a feeling that he wasn't nearly as linear as he was trying to portray, but she let the subject drop. She was far too exhausted to conduct a debate to attempt to unearth the inner man she *knew* had to exist beneath the No Trespassing signs and barbed wire strung up around him.

Kane pulled up the car before a single-story building with rooms that were positioned next to one another like white sugar cubes lined up on the sand. An archway in front proclaimed it to be the Happy Inn.

It needed a new coat of paint. "Doesn't look very happy to me," Kane muttered.

"Must be the lighting." She got out of the car and stretched. Her body ached from the vicelike grip tension had her in. The air felt as if it were physically pressing on her. "Doesn't it ever cool off in this place?"

He half smiled. "Lady, this *is* cool for Phoenix."

"How do they stand it?" Jennifer followed him to the first building. The Vacancy sign over the word Manager was lit up in bright red neon letters.

"Air conditioning." He pushed open the door. "And they wrinkle a lot."

The room was tidy. A man with a slight build who looked like one half of a parenthesis turned and glanced in their direction when they entered. Behind him on the small television a classic black-and-white comedy program played.

"What can I do for you folks?" He was a soft-spoken man whose sentences all ended in a whisper, as if he had run out of energy before he came to the last words.

"I'd like a room, please. Two," Kane corrected. Habit had him asking for one. It was difficult for him to think in anything but the singular.

The man inclined his head speculatively. "Anything you say, mister." He jotted a note on the registration book, then turned it around for Kane and Jennifer to sign. "No computer," he said in answer to the question he was anticipating. "We're old-fashioned around here."

Translation, Kane thought, they were too cheap to invest in computer equipment. Electronics were catching up on all of them, though. Sometimes he wondered if that was a good thing. It made the world smaller. Easier, at times, to apprehend a criminal, but harder for a man to stay lost if he wanted to.

"Luggage?" the desk clerk asked, leaning over the counter to see for himself. He smiled at the single case in Jennifer's hand. Marmalade eyebrows rose high on the wide forehead. "Short stay?"

"Remains to be seen," Kane answered. He took both of the keys the man handed them.

"I put you right next to each other," the clerk informed Kane as they began to leave.

"Thanks," Kane bit off.

"Makes things easier," the clerk added with a pronounced wink. "We like 'em happy around here."

"Sleaze bucket," Kane muttered under his breath as he ushered Jennifer quickly out into the heat again.

He didn't like being paired off, Jennifer speculated. "I guess he thought we were having an affair."

Kane glanced at the numbers on the keys, then at the corresponding numbers on the doors. Theirs were located two rooms down from the end.

"Man like that in a place like this isn't capable of thinking anything else."

Without another word, he brought her to her room, then paused. He had avoided looking at her as much as possible for the last few hours. Now, he couldn't help it. Somehow, though she wasn't small in stature, she gave the impression of being small. Lost. Vulnerable.

"Will you be all right?" He thought the question sounded incredibly lame. "In the room, I mean." That, he congratulated himself, was even worse. He blamed it on a complete lack of sleep.

She started to answer that she'd be fine. But she wasn't going to be fine, not until they found her baby. She shrugged. "As well as can be expected." Taking her key from him she pushed it into the lock and turned it. The door creaked open before her.

The room was cheerier than she had anticipated. But she still felt cold inside. To her surprise, Kane walked in with her, leaving his briefcase by the opened door.

Kane looked past her shoulder. There was a large window looking out on the empty back lot. Twilight was just setting in over the desert. The sky was a mass of purple bleeding into blue, dripping down a huge canvas into the darkening sand below. It captured a feeling of loneliness and tied it up with a ribbon of despair.

"You have a nice view," he commented.

Jennifer realized she had been oblivious to it, though she had been staring straight ahead. She looked at it now. The starkness of it filtered into her soul. She ran her hands up and down her arms.

"It looks so desolate to me." She let out a sigh. "And so huge."

Jennifer was doing her best to hold on to her courage, but it was becoming more and more difficult to maintain a front, even for herself. Panic kept sparring with hope within her and right at this moment, hundreds of miles from home, with night setting in, panic was winning the round.

"Oh Kane, she's out there somewhere." Jennifer turned to face him, struggling with desperation. "But she's such a little thing. How are we ever going to find her?"

He rubbed his hand along the back of his neck to keep from touching her. He wanted to comfort her, but didn't know how to even begin. "It's a little easier than finding a needle in a haystack."

She laughed to herself. The man was nothing if not steadfastly honest. "But not much," she concluded.

It was tantamount to handing a lead pipe to a woman who was drowning. He struggled to make what he had said seem more encouraging than it sounded. "Well, we know who took the needle and where she might be likely to sew."

Jennifer ran her hand along the foot of the bed. It was cracked in three places. "Three states," she murmured. "Three large states."

"Odds are better than if the territory was spread out over fifty," he pointed out.

Kane surprised himself by serving up this platter of hope. He had sworn to himself that he would never get emotionally involved with anyone, yet it felt almost inhuman to remain stoically silent in the face of the pain he saw in her eyes.

He placed his hands on her shoulders. He had no idea how they wound up slipping around her, how he wound up holding her to him. Perhaps it was orchestrated by a force that existed within everyone which instinctively offered physical comfort.

"We'll find her, Jennifer. It's just going to take time."

She squeezed her eyes shut to keep the tears from flowing and nodded, grateful for the words. "I know, it's just that sometimes, I feel so scared, so hopeless. I don't mean to take it out on you."

He released her, backing off before the contact blossomed into something that frightened him more than the possibility of having to stop a bullet. "It's okay. I guess everyone needs to let off steam once in a while."

"Except you." She didn't know whether or not she believed that but knew instinctively that he did.

All through the flight to Phoenix, she had felt his dark, probing eyes absorbing her every move, almost pulling out her every thought. She felt as if she were an open book that he was evaluating both mentally and physically. But she had gotten very little insight as to who or what Kane Madigan was, except that he did possess a heart that could be moved, no matter how he acted to the contrary.

"Except for me," he agreed.

She sat down on the bed. It sagged, fitting around her hips like hands molding around a smooth vase. She rose. "Why is that?"

Kane shrugged. "It just is. It makes things neater, tidier." He didn't like explaining himself. He didn't know why he was doing it with her.

She smiled as she took in his faded jeans and work shirt. His windbreaker looked as if he slept in it, not once but every night. The boots on his feet were worn at the heel and looked as if they were carrying the dust of all three states on them.

"You don't exactly look like someone who'd concern himself with neatness."

He looked down at his attire. "Life should be neat," he amended. "The way I look going through it, well, that's another matter." He frowned. What was it about her that always had him straying mentally? "How'd we go from talking about you to talking about me?"

She sensed that the topic was taboo. "Why can't we talk about you?"

"Because the conversation would get boring. There's nothing to say." The look on his face told her that the discussion was terminated.

But she didn't want to give up so easily. She wanted to know who he was. And why talking about it was so painful for him. It wasn't his life story she was looking for, just a little insight.

"You've got to be somebody's son, lover, brother?" To each label, Kane shook his head. "No family?" she asked. A sadness pervaded her. Having been lovingly cocooned within hers, it seemed almost inconceivable to her what it would be like to go through life without a family. Alone. How awful for him.

"None." His voice was hard. Kane had no idea where his mother was. His father had died the way he had lived, in a drunken stupor, over ten years ago.

She touched his arm. "I'm sorry." It seemed like pitifully little to say.

He didn't want her pity, or her compassion. "There's no reason to be." He remembered cowering in the closet, a frightened boy of five, while loud voices belonging to his parents said horrid things to one another. "Not all families are as close as yours. Sometimes they just take pieces of each other instead of giving them." He shored up the slight chink in his shield, damning himself for letting it happen. "Then you're better off without them."

She didn't want to be shut out. In his own way, he was as hurt as she was. "Tell me about it."

He lost his temper for a minute. What gave her the right to probe, to dig up fresh wounds?

"Lady, you have no place in my mind, or under my skin." He dragged calm back to him like an errant thief who had tried to slip away. "I'm just the police detective who's going to bring your baby back to you, nothing else."

Jennifer retreated. But not without offering him a slice of her gratitude. No matter what he thought, his self-esteem needed it.

"That's far from nothing. Do you really think that woman is coming back here to sell Katie?"

It was a foregone conclusion that the woman was going to have to sell the babies she stole somewhere. "We've pulled in every known connection to a baby black market in the California area. By process of elimination, I'd say it's got to be here or in Nevada." *Unless it's somewhere else.*

Jennifer could see the slight doubt. There was a tiny line running down between his eyes. She'd noticed it only formed when he had doubts. "What if it's a whole new organization?"

She was sharp. He'd give her that. "We'll cross that bridge when we come to it." He remembered that the last time he had put anything into his stomach was around noon. "Want something to eat?"

She shook her head and passed her hand over her belly. It felt like a cement mixer in perpetual motion. "I wouldn't be able to hold anything down."

He cast a disparaging eye on her frame. Slender, she would be on her way to skinny in less than a month's time. "Your sister's right. You don't eat enough. You've got to keep up your strength. C'mon." He motioned toward the door. "I'm buying."

Jennifer looked around the room. She knew she wouldn't be able to rest and the hours between now and tomorrow stretched out endlessly before her.

"All right." She walked out and heard him lock the door behind them. "What is it you're buying?"

He had seen a taco take-out place on their way over here. "What else? Fast food." He guided her away from the car, where she was heading, and toward the sidewalk. The restaurant was only down the street.

"Okay." She fell into step next to him. "But on one condition."

He was mildly intrigued that she was setting up conditions on this. "What?"

"You have to swear you'll never tell Nik. He'd probably disown me." They stopped at the corner, waiting for the light to change. She glanced at their reflections in the darkened window of a florist. There was a halo of white carnations around them.

"Done." He managed a smile. "That sandwich your brother threw together for me today almost succeeded in breaking my jaw. I don't think an anaconda could have taken a regular bite out of it."

She laughed, envisioning the look on her brother's face when Julia told him what Kane had selected for lunch. To go, yet. "Nik doesn't make sandwiches very often. I guess he got carried away."

"Either that, or he was trying to get even with me for insulting his restaurant."

"There's that, too." She turned and smiled at him. "Thank you."

He hadn't done anything for her to be grateful for, yet. "For what?"

"For talking to me. For letting me come along."

"Lady, if I hadn't, you probably would have handcuffed yourself to my side."

Jennifer grinned. "Maybe. If I had found a pair of handcuffs." She knew that if he really hadn't wanted her to come along, he would have found a way to keep her from going. "Thank you for understanding."

"Yeah, no problem." Except that, he thought, it probably would be. Eventually. He kept his mind focused on now and walked up to the taco stand with her.

He was nice, she thought, stealing a side glance at him. He made her feel safe. Nervous and safe at the same time. It was an odd combination, but one that seemed somehow to fit the situation.

Chapter 8

Fajita Olé! was part of a chain of fast-food restaurants that specialized in Mexican food. Its logo, a Mexican hat sailing high through the air, had been faded by two shades from its original colors by the intense Phoenix sun. It appeared to Jennifer that the entire exterior needed a new coat of paint.

The interior, mimicking a cantina recreated in hard plastic and vinyl, still managed to look festive and bright. The restaurant was fairly empty because of the hour. There were only three other people in the restaurant, not counting the crew behind the counter.

Kane pointed out the menu board to Jennifer and asked what she wanted. She chose the most edible-looking item depicted and ordered a beef burrito with a diet soda. Kane echoed the order and added an extra burrito as an afterthought. He was hungry.

Their order was on their tray before Kane had a chance to take money out of his wallet.

"Pick a table," Kane told her. He followed behind Jennifer with the tray in his hands.

She chose one in the center of the room, midway from the door and counter. Lively music from five overhead speakers, bright and airy, swept through the dusty corners of the room.

Jennifer watched in fascination as Kane wolfed down two beef burritos in the time it took her to consume half of her own.

She leaned her head on her hand and smiled. "How do you taste it that way?"

He crumpled up the paper wrapper and tossed it on the tray, then reached for a napkin to wipe his fingers. "What do you mean?"

She indicated the two wrappers wadded up into tiny balls next to one another. "If you wolf your food down like that, how do you taste what you're eating? How do you savor anything?"

He laughed, amused at her question. Only she would ask that. "Savor?" The word was etched in disbelief. "You're talking about a dollar forty-nine burrito, Jennifer, not filet mignon or caviar. I eat to kill the hunger, that's all."

She tossed her hair over her shoulder and smiled ruefully. "Sorry, early training." She took a sip of the diet soda. It tasted watered down, but it was cold, which was all she cared about. "I was raised to chew everything very carefully before swallowing."

He couldn't remember conversation at the table when he was a boy, much less hearing any attention spent on etiquette. "You have rules for everything when you were growing up?"

She hadn't thought of them as rules, exactly. Just as things she did or didn't do. They had never been handed to her as mandates from her parents. It was just the way things were done. She supposed, from his point of view, they could be looked at as rules.

"A lot." Every conversation they had seemed to raise questions in her mind about him. "Didn't you?"

His lips twisted into a cynical smile. "Yeah, just one. Grow up. Fast." He stuffed his napkin into the empty soda container. He knew she was in the mood to talk but he wasn't, not about himself. He eyed the last bit of burrito she still held in her fingers. "You about finished with that?"

She nodded, carefully folding the wrapper around the remainder of her burrito. She placed it on the tray. It hadn't been very good to begin with and now it was cold on top of that. Maybe he had a point, eating his food quickly, she thought.

He rose with the tray in his hands and threw out the contents into a trash can shaped like a small adobe house by the door. He noticed the way she had picked at her meal. "Don't you like Mexican food?"

Actually, she did. Good Mexican food. But she didn't think it would be prudent to word it just that way.

Jennifer walked through the door he held open for her. "Thank you. Yes, I do, but it's just as I told you. I can't really eat. My stomach feels like there's this huge coiled cobra inside of it, waiting to strike. It's taking up all the available space."

They walked along the darkened street. Traffic was light. Foot traffic was almost nonexistent. It felt as if they were the only ones out. Anyone who had somewhere to go was doing it in a car.

It felt nice, she thought, walking like this with him, even with silence between them. If only circumstances were different, she could let herself enjoy this moment.

Kane struggled against an urge to slip his arm around her. Where it had come from, he had no idea. It was as if something were compelling him to act against type. Or to revert to something, some*one* he had once been.

"You're not going to do Katie any good by not eating and getting yourself sick." He realized he was making overprotective noises and pressed his lips together. What she ate, how she acted, that was her business. It should have absolutely no bearing on his life, he thought. So why was he even bothering to comment?

Jennifer sighed as they approached the hotel. "You're right, it won't." She lifted one shoulder and let it fall. "Maybe I'll feel more like eating in the morning. Breakfast is my favorite meal, anyway." She looked at him. "What's yours?"

"I don't play favorites," he muttered.

He didn't have a favorite meal. He ate when he was hungry and called it nothing in particular. She had had structure when she was growing up. Structure and love. He had had a void, one long struggle to reach an age when he could legally get out on his own. There were moments when he felt he shouldn't even be standing in the same room with her. They were from two very different worlds, *of* two very different worlds.

And this attraction he felt for her had no business existing.

But it did.

They walked across the last long block in silence. Gravel crunched like tiny shells popping beneath his boots as he crossed the parking lot, taking Jennifer to her door at the hotel.

Kane waited until she took out her key and opened the lock. Then he turned to leave. "I'll see you in the morning."

Jennifer hesitated. "You won't leave without me, will you?"

Damn, she had second-guessed him, he thought. He couldn't help the rueful, grudging smile that rose faintly to his lips. "No, not any more."

She felt disappointed. She had begun to feel that they were becoming friends. Perhaps even more than that. And now he was admitting that he had planned to leave her behind in the morning when he went to the precinct. "But you would have?"

He saw the flicker of hurt in her eyes, even in the dim lighting from the street lamp across the parking lot. He told himself that it shouldn't bother him. But it did. He shoved his hands deep in his pockets, as if digging for an excuse that would work.

"I don't want to see you dragged around needlessly. Or needlessly hurt, either." Somehow, though he knew it shouldn't, keeping her from being hurt had become important in the last few hours. He looked past her head, not wanting to hazard a glance into her eyes. "If you want to be in on the end, fine, it's just that—"

He wasn't going to talk her out of it. She wouldn't allow it. "Kane—"

Kane raised his hands in surrender and to ward off the words he saw coming. "Yeah, I know, we've had this dance before." He sighed. "All right, I'll give you a wake up call."

She appreciated his concern, even though it took this form. At least he listened to reason. *Her* reason. "Thank you."

He frowned, annoyed at her, himself and the world in general. "You've got to stop doing that."

She didn't understand. Why did he look so angry when she was just attempting to be grateful? "Doing what?"

"Thanking me," he snapped.

It made him uncomfortable, as if he were obligated to do something in return. Something he might not be able to do. They had leads, but he wasn't Supercop. The Ward woman might still disappear between the cracks. He'd seen it happen more than once.

"I haven't done anything yet," he reminded her.

"No, but you will, Kane." She was never more certain of anything in her life. Somehow, she *knew* he'd be the hero she was holding out for. The man to return her child to her. "You will."

There she went again, placing a burden squarely on his shoulders that was so heavy, he could hardly stand up beneath it. Didn't she understand that? Or did she? Was that innocent, vulnerable look in her eyes there by devious design? He'd spent so much time with people who deceived, who lived by their wits and would lie their way out of anything that he had trouble believing that she was as straight and sweet as she seemed.

No, that wasn't fair, he thought. She was exactly what she seemed. Trouble.

As he opened his mouth to tell her that he was only a man, nothing more, another emotion washed over him. He *was* only a man and nothing more. And the man within the burned-out shell ached to kiss her again. To hold her. The urge had been within him, alive and thriving, since he first kissed her. He wanted that tangy taste back. He wanted to lose himself in a mine field of emotion and not really care that he was in danger of being blown to smithereens.

He was tired, he thought. And unable to resist the temptation before him. Sighing, he took her face in his hands.

"Damn it, I'm going to regret this," he muttered to himself as he lowered his mouth to hers.

Excitement rippled through her as her heart imitated the rhythm of the music they had just heard in the restaurant.

"What a lovely thing to say."

The last word she murmured brushed against his lips. The erotic flavor it generated sent telegraphs of pending disaster throughout his system.

He didn't care.

Her mouth still carried the spicy, tangy flavor of the meal she'd just had. He'd always had a weakness for Mexican food. The taste he found there blended with the sweetness that he knew to be hers alone. Kane had no power within him to resist.

It was a minor infringement, he insisted to himself. Only minor. If he let his guard down for a second, it carried no consequences. None.

Kane cupped the back of her head in his hand and tilted it, drinking deeply of her mouth and the cauldron of tastes he found there. His tongue lightly brushed against hers. When she moaned, he had to struggle to keep from giving in to the rest of his desire.

He hated this state he found himself in, too weak to turn from her. All he wanted was to find a haven for himself within her goodness, within the sweetness and purity that she represented. Purity he had never known in his own life.

This time, the kiss was gentle, almost worshipful. But the intensity was there nonetheless, pulsating beneath the gentle brushing of lips.

He wanted to make love with her.

Abruptly, as if a silent alarm had gone off in his head, Kane dropped his hands to his side and stepped back, shaken. It took every fiber of his being not to show it. Her eyes were wide, the pupils huge, as if she had been falling into a drugged state. She struggled to focus on him. When she did, he was turning from her.

The words *Good night* hung in the air in his wake.

Jennifer ran her hand through her hair and stepped inside her room. It was going to take a while, she thought, for her heart to settled back down into a regular beat.

She spent a horrible night.

The bed, despite its sag, had been relatively comfortable. It didn't matter. She could have been sleeping on a bed of cacti for all the rest she got. Because of her baby and the man she trusted to help her, Jennifer was too keyed up to sleep. She tossed and turned most of the night, dozing off only to snap awake abruptly, a fragment of a nightmare clinging to the fringes of her mind. Then she'd lie there, waiting for her heart to settle down.

And she'd think.

The pattern repeated itself several times through the night. By three a.m. she was worn out. In the wee hours before dawn, Jennifer finally managed to drop off into a fitful sleep.

She had no idea what woke her this time. An oppressive bereavement washed over her as soon as she was conscious. The feeling had been her constant companion ever since Katie's abduction. The second feeling she experienced was disorientation. It took her a moment to remember where she was, and why.

And then another feeling pervaded her, a soft feeling, like a rose petal being carried off in a gentle breeze. It was born out of the memory of Kane's kiss. The kiss last night had been gentle, a complete contrast to the first kiss. That had been one full of anger, of warnings. Last night's had made no less of an impression on her for its tenderness, perhaps even more so. Jennifer felt his need even more this time. His need and his confusion. It was as if while he was kissing her, there was a war raging within him at the same time.

She dragged a hand through her hair and looked at her wristwatch on the nightstand. Seven a.m. The strong Arizona sun was already pushing its way through the curtains.

Her heart skipped a beat as she wondered if Kane would re-nege on his promise to wake her before he left.

Jennifer had just kicked the tangled sheet aside when there was a knock on her door. She pulled her short robe out of the suitcase on the floor. Throwing it on over the base-ball jersey she wore as a nightshirt, she hurried to the door.

"Who is it?"

"Detect—" Kane stopped. It was absurd to refer to him-self as Detective Madigan after he had kissed her twice. "Kane," he amended, uttering the name as if it were all sharp edges and cut his tongue to say it.

She smiled to herself. Maybe the walls were finally tum-bling down just a shade. She opened the door quickly, be-fore he found an excuse to leave.

"Good morning." She noticed the way he looked at her, as if he had expected her to be dressed and ready. "I was up until three, then I guess I must have fallen asleep." She opened the door wider to admit him in. "I can be ready in a minute."

Her legs were long, he thought, following her in. Too long. He looked at the faded wallpaper instead. "No woman can be ready in a minute." Kane placed the take-out bag he was holding on top of the bureau.

"I can," she assured him. She stooped down and rum-maged through her suitcase, then noticed the bag he had brought in. "What's that?"

He shrugged self-consciously. "I remembered what you said about liking breakfast. So I brought you some." His tongue felt awkward in his mouth, as if it had just swollen to twice its size.

She left the clothes she had chosen on the bed and moved to the bureau. "That was very kind of you."

"Practical," he contradicted, feeling progressively more awkward by the second. "I was up early, you weren't. I got breakfast." He made it all sound very logical. "We should be at the precinct by eight."

His initial comment caught her attention. "How did you know I wasn't up?"

He shrugged again, feeling at his breast pocket. "Thin walls. I didn't hear you stirring." Damn, why wasn't there a pack of cigarettes in his pocket?

Jennifer stared at him incredulously. "You *listened* for me?"

She made it sound like more than it really was. Like more than he wanted to admit that it was.

"There isn't much on television this hour of the morning." He dropped his hand, swearing to take up his vice at the first cigarette machine he passed. "Besides, I'm not much for artificial drama. I get enough of it firsthand."

He felt as if he had walked into somewhere he hadn't intended on being. Damn, it was only breakfast, not a lifetime commitment. He jerked an impatient hand toward the bag. "Do you want to eat, or what?"

Jennifer grinned at his discomfort. It reminded her of a puppy who hadn't grown into his paws yet and was tripping over his own feet. "By 'or what,' do you mean get dressed?"

Kane's eyes couldn't help taking in the way the jersey seemed to flirt with the tops of her thighs. He shoved his hands into his pockets to keep from doing something he'd regret. Again.

"Yeah. That's not a bad idea." He waved a hand at her attire. "It's distracting."

He had fairly growled out the words, but she took them at their worth. "Thank you."

He let out an exasperated sigh. "It wasn't meant as a compliment."

"I know." He wasn't the type to give compliments. But she could read between the lines. Jennifer picked up the clothes she had selected from the bed. "But I'm taking it as one."

Something goaded him into asking even though he thought he didn't care what the answer was. "Old boyfriend's?"

She stopped short of the tiny bathroom, her arms full. "Excuse me?"

"The jersey," he said impatiently, wishing he hadn't said anything at all. "Does it belong to an old boyfriend?" He wouldn't have wanted her to pry into his life. Wouldn't have answered if she had. Yet something drove him to venture on the path into hers.

Jennifer grinned in response. That he was curious, for whatever reason he might give, pleased her. "Actually, it's Nik's."

He raised his brow in surprise. "The chef played baseball?"

She nodded. "In college." She remembered how proud she was of him, sitting in the bleachers, cheering him on. "Until his senior year."

He leaned against the bureau. Somehow, it didn't seem right, sitting on her bed, not with her sheets still fresh from the warm imprint of her body, her scent still clinging to the pillow.

"What happened in his senior year?"

"He dropped out to take care of Julia and me."

He didn't say it, but the word *why* was there in the room with them.

The memory was painful, like a briar patch scratching at her legs as she made her way, but she managed to work through it.

"Our parents died within seven months of each other. Julia and I were still in high school. Nik went to work to support us." She smiled fondly as she glanced down at the jersey. "He finally managed to go back to college eighteen months later, but just at night. He didn't have time to play ball any more. It was a shame because he was good at it. Even thought about playing professionally. He gave up his dream for us."

Jennifer hugged the clothes against her as if that would stave off the sadness that threatened to come forward. She looked up. "I'm sorry, I'm rambling again."

He saw her need to distance herself from the subject and played along. "You do that fairly often?"

"No." She shook her head. "Only once or twice a day."
There was an apology in her smile. "I'm sorry, you really
haven't seen me at my best."

His eyes skimmed along her legs. The side of the jersey
kept hiking up whenever she moved. "I don't know about
that."

Her smile was replaced with a grin. "I'll be right out," she
promised, disappearing into the bathroom. The door
creaked and resisted being closed, then groaned as she pulled
it shut.

He had his doubts if she'd be "right out." In his limited
experience, women went by a different timetable than men
did. A few minutes to them seemed closer to an eternity to
him. His cup squeaked as he pulled off the plastic lid. The
coffee within was black. It was basically all he required of
it. Hot was a bonus he hadn't been expecting.

Holding the cup in both hands, he let his mind wander
back to the case as he examined each piece of information
he had available to him from every angle he could think of,
searching for any perspective that he might have missed, the
one that could help him untangle the skeins of confusion
that lay before him.

Kane had only managed to take a few meditative sips before Jennifer came out of the bathroom, dressed.

He looked at her, surprised. "You have a magician in
there?" He nodded toward the tiny room.

"No, I told you I'd only be a minute."

He looked at her face and tried to discern if she was
wearing no-makeup makeup, or whatever women were doing to their faces these days. Whatever it was, Jennifer
looked good. Too damn good for this hour of the morning.
Or any hour.

"I didn't think you meant it literally." He indicated the
bag with his cup. "That's for you. I wasn't sure what you
wanted so I had them fix a few things."

She looked inside the bag. There were three different
containers inside. The man must have thought she ate like a
horse once she got going. The sweetness of the gesture

touched her heart, but she knew better than to say anything. He'd hand her head to her.

Jennifer began taking things out and arranging them on the bureau. "How much do I owe you?"

He took another swallow to wash the bitter taste of cynicism from his mouth. "If I had wanted you to pay for it, I would have asked."

He sounded annoyed. Whether it was because of her offer to pay, or because he had done a good deed to begin with, she didn't know. She only knew she wanted to smooth out the rough waters between them. "I didn't mean to offend you. I just don't want to impose."

"Lady," he began, his temper short, "if that was true—" His voice trailed off, strangled by impatience. "Never mind."

He exhaled. He didn't want to put anything into words, not even in his own mind, that would add further fuel to this swirl of feelings that was trying to rise. If it was within him, he wanted it excised. Didn't want to impose. She was *already* imposing, in the worst possible way. She was imposing on his mind, irritating him far more than his craving for cigarettes ever had or would. Because, he realized, he was beginning to battle with an entirely different craving.

"Eat your breakfast, we have to get going."

Jennifer looked at the assortment spread out before her. "I can't finish all this. You're going to have to help." She pushed one container marked hot cakes and sausage toward him. "But then, you do that very well."

Her mouth was soft as she formed the words. He had to force himself to look elsewhere. Staring at flowers on the wall was getting damn old.

He yanked the lid off and tossed it aside. "Don't flatter me."

"Why?" She unwrapped something that resembled an omelet housed within a biscuit. A variety of different diced vegetables pockmarked it. It tasted surprisingly flavorful. "I get the feeling that you haven't received enough flattery in your life."

He let his plastic fork sink into a dark brown river of syrup puddling on the side of the plate. "And don't analyze me."

She tried to ignore the hurt that nipped at her, reminding herself that it was just his manner and she had gotten in the way. "I wasn't analyzing. I was just observing."

He'd lost his appetite and pushed the container away. "You were probing."

Why did he insist on maintaining this cloak of mystery around himself? He'd kissed her, hadn't he? And it wasn't casual. That meant that he wanted to have some sort of a relationship between them, however cursory. Relationships involved communication. "It's called getting to know someone."

He knew exactly what it was called. "Do us both a favor and don't."

She finished her biscuit and threw the wrapper away. "Don't what?"

She was entitled to a whitewashed world. He knew a world that was nearly black. It was his beat. "Don't get to know me."

"Too late," she answered as she hastily cleared the room, stuffing the wrappers and containers into the bag. "I've already started."

He took her arm, as if the momentary contact would make her come to her senses. They would never even remotely be two of a kind. If she became involved with him, it would only end badly for her. "Then stop."

She didn't know what surprised her more, that his grip was cruel or that his tone was.

"It's not something that I can just turn off and on like a faucet, Kane." She looked down at his hand, waiting. He released her. "Besides, we're going to be together for at least a few days, until we locate Katie." She said the last phrase as if it were a prayer. "I thought we could be friends."

He suddenly felt caged, trapped, as if there were a storm coming and he didn't know which direction it was coming from. Just that it would be here soon. "I don't have any friends."

She didn't take it as a warning, but an invitation. "Then I'll consider myself the first."

Why was she trying so hard? What was wrong with her? "Don't you get it? I don't need any friends." And he meant it sincerely.

It was as if he were speaking in another language to her, one she could never begin to understand. "Everybody needs friends."

"I don't."

His adamant response had her studying him. "What are you afraid of?"

Kane scowled at her. He'd spell it out for her, just this once. "Needing a friend. Okay?" He moved toward the door. "Now let's go."

He was almost out when she called him back. "Kane."

Kane spun around. "What?" he shouted at her, then ran his hand over his face. "What?" he repeated several decibels lower. She was making him lose his control. If he lost that edge, he'd be no good to either one of them in the only capacity that really mattered. A cop.

The look on her face made him feel as if he were in a no-win situation. She made his mouth water, but if he gave in, he'd still lose. And so would she.

"I didn't mean to make waves."

He snorted. "You have a funny way of showing it."

"I appreciate everything you're doing for me—" she began.

Not again. "I'm just doing my job," he cut in.

Jennifer remained undaunted. She was beginning to see through his stubborn manner. And she could be just as stubborn as he, if necessary.

"—you're doing for me," she repeated. "Letting me come along."

They didn't have time for this. *He* didn't have time for this. Not ever. "Well, if you want to keep coming along, you better hustle because I'm leaving.'' With that, he walked out the door.

"I'm right behind you." Jennifer grabbed her purse and hurried after him.

"I know," he muttered as he crossed the lot to the car. *And that's my problem.*

Chapter 9

Kane looked at Jennifer as she sat across from him at the Captain's desk. She looked tired and discouraged, he thought. Her expression matched the frustration he felt himself. It had been a long two days that had gone nowhere. They had both accompanied Redhawk when he went to question the one relative who still lived in Rosalind Ward's old neighborhood, her brother Ralph. As it turned out, he was living in the house where she was born. Kane had theorized that bringing Jennifer with them might strike a sympathetic chord with whomever they talked to.

He took her along because of that, but mostly because she refused to say behind.

She was a fighter. Grudging admiration touched the corners of his being. There were other emotions, as well, that he was having an increasingly difficult time ignoring. Usually, he had no trouble keeping himself separated from anyone who crossed his path, be it victim, criminal or another policeman. They all comprised different shades of "them."

And he remained alone.

But this time, his aloneness felt just that. Lonely.

He'd grown comfortable with his state, accepted it. Now, because of her, he was becoming increasingly aware that there was something missing from his life. She represented things that he had tried to forget existed.

Kane struggled to refocus his mind on the case and not have it linger on her, on the brief moments they had shared when his guard had temporarily deserted him. He would do neither of them any good if he dwelled on things that had no right to be.

Their one possible lead had crumbled. If Ralph Ward knew where his sister Rosalind was, or had seen her during the time that the Arizona abduction had taken place, he wasn't saying. He disavowed any knowledge of Rosalind's whereabouts.

Another dead end waited for them at the hospital where a baby had been abducted a few months ago. No one at Phoenix General recognized the photograph that Kane and Jennifer showed around the maternity ward. And when they had passed by the glass-enclosed nursery with its tiny occupants lined up for viewing like so many small miracles on parade, Kane had felt Jennifer's anguish. He had wanted to take her into his arms and hold her then, promising her that he would exhaust every possible avenue of approach until they found Katie.

But he didn't hold her. He only gave her shoulder a squeeze and ushered her along, away from the nursery. He had murmured some words to the effect that it would be all right. He had never felt as impotent, as helpless as he had at that moment.

He had left a copy of Rosalind's photograph at the hospital on the slim hope that someone on a different shift might recall seeing the woman.

Captain Hernandez was in conference with two of his men and Redhawk was occupied in another part of the precinct. Phones rang, men spoke. Everything provided background dissonance. They were alone, he and Jennifer, on this island of despair.

Redhawk walked in and silently handed Jennifer a cup of coffee. She looked as if she needed a lot more than that, Kane thought.

Kane rose, running his hand through his hair. Impatience danced through him like summer raindrops bouncing about on a tin roof. He wanted to do something for her, to end her misery. He had never wanted to solve a case more in his life.

"I told you it was going to get discouraging," Kane told her, biting off the words.

Jennifer nodded her thanks to Redhawk for the coffee. "I didn't expect to find her sitting up and waiting for me." Her voice quavered. She wrapped shaky hands around the cup and she held it to her. "I know it's going to take time. But we'll find her." She said the words so fiercely, her emotions vibrating through every part of her, that she squeezed the paper cup. Coffee threatened to brim over. Jennifer took a breath to steady herself. "We're going to find her." She repeated the words as if they were bound in an oath.

"Hey," he said softly, his voice a contrast to hers in an effort to soothe her, "I didn't say we wouldn't."

God, he thought, now he was actually making unsubstantiated promises to her. Moved by the tears he saw shimmering in her eyes and filling her voice, he was breaking his own rules.

The phone jangled on the captain's desk. Kane moved aside as Redhawk reached over the desk to answer it.

"Look," Kane began, trying to regain control over his own ragged emotions, "let's get something to eat, and then—"

She shook her head, watching the telephone, willing that whoever it was on the other end was calling about her baby. "I'm not hungry."

It was time to use a little force before she completely wore out on him. Kane placed his hands on the back of her chair as if to urge her up. "But I am."

One hand on the telephone, Redhawk signaled for them to stay where they were, then continued taking notes. The lackluster look in Jennifer's eyes disappeared, pushed aside by hope as she strained to make sense of Redhawk's end of the conversation.

"Sounds good," he declared. "We'll have someone down within the hour to take your statement in full. Thanks for calling in." He hung up.

"What d'you have?" Kane asked before the receiver had touched the cradle.

The broad Indian face was split by a grin. "One of the night shift orderlies remembers seeing someone who looked like Ward." He tapped his pencil on the photograph on the desk. "Swears to it. Says he remembers because when he saw her holding a baby in the nursery, she was jiggling her other hand, like she had something in it. He thought she'd drop the baby. When he said something to her, she told him she'd been holding babies for twenty years and had never let one of them fall."

Jennifer's head snapped up, a memory suddenly flashing before her. "What did you say?"

Redhawk turned toward her. "That she never dropped one."

She shook her head, trying to catch the memory. She needed his words. "No, before that. About—about the jiggling."

Redhawk paused, remembering. "The orderly said she was jiggling her hand."

The memory solidified. Jennifer could see the woman, standing by the door, Katie in her arms. She was jiggling her right hand. Jennifer turned to Kane. The sudden vividness of the image made her almost feel as if he could see it as well. "It's her. The orderly saw Ward."

Redhawk looked doubtful. "I don't know. Sometimes people make things up, just to snag a little attention. Maybe he's lying."

But Jennifer remained adamant. "No, she did the same thing in my room with her hand. It's like a nervous habit. You know—" Jennifer looked at Kane for support "—like you feeling your pocket for cigarettes every time you get agitated."

PLAY
£600,000 LOTTO!

NO COST... NO OBLIGATION...

NO PURCHASE NECESSARY!

IT'S FUN

IT'S FREE

FREE! This cuddly teddy bear with the compliments of Silhouette.

FREE BOOKS! CASH PRIZES!

OFFICIAL RULES
MILLION DOLLAR
SWEEPSTAKES (III)

NO PURCHASE NECESSARY TO ENTER

To enter, follow the directions published. Method of entry may vary. For eligibility, entries must be received no later than March 31, 1996. No liability is assumed for printing errors, lost, late or misdirected entries.

To determine winners, the sweepstakes numbers on submitted entries will be compared against a list of randomly, pre-selected prizewinning numbers. In the event all prizes are not claimed via the return of prizewinning numbers, random drawings will be held from among all other entries received to award unclaimed prizes.

Prizewinners will be determined no later than June 30, 1996. Selection of winning numbers and random drawings are under the supervision of D. L. Blair, Inc., an independent judging organisation whose decisions are final. Limit: one prize to a family or organisation. No substitution will be made for any prize, except as offered. Taxes and duties on all prizes are the sole responsibility of winners. Winners will be notified by mail. Odds of winning are determined by the number of eligible entries distributed and received.

Sweepstakes open to residents of the U.S. (except Puerto Rico), Canada, Europe and Taiwan who are 18 years of age or older, except employees and immediate family members of Torstar Corp., D.L. Blair, Inc., their affiliates, subsidiaries, and all other agencies, entities, and persons connected with the use, marketing or conduct of this sweepstakes. All applicable laws and

regulations apply. Sweepstakes offer void wherever prohibited by law. Any litigation within the province of Quebec respecting the conduct and awarding of a prize in this sweepstakes must be submitted to the Regies des Loteries et Courses du Quebec. In order to win a prize, residents of Canada will be required to answer a time-limited arithmetical skill-testing question to be administered by mail.

Winners of major prizes (Grand through Fourth) will be obligated to sign and return an affidavit of Eligibility and Release of Liability within 30 days of notification. In the event of non-compliance within this time period or if a prize is returned as undeliverable, D.L. Blair, Inc. may at its sole discretion, award that prize to an alternate winner. By acceptance of their prize, winners consent to use of their names, photographs or other likeness for purposes of advertising, trade and promotion on behalf of Torstar Corp., its affiliates and subsidiaries, without further compensation unless prohibited by law. Torstar Corp. and D.L. Blair, Inc., their affiliates and subsidiaries not responsible for errors in printing of sweepstakes and prize winning numbers. In the event a duplication of a prize winning number occurs, a random drawing will be held from among all entries received with that prize winning number to award that prize.

This sweepstakes is presented by Torstar Corp., their subsidiaries, and affiliates in conjunction with book, merchandise and/or product offerings. •The number of prizes to be awarded and their value are as follows: Grand Prize - $1,000,000 (payable at $33,333,33 a year for 30 years): First Prize - $50,000; Second Prize - $10,000; Third Prize - $5,000; 3 Fourth Prizes - $1,000 each; 10 Fifth Prizes - $250 each; 1000 Sixth Prizes - $100 each. Values of all prizes are in U.S. currency. Prizes in each level will be presented in different creative executions, including various currencies, vehicles, merchandise and travel. Any presentation of a prize level in a currency other than U.S. currency represents an approximate equivalent to the U.S. currency prize for that level, at that time. Prize winners will have the opportunity of selecting a prize offered for that level; however, the actual non U.S. currency equivalent prize, if offered and selected, shall be awarded at the exchange rate existing at 3:00 P.M. New York time on March 31, 1996. A travel prize option, if offered and selected by the winner, must be completed within 12 months of selection and is subject to: travelling companion (s) completing and returning of a Release of Liability prior to travel; and hotel and flight accommodations availability. For current list of all prize options offered within prize levels, send a self-addressed, stamped envelope (WA residents need not affix postage) to MILLION DOLLAR SWEEPSTAKES (III) Prize Options, Silhouette Reader Service, PO Box 236, Croydon, Surrey, CR9 3RU.

For a list of prizewinners (available after July 31, 1996) send a separate, stamped, self-addressed envelope to: Million Dollar Sweepstakes (III) Winners, Silhouette Reader Service, PO Box 236, Croydon, Surrey, CR9 3RU.

•U.K. equivalent prize values at the time of printing. Grand Prize - £600,000; First Prize - £30,000; Second Prize - £6,000; Third Prize - £3,000; 3 Fourth Prizes - £600 each; 10 Fifth Prizes - £150 each; 1,000 Sixth Prizes - £60 each.

Silhouette invite you to play
£600,000 LOTTO!

LOTTO CARD No:

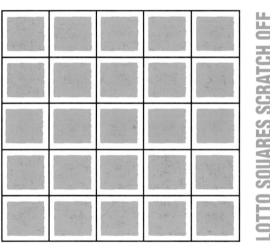

LOTTO SQUARES SCRATCH OFF

Instructions: Using a coin scratch away 4 or 5 silver squares in a straight line to see the maximum you could win in our Grand Prize Draw. 5 hearts revealed means this card is eligible for the £600,000 Grand Prize; 4 hearts revealed… the £30,000 First Prize; 3 hearts… £6,000; 2 hearts… £3,000; 1 heart… £600. VOID IF MORE THAN 5 SQUARES ARE SCRATCHED AWAY.

AND… YOU CAN CLAIM UP TO 4 FREE SILHOUETTE SPECIAL EDITIONS A CUDDLY TEDDY AND A MYSTERY GIFT ABSOLUTELY FREE.

To register your entry in the £600,000 Prize Draw and to claim your free books and gifts simply return this card. See the coupon overleaf for more details.

We are sure that once you have read your free books, you'll want more of these exciting Silhouette Special Editions. So unless we hear otherwise, every month we will send you 6 of our very latest Silhouette Special Editions for just £1.95 each. Postage and packing are free - we pay all the extras! Your satisfaction is guaranteed! You may cancel or suspend your subscription at any time, simply by contacting us. Any free books and gifts will remain yours to keep.

DON'T HESITATE REPLY TODAY!

FREE BOOKS CERTIFICATE

YES! Please send me the free books and gifts to which I am entitled and enter me in the £600,000 prize draw. Please also reserve a Reader Service subscription for me. If I decide to subscribe, I shall receive 6 brand new Silhouette Special Editions every month for just £1.95 each. If I decide not to subscribe I will contact you within 10 days of receiving my introductory parcel. The free books and gifts will remain mine to keep in any case. I understand that I am under no obligation whatsoever and that I may cancel at anytime simply by writing to you.

If you would like to enter the £600,000 prize draw but would prefer not to receive books please tick box. ☐

Ms / Mrs / Miss / Mr _____

Address _____

_____

_____ Postcode _____

1OS4SE

Signature _____

MAILING
PREFERENCE
SERVICE

SILHOUETTE READER SERVICE
FREEPOST
P.O. BOX 236
CROYDON
SURREY
CR9 9EL

NO
STAMP
NEEDED

Kane opened his mouth to deny her assessment, then let it go. Though he didn't like his private habits brought to light or examined in any fashion, this wasn't the time to say anything. Something was developing in the back of his mind and he pulled at it like a baker kneading dough until the loaf was finally formed.

"Describe it," he instructed Jennifer.

His tone had both Redhawk and Jennifer looking at him.

"Describe what?" she asked.

"The jiggling motion." Kane pointed to Jennifer's hand. "Describe it." Words meant different things to different people. For all he knew, she might be talking about a nervous tremor. If she was, his theory fell as flat as bread without yeast.

She shrugged, not knowing what Kane wanted from her. "I don't know. Jiggling. You know, shaking. As if there were coins in her hand and she was rattling them around."

"Or maybe a key?" Redhawk suggested.

She shrugged. "I suppose." She looked at Kane, waiting. "But I don't—"

"How about dice?" Kane said slowly, watching her face as he asked.

"Dice?" She hadn't thought of that.

Kane nodded. It might give them something more to go on. "Dice, like at a Las Vegas crap table."

Jennifer turned the thought around in her mind as she replayed the image in her mind again. "Yes, it could be like getting ready to throw dice."

Redhawk was pleased that they were making headway, though he had no idea where Kane was going with all this. "Looks like we've got a positive ID in three different places." He checked off the list of eleven hospitals Kane had faxed the day before. "Queen of Angels, Harris Memorial and Phoenix General."

Jennifer scarcely heard him. Her eyes were on Kane. He was working on something. She could see it. "What are you thinking?"

It was a long shot, but stranger things had paid off. "That we've got a gambler on our hands." He turned to Redhawk. "I think we need to pay her brother another visit and find out if the Ward woman likes to gamble."

Redhawk nodded. "Let's go." He led the way out of the room.

Jennifer was trying to piece things together as she hurried to the parking lot behind Kane. "What does all this mean?" She could tell that he was already at the next step in his mind and she wanted to be there with him, not trail behind.

Kane held the precinct door open for her. "Where do you go if you like to gamble?"

Jennifer shrugged. She had never even bought a lottery ticket. Betting was something entirely foreign to her. "The racetrack?"

"That's if you play the horses." Kane thought of the newspaper he had found in the trash. "If you play dice, you go to Vegas and play the crap tables."

Jennifer felt like Hansel and Gretel, following a trail of bread crumbs. Would she finally reach the end, or would there be something to sweep the bread crumbs away before she got there? There was enough tension within her now to fill a stadium. "You think she's gone to Las Vegas?"

"She's been there at least twice already," he told her. "We have the kidnapping and the old newspaper I found. Maybe she's gone there to lay low for awhile, or enjoy herself. If we get the right answers from her brother, it's worth a shot."

Jennifer climbed into the back of the car and leaned forward, her arms on the back of the seat. Redhawk waited until Kane was seated, then took off before the passenger door was completely shut. "But what if she doesn't have Katie with her?"

The thought had plagued Kane all along. He put off exploring it. "First we have to find her," he told Jennifer.

Ralph Ward was annoyed at being disturbed twice in two days about the sister he swore he had lost touch with years ago. He stood in the doorway of his two-story house, a white-haired, grizzled centurion whose sturdy arm barred access into his home as he kept his hand on the door frame.

"Look, we were never what you call close to begin with. She was ten years older and almost gone out of the house by the time I started having any memories to speak of." He snapped out the words. "Why can't you people leave me be? I ain't done nothing wrong."

But Kane wasn't about to be turned away. "Does your sister like to gamble, Mr. Ward?"

"Gamble?" the old man snorted. "Rosie would bet on anything if the odds were right. Sometimes even if they weren't." Self-righteousness puffed out the wide cheeks beneath the spiky white stubble that covered his face like tiny quills on a baby porcupine. "That's what got her into trouble in the first place. She was hooked on it. Always thought she could make it back the next time around. Except for once or twice, she never did."

Jennifer and Kane exchanged glances. "Did she ever go to Las Vegas?"

A superior smirk spread along the fleshy lips. "Does a cat have kittens?"

Kane pushed a little more. He wanted to pin this down, not play with metaphors. "Not if it's a male cat."

"Well, this cat had kittens. Lots o' them. She *used* to go there every chance she got. I was surprised she didn't live there." He shrugged. "Maybe she does. Now I don't know nothing else. You guys gonna leave me alone, or do I have to file a complaint about being harassed?"

"You've been very helpful," Redhawk told the man, stepping off the porch.

A little more of the path leading to her daughter had been cleared away. Grateful, Jennifer touched the man's arm. "Thank you, Mr. Ward."

"Yeah, sure." He slammed the door on them. It trembled as it hung precariously on rusty hinges.

"Vegas?" Jennifer asked Kane as they hurried to the car.

"Vegas," he confirmed. "We'll make a detective out of you yet."

She liked the momentary smile that crossed his lips. It gave Kane's face a kindly expression that he was obviously unaware of. Jennifer felt heartened in more ways than one.

Kane phoned Henderson in California to let him know what their next step was. He asked the man to telephone ahead to the police precinct in Las Vegas and forward the same information to them that had been sent to the Phoenix department. Airline tickets were secured, the hotel paid up, and they left Redhawk with a promise to be in touch if anything bore fruit. The latter promised to have a patrolman keep an eye on Ward's house on the outside chance that Rosalind might return.

Despite the tension ricocheting through her body, Jennifer dozed on the flight to Las Vegas for a few minutes, her head leaning against Kane's shoulder. He sat very still, absorbing the sensation of having her so close to him. Having her so near created a small beacon of light to be stored up against the darkness that always filled his soul.

It made him ache to have her so close and yet know that he couldn't have her at all. It wouldn't be fair to intrude on her life. She had enough grief to deal with. Becoming involved with him would only make things worse for her. Because there was no future in it. She deserved things that were good and pure and filled with the hope she seemed to be able to cling to so tenaciously. He dealt with the dark and found comfort in it.

Or had, until she had wandered across his path.

Jennifer's eyes flew open as the plane began its downward descent. She jerked up.

"Easy." Kane placed his hand over hers on the armrest. "We're just landing, not crashing."

She blinked the sleep from her eyes, then smiled ruefully. "I dreamed that we found her."

The soft curve of her mouth made it unnecessary for Kane to ask which "her" she meant, Katie or Ward.

"We will," he told Jennifer, then turned to look out the small window as the ground below rushed up to greet them.

Jennifer wondered if he believed it now, or if he was just saying the words for her benefit. A day ago, she knew there would have been no question in her mind. Things had been very cut-and-dried with him and he wasn't able to offer hope, only the truth. Now he had gotten even harder to fathom. Either way, she was grateful to him for so many things.

They deplaned in Las Vegas. As before, there was a squad car waiting to pick them up. This time the vehicle was driven by a sleepy-eyed plainclothesman named Bill Reed. His red hair and freckles looked a great deal more lively than he did at this early hour of the morning.

"Things really start jumping here at sundown," he informed them, mumbling into his wrinkled shirt as he waited for them to get into the car,

Kane buckled his seat belt, wondering if the man was awake enough to drive.

"Midmorning might be a good time to question dealers," Kane said to Jennifer, thinking out loud. "Before the crowds get them too busy." He saw that his statement had no effect on the policeman. Maybe he hadn't been briefed yet. Before he launched into any explanations, he thought it best to talk to the officer in charge. "Why don't you take us to the precinct and we'll go from there?"

Reed shrugged. "Those are my orders, anyway."

Captain Theodore Roosevelt Jameson was a stocky man with a permanently flushed face, as if he were perpetually in the midst of carrying on an argument. It took Kane only a few sentences to ascertain that the man was hostile to the idea of having outsiders come into his territory "with their problems."

They were on their own here, Kane thought. "The way I see it, captain—" he began, leaning back languidly. He looked relaxed, but Jennifer knew better. "It's your problem, too. A baby was stolen from a hospital in your city."

"We've only got one hospital in the area. According to what *you* say—" Jameson's expression clearly showed what he thought of the theory "—the Ward woman never strikes twice in the same hospital. For us, that makes this an isolated incident." He lifted his large shoulders and let them drop. "Maybe it's not even the same woman. I can't have you coming in, bothering people because you *think* they might be kidnappers.''

Lack of sleep and frustration had Jennifer's temper flaring before Kane could answer. ''I don't think the parents of the baby who was kidnapped from your hospital think of it as just an 'incident.' ''

Jameson frowned as he studied the interior of his coffee cup. ''What is it you want from me?''

Kane had been up against men like this before, so enamored with their own authority that they attacked anyone whom they perceived as challenging it. He had no time for head games. There was a child at stake. Perhaps, if they were lucky, several of them, not to mention their parents.

''Cooperation,'' Kane told them. ''I need one man to take her photograph to the hospital and show it around, see if anyone recognizes her. I don't have jurisdiction. If we find her, I'm going to need one of your people to make the arrest.''

Jameson crossed his arms before him and used his stomach as a perch. Jennifer could remember doing the same thing when she was pregnant. She felt a pang seize her heart.

''Evidence?'' Jameson demanded.

Kane nodded. ''Enough to put her at three of the kidnapping sites at the time of the abductions.''

Jameson paused dramatically, milking the moment as he pretended to roll over Kane's words in his mind. The two men knew that logically there could be only one outcome.

''Okay.'' The captain rose to his feet, a mountain rising from the sea. ''What are you going to do?''

Kane placed his briefcase on the desk, snapping the lock open. ''I've got copies of her mug shot taken ten years ago in Phoenix. We want it shown around to the dealers at the various casinos.'' He took them out and placed them on the desk.

Jameson fingered one of the photographs. ''She steal chips on the side?'' he asked with a disparaging laugh. The look in Jennifer's eyes made him feel guilty. ''Sorry.'' He dropped the photograph on the desk. ''I didn't mean to make that sound the way it did.'' He sucked air in between his teeth and looked at Kane. "I suppose you want a little manpower?"

Just the faintest hint of a smile crossed Kane's lips. "That comes under the heading of cooperation."

Jameson glanced at the duty roster on the board. "I can spare three men for a couple of hours," the man said grudgingly.

Kane nodded. He would take what he could. This was the city of luck. Maybe they would finally find theirs. He glanced at Jennifer. They were certainly due.

She felt as useful as a bump on a log. Jennifer knew that everything that could be done was being done, yet she felt that she should be doing more, contributing somehow. They had separated at each casino they hit, showing Ward's photograph and questioning dealers. But no one recognized the woman depicted so angelically in the photo.

"Tired?" Kane asked as they walked into their third casino.

She had gone past tired and was on her way to numb, but she shook her head. "Even if I was, I wouldn't know it." She looked around the huge area. "They don't have any clocks around here." The fact amazed her.

The reason was perfectly obvious to Kane. The casinos didn't want people aware of how much time they had spent or when it was time to leave.

Kane took Jennifer's elbow as they walked across a lush red carpet that led past a double guard of slot machines. "That's because time is supposed to stand still while you wait for fate to blow on your dice."

She wondered if he spoke from firsthand experience. "Do you gamble?"

He slanted a look in her direction. "Every day of my life." *And never so much as now.*

The front lobby with its slot machines was filled with far more activity than the casino was at this hour. They started to separate, but Jennifer stopped when she saw the voluptuous woman at the long dice table brighten noticeably. The woman had turned luminous turquoise eyes in Kane's direction.

The woman appeared to sum Kane up with the long, languid stare of a predator. Her teeth were white and perfect as she smiled at him.

"Out to make your fortune early, handsome?" She jiggled the dice and blew on them.

Jennifer moved toward Kane. An emotion akin to jealousy pricked at her. She had no business feeling it, especially at a time like this. But it was there, refusing to be erased or dismissed.

Kane gave the woman at the dice table a thorough, appraising look. "That all depends."

The hostess, dressed in a royal blue dress that looked as if it were painted on, drew closer to Kane. She reminded Jennifer of a shark circling her prey just before striking. "On what?" the woman asked, her voice breathy.

Kane ignored the blatant invitation in her voice. "On whether you've ever seen this woman." He produced Ward's photograph from inside the manila envelope.

The blonde's eyes flickered over the four-by-five inch black-and-white photo, apparently ready to dismiss it in deference to something that had captivated her fancy more keenly: Kane. But the face caught her attention and the woman took a second look. She took the photograph from Kane and studied it to make certain that it wasn't a mistake.

"What are you doing with Rosie's picture?"

Bingo. "You know her?" Kane asked. He didn't have to turn around to look. He could *feel* Jennifer tensing behind him.

"Sure, she turns up here every so often." The hostess returned the photograph to Kane. "Worse case of hard luck I've ever seen." She laughed and for a moment, her edges seemed to mellow slightly. "We've even tried to get her to stop, you know." She leaned closer to Kane, her low neckline dipping even further down as she entrusted him with the secret. "Against the house rules, but hell, she looks like my grandmother. I don't figure retired nurses have that kind of money to blow.''

A retired nurse. Kane wondered if that was true, or part of Rosalind Ward's scam. It would help explain the ease with which she infiltrated maternity wards without arousing suspicion. Someone who was versed in hospital routines would have an easier time of it, Kane mused.

Jennifer pressed forward. "Does she live around here?"

The blonde glanced at Jennifer as if noticing her for the first time. Some of her friendliness abated. "Not too far from the strip. She's got a little bungalow there, I think." The woman shrugged as if the detail were far too trivial for her to bother with. "Randy drove her home one night after she'd lost everything. He'd be the one to ask."

"Randy?" Kane probed.

The woman's eyes were all over him, as if already declaring possession. "Randy Hudson. He works one of the other tables." She nodded in the general direction where Randy usually worked. "Hey, what do you want Rosie for?"

Jennifer began to answer, but Kane interrupted. "One of her relatives left her some money. We're from the lawyer's office."

It seemed all right to the woman. "Randy's on vacation," she volunteered. "But I think he's due back today. His shift usually starts at two." There was an open invitation in her words a deaf man couldn't miss. "You might want to test your luck until then."

Jennifer had no idea what possessed her, but she hooked her arm through Kane's. "He has all the luck he can handle at the moment." With that, Jennifer turned on her heel, forcing an amused Kane to follow.

She had taken him completely by surprise with her intervention. "Oh? And what kind of luck is that?" Kane asked as they moved away from the dice table.

Jennifer looked over her shoulder at the woman who was still watching them intently. "The luck of being saved from a piranha. She looks as if she could have you for lunch and spit out the bones without blinking."

Her cheeks were mildly flushed and there was a spark in her eyes he hadn't seen before. He found himself more than a little attracted to this fiery aspect of her. "Don't you think I can handle myself?"

He was laughing at her, she thought. Maybe she had interrupted something after all. The thought annoyed her. "Why, is she your type?"

He shook his head. "No. Too brassy and flashy. Anyway, I don't have a type. But if I were to have a type," he said softly as he rubbed his thumb slowly along the hollow of her cheek. "It would be you."

Jennifer felt her heart lodge itself in her throat, pounding so hard, she was having trouble hearing the buzz of voices all around them. Everything seemed jumbled up. She felt as if her emotions were stretched out to the limit, like a tightrope about to snap. This was happening to her at the worst possible time. And yet, if it wasn't this time, if her baby hadn't been abducted, she wouldn't have met Kane at all.

She looked around, trying desperately to clear her head. "What do we do until he gets here?"

Now that they had found someone who knew where Ward stayed, there was no point in remaining here until he arrived. They could return at two.

"Get a room to stash our belongings, maybe get a few hours' sleep." That was all he really wanted right now, he thought, to get some sleep. And to have her laying beside him. Nothing else, just her body near his. It was little enough to ask for, but much too much.

She shook her head. "I can't sleep."

The woman was the last word in stubborn, Kane thought. In that, he seemed to have met his match. Too bad there were so many other things in which they were light-years apart.

"That's what you said before you dozed off on the plane," he reminded Jennifer. "You can't keep going like this."

"You are," she pointed out.

He frowned. He was trying to make a point for her own good, not get into another debate. ''That's different.''

She looked up at him innocently. ''Why?''

She was a difficult woman to keep his temper around, he thought. ''Because it is.''

She linked her arm through his again as they turned to leave the casino. ''You do tend to run off at the mouth, don't you?''

''On occasion—'' he looked down at her lips ''—my mouth has been known to get me into trouble.''

Jennifer felt a small ripple send sparkles through her. She knew exactly what occasion he was referring to. She was, she realized, beginning to understand the way he thought.

Chapter 10

Jennifer and Kane were about to leave the main casino when the blonde at the dice table called out to him. "Hey, handsome."

When Kane turned in response, Jennifer murmured, "And here I thought you were modest."

The teasing grin on Jennifer's face struck a kindred chord he didn't even realize he possessed. "Honest," he told her. "Always honest." He looked inquisitively over his shoulder at the blonde.

The woman was pointing toward someone only a few feet away from them. "If you want to talk to Randy, that's him coming in now. I guess he's taking over an earlier shift."

The man just entering was tall and sturdy looking. He reminded Jennifer more of a bouncer than a man who earned his living by making a roulette wheel spin for eight hours a day. He looked a little apprehensive at being singled out.

The woman at the dice table beckoned to him. "Randy, these two want to talk to you about Rosie."

Randy appeared to assess Kane and Jennifer before saying a word. A suspicious scowl lightly furrowed his brow even though his plastic smile remained in place. It was a prerequisite for working at the casino. "What about Rosie?"

Kane removed the woman's photograph from the manila envelope and held it up to him. "Are you acquainted with this woman?"

Randy didn't touch the photograph, as if doing so would somehow implicate him in something he wanted no part of. "Yeah. She plays at Joely's table, mostly." He nodded at the blonde.

Kane glanced at her and the woman's smile widened. "Joely told us you took Rosalind Ward home one night."

Randy's shoulders stiffened, giving the impression of a cat whose back was arched just as it readied to do battle. "So, I'm a nice guy. What of it?"

The man was hiding something, Kane thought. But whether it had to do with his own life or Ward's, Kane had no way of ascertaining yet. "Do you remember where she lives?" he asked evenly.

Randy cocked his head, his body appearing to relax slightly. "Maybe." A greedy glint entered his eyes. "What's it worth to you?"

First impulse had Jennifer wanting to say, "Everything." But she stifled it. He looked like the kind of man who would take advantage of the situation if he could. She felt Kane's hand tighten on hers, as if warning her to remain silent.

Kane didn't want to take a chance on word that the police were looking for her getting back to Ward. "Might be worth a lot to Miss Ward," Kane said easily. "We represent a law firm that's trying to find her. A relative died, leaving her a small inheritance. You could settle up with her when the time came." Kane could see instantly that he had played the man correctly.

Randy looked as if he were tempted to take them to Ward himself. But the sight of a smiling, dark-suited man slowly approaching him from the rear of the casino had him suddenly frowning.

"Damn supervisor comes out of the walls," Randy muttered. "Look, I've got to get to work. I took her to The Lucky Lady Arms on Bearpaw Way. I think it was apartment nine." Randy paused for a moment, thinking, then nodded. "Yeah, it was nine."

"You're sure?" Kane pressed.

The man shrugged carelessly, as if it had never occurred to him that he might be mistaken. "Hey, numbers are my life." Glancing again at the man in the distance, Randy muttered a curse under his breath and left them.

Jennifer waited until they were out in the daylight again before asking. "Why didn't you let me tell him the truth back there?" Though she had hesitated herself, Jennifer was curious to see what Kane's reasoning was.

"Two reasons. I didn't want to take a chance on word getting back to Ward that the police are looking for her. And, because in this case, the truth wouldn't have helped us." Kane had made an immediate assessment of the man. In his line of business, Kane didn't always get a second chance to make a judgment. "He's not the type to care about babies being stolen, Jennifer. If he knew this was a police matter, it might have made him clam up altogether."

Kane stopped at the vehicle Jameson had lent them. "Jennifer, not everyone is ready to do the right thing."

Did he think she was a complete imbecile? "I know that."

"No, I don't think you do." Kane held the door open for her. He could see that his observation annoyed her. Probably because it was true. He got behind the wheel and started the car. "I think you feel that evil is an aberration and that goodness is the norm."

She knew he was a policeman, but was his view of the world really as black as all that? How awful for him. "You make it sound as if I'm an idiot."

"No." There was even a spark of sympathy in his voice for the condition she was laboring beneath. "Just not a realist."

Even with her baby stolen, Jennifer refused to subscribe to the philosophy that he seemed to espouse. She could never survive that way. People were good, given the chance.

Not all people, but most. "I prefer to believe in the best in people."

He laughed shortly. She was a dreamer. Perhaps that was what fascinated him about her. That she could still dream, even after all this. "And be disappointed."

"No, not usually." She turned and looked at him, wanting him to believe the way she did. "People tend to live up to expectations."

He shook his head. What would it take for her to learn? "Only in half-hour sitcoms."

"You're too cynical, Kane."

The genuine sorrow in her voice had him turning momentarily to look at her. "I'm realistic. I've carried a shield for a long time, and seen the underbelly of society too often not to be." He thought of the restaurant. She didn't travel, she was young, maybe the people there defined the boundaries of her world. "You've only seen people with their table manners in place."

His voice was hard, impenetrable, but Jennifer had a feeling that Kane's hurt went far deeper than hers, if possible. And beyond what he had seen as a policeman. Her child had been stolen from her. God willing, they would get her back. Kane sounded as if his entire life had been ripped away from him before he had ever had a chance to live it and enjoy it. There was no getting that back, no way of having restitution made.

She wanted to know. She knew she couldn't erase it, but perhaps sharing it with someone might help him shoulder the pain and finally bury it.

For a second, she hesitated. She knew he was probably going to bite her head off for this, but she had to try. "When this is over—" she began, then paused.

Kane stepped on the gas and just made it through a light as it turned red. "Yeah?"

She took a breath, then pushed the words out. "Will you talk to me?"

He didn't quite understand her point. "You mean, will I come and look you up and talk about the case over brunch? I don't think so." When this was over, it would be over. And he would go back to his life and she to hers. And that would be best for both of them.

She shook her head. He didn't understand. Or perhaps refused to. She knew that she should just let it drop, but the man who sat next to her had reached out and she couldn't turn her back on him. Reached out not with words, but through the kisses they had shared. Both the ruthless one and the gentle one that followed.

"No," Jennifer persisted. "I mean after we find Katie, will you tell me what happened to you?" The expression on his face grew dark, but she refused to back away. "What hurt you?"

His hands tightened on the wheel as he took a turn. "What makes you think I was hurt?"

There was an icy distance in his voice, but she wasn't going to be put off. "Everything. The way you lash out when I try to ask questions—"

Did she need the words written down for her? No trespassing. Ever. And she had already jumped the fence and left fresh tracks on his private field. He didn't want her coming any further. He wanted her back over the fence again.

"That's just self-preservation."

She studied his face as she continued. "The way you back away from any intimacy."

His jaw hardened. "See reason number one." Kane pulled the car in at the precinct. Turning off the engine, he made it clear that he was turning off the conversation as well.

Kane got out. "Time to convince the good captain that we are going to need his help."

He walked ahead of her into the precinct. The message was clear. He wanted distance to remain between them, no matter what momentary aberration had occurred. And she was not to cross the line.

Like hell she wasn't, Jennifer thought, hurrying to catch up.

Kane knew better than to try to talk to Ward on his own. He needed authority on his side if the case against the woman was ever to get to court. As quickly as possible, he relayed the details to the captain and asked for a uniformed policeman to accompany him when he went to The Lucky Lady Arms to see Rosalind.

"On the say-so of some guy who's probably drifting through?" Jameson scoffed. "It's probably just some wild goose chase."

"It's a lead," Kane answered. His tone was mild, but there was no arguing with it or the unspoken words behind it. Jameson had to have the lead checked out or Kane would take the matter up with his superior.

"Okay, I'll give you a man." He glanced in Jennifer's direction. "But no civilians," he specified. "I've already got too much to handle without worrying about hysterical women coming along on so-called busts."

"I am not hysterical and this woman has my daughter," Jennifer retorted.

Jameson was only saying what Kane had maintained all along. But hearing the man put Jennifer down had Kane balking. The man definitely had a way of rubbing him wrong. Besides, Kane had caught the look in Jennifer's eyes. Disappointment mingled with determination. There was no telling what she would do if he left her behind. He could just see her hailing a cab and following them. She knew the address as well as he did.

"Look, little lady—" Jameson began.

"I'll take responsibility for her," Kane cut in quickly.

Jennifer didn't know whether to be grateful to him for taking her side, or annoyed that she was being treated like some kind of unhousebroken puppy he had to "take responsibility" for.

Jameson frowned, but he was obviously tired of arguing the point. "Great. She fouls things up, it's on your head." The captain looked at his duty roster. "Okay, I can give one uniform. Take Kaminsky. If your suspect's not there, I can't help you any more. Agreed?"

Kane agreed. If Ward wasn't there, he would go back to hitting the casinos. He had a gut feeling that Ward was in Vegas somewhere. His hunches were few and far between, but they usually paid off.

"Thanks for riding to my rescue," Jennifer said to Kane as they waited for Officer Kaminsky to join them.

He shrugged off her thanks. "Also self-preservation. I know you by now. You won't stay put. You'd turn up there ahead of us and maybe blow the whole thing wide open. I'd rather have you at my side." He saw the small question growing in her eyes. "Professionally," he added.

"I knew that," she answered.

Jennifer sat in the back of the police vehicle. She was so tense, she had to remind herself to breathe. Kane exchanged a few words with the young officer driving them. He sounded as if they were just going for a tour of the city instead of possibly finally cornering their quarry. Jennifer knotted her fingers together and stared straight ahead. She prayed harder than she ever had before that the trail would end here and that she would be holding her baby in her arms by nightfall.

Kane maintained his deceptively relaxed tone. It sliced through the thick air like a sharp knife, intent on subdividing the anxiety that was almost palpitating within the vehicle. Aware of what he was doing, Jennifer struggled to keep her feelings under control.

The Lucky Lady Arms was a rundown cluster of single-bedroom dwellings arranged in a semicircle around the arched entrance. Over a quarter of a century since they had been constructed, the attached apartments had weathered poorly in the broiling desert sun. Maintenance was obviously minimal and of low priority. Wood trim around the archway peeled and curled like burned potato chips.

Jennifer's heart ached to think of her baby in a place like this.

The patrolman pulled up before the entrance. Kane turned in the front seat and looked at Jennifer. "I want you to stay in the car."

Jennifer already had her hand on the door handle, about to turn it. He couldn't possibly be telling her to remain behind. Not now, not when they were so close. She stared at him, stunned. "But—"

"Stay, Jennifer." There was a warning note in his voice.

The patrolman had already gotten out. Frustration vibrated through her. "I'm not a dog, Kane."

Leaning over, he placed his hand over hers firmly. "No, a dog would listen. But you're staying, do you hear me? I don't know what's going down, but I don't want it to be you, understood?"

They were wasting precious time arguing. Jennifer nodded, hating the impotent feeling that flooded through her.

Kane would have felt more confident if they left her handcuffed to the steering wheel. He only hoped that Jennifer's common sense would kick in for a change as he accompanied Kaminsky to the first apartment.

The man who opened the door a crack in response to the third knock was as seedy looking as the apartments he cared for. His bloodshot eyes narrowed as he studied the police shield that Kaminsky held up to the door. With a belabored sigh, he closed the door and took off the chain, then reopened it again. He was dressed in brown, stained pants and a dirty T-shirt.

"What can I do for you boys?" His voice was too agreeable. The wide smile didn't match his eyes. They were wary as they darted from Kaminsky to Kane, a wolf guarding his small territory from being overrun by members of a neighboring pack.

"Do you have a Rosalind Ward living here?" Kane held up Rosalind's photograph for his benefit.

The man squinted as he regarded the likeness before him. "Yeah, that's number nine." He sneered. "She's late with her rent again this month. Why? She bounce some checks or something?"

"Or something," Kane repeated. He motioned for the tall officer to follow behind him.

The superintendent looked torn for a moment between wanting to follow them and wanting to protect his privacy. Privacy obviously won. Kane heard the door to apartment one being firmly shut in their wake. One less thing to worry about, he thought.

Jennifer tried, she honestly tried to remain in the car. For a whole three minutes she tried. She sat in the car and watched as Kane and the officer crossed the front courtyard, heading for an apartment in the center of the semicircle. She'd had enough. Quietly, she slipped from the car and slowly made her way over toward the apartment. She could no more sit still, waiting for Kane to return with news of her daughter, than she could have sung all the arias from *Madam Butterfly.*

Not when she was so close.

Jennifer held her breath and watched as she saw Kane knock on the door.

An old woman with the face of a benevolent angel opened the door to the apartment just the slightest crack, holding the world at bay by virtue of the metal chain barring admittance.

"Ms. Ward?" Kane asked politely.

"Yes?" The smile was still bright, but the gray-blue eyes were just the slightest bit cautious as they flickered over the patrolman's uniform.

"We'd like to speak to you a few minutes, if you don't mind. Las Vegas P.D., ma'am." The young patrolman showed her his identification.

Rosalind shook her head. The slightly befuddled expression took on a skeptical cast. She kept her hand over the chain protectively.

"You could have stolen that, young man, along with your uniform. I'm afraid you're going to have to come back when my son is here. He'll be home at ten," she added helpfully. "Why don't you both come back then?"

She began to close the door. Kane quickly shoved his foot in the way, then braced the door with his shoulder. Rosalind gasped in surprise.

She played the addle-brained woman well, Kane thought. Too well. "We have a warrant for you, Ms. Ward," he lied. "You're only making it hard on yourself by resisting."

The cherubic expression shifted slightly on Rosalind's softly wrinkled face. The light in her eyes changed subtly. Kane had seen the same look in the eyes of other criminals when they had been cornered. Veiled desperation. He could almost see her struggling to contain it.

"A warrant?" Her voice squeaked an octave higher. "For gambling?" She shook her head, looking like a lost soul just turned out on the street by her children. "I thought that was legal in this state."

Kane could see why the woman managed to deceive so many people. She looked harmless, trustworthy. A sweet old lady who, twenty years ago when such things were in vogue, might have been aided by a Boy Scout while crossing the street.

"No, not for gambling," Kane told her. "For kidnapping."

"Kidnapping?" Rosalind echoed, her voice dropping to a whisper. The pale look appeared genuine, Kane thought. "You must be mad."

Jennifer finally ventured out far enough to get a good look at Rosalind. The words broke free without forethought. "That's her," she cried. "That's the woman who took my baby."

Kane spun around while Kaminsky kept his eyes on Rosalind. "I thought I told you to stay in the car," he snapped. Damn, why couldn't the woman stay put?

But Jennifer wasn't listening to him. Confronting the woman who was responsible for her nightmares, it took everything for Jennifer not to lunge at her.

"Where is she?" Jennifer demanded. "Where's my daughter? What have you done with her?"

"I don't know what you're talking about," Rosalind cried, alarmed.

The rickety chain gave way, breaking loose from its casement under the weight of Kane's shoulder. The door flew open, banging against the opposite wall. Plaster chips fell like discolored rain onto the cheap rug that covered an even cheaper floor.

Rosalind Ward backed away, clearly afraid of the woman who was advancing on her. "Wait, wait." She raised her arms before her defensively. "I can explain."

Jennifer grabbed Rosalind by the shoulders, shaking her before either Kane or the officer could make a move to stop her. "Explain what, that you waltzed into my hospital room, knowingly lied to me and took her? That you stole my baby to pay off gambling debts? Where is she, damn you? Where's my daughter?"

"Jennifer, let her go!" Kane ordered. He felt for her, something that would have shaken him had he had the time to examine the emotion. But she couldn't go about it this way.

"Ma'am, you can't do it like this," the policeman told her gently, obviously sympathetic to what Jennifer was going through.

Jennifer released Rosalind, uttering a strangled cry of exasperation, and ran off to search the small apartment.

"Watch her," Kane ordered the officer, following Jennifer. "Don't touch anything," he cautioned her, coming into the bedroom. There were a myriad of rules to observe, rules that could trip them up and have the case thrown out of court on a technicality. Rules that Jennifer didn't want to hear.

"She's not here," Jennifer whispered in disbelief, raw emotion throbbing in each syllable. "Kane, she's not here." The small, unkempt apartment was devoid of any trace of an infant ever having been there.

Kane slipped his arm around her as they returned to the living room. "Where is she?" Kane demanded, his voice low and dangerous.

Rosalind ignored his question. The officer was reading her her rights.

"You have no proof of anything," the older woman informed them haughtily. Silver bracelets held her wrists together. The kindly grandmother had faded into the shadows, supplanted by the savvy woman Rosalind Ward had always been.

Kane's arm dropped from Jennifer's shoulder as he faced down a criminal in orthopedic shoes. "We have three witnesses who put you at the site of three of the kidnappings."

Rosalind shrugged, never wavering. "Circumstantial evidence."

Kane's smile unfolded a fraction of an inch at a time. It was a cold smile that could have chilled the heart of a mugger in a dark alley. It was a smile that knew no humor and no mercy.

"You'd be surprised how far that kind of evidence can go in convicting someone. Prison for someone your age isn't something to be lightly tossed off."

At the mention of prison, terror entered the woman's eyes. Her breathing had turned shallow at the thought of being caged. "I can't go to prison."

"Sorry."

A line of perspiration beaded along her brow, mingling with the wisps of gray hair that fell there. Rosalind licked her lips nervously. They dried before the action was completed. Her eyes darted toward Jennifer. "What if we make a deal?"

"Sorry." Kane shook his head, unmoved. "No deals." He looked at Kaminsky. "Take her to the car, Officer."

Kaminsky began to take hold of Rosalind's arm. She jerked it away.

"Wait," she implored Kane. "I can tell you where the baby is." Again, she looked at Jennifer. This time she spoke to her. "That has to be worth something."

Kane paused, as if weighing the matter. "A cooperative witness might be entitled to some leniency," he speculated.

"Not leniency," Rosalind retorted adamantly. "I want to go free."

He wanted the information quickly, but he wasn't about to lie about cutting a deal with her. A good attorney would jump on that. He had to be careful. "You know I can't do that."

"Kane," Jennifer pleaded, moving between him and the woman.

Encouraged at the display of dissent before her, Rosalind pressed on. "I'll give you the name of the organization that has her now in exchange for my freedom," she bartered, giving a symbolic yank on the handcuffs as she held them aloft.

Kane remained firm. "The name and location of the organization in exchange for a recommendation to the court for a commuted sentence." It was the best he could do on his own authority. He placed a restraining hand on Jennifer. She looked as if she were ready to choke the name out of Rosalind at any second.

Rosalind shook her head. "Not good enough."

She was bluffing, Kane thought. In the end, she would do anything to lessen her sentence. But she had to try. Once a gambler, always a gambler, he supposed. "Will you testify against them?"

Terror rose in her eyes. "I can't."

Whoever she was involved with had to have a long reach, he thought. His expression remained nonchalant. "Back to square one, Rosie." He half turned from her, playing out his line in order to reel her in.

Rosalind sagged, her handcuffed hands clutched her chest. "Oh, my heart, my heart," she gasped.

Kaminsky moved quickly to catch her before she fell. In the blink of an eye, Rosalind wrapped her hands around his exposed service revolver. Jennifer saw the intent in the woman's eyes. Jennifer knew her body was blocking Kane's view, but not Kane.

Though it all happened so fast she only acted on instincts, Jennifer saw it unfolding in slow motion. The gun being raised, pointed toward Kane. She heard her own scream, felt the impact of her body against his as she knocked him out of the way. And then felt the flash of fire as it ripped against her shoulder.

Recovering himself instantly, Kane had his revolver trained on Rosalind. Faced with the look in Kane's eyes, the woman made a calculated guess and dropped the officer's gun to the floor. Kaminsky was quick to recover his weapon.

"All right, I'll testify," Rosalind said in a broken voice.

With Kaminsky's gun on the woman, Kane turned to Jennifer. Concern almost closed off his throat. But she was on her feet, clutching her arm. There was blood seeping out from between her fingers. "Are you out of your mind?" Kane demanded.

It stung like hell, but at least he was all right. "A simple thank-you will do," she muttered. Now that it was over, she had to concentrate to keep from fainting.

"Thank you?" he thundered incredulously. God, what if—?

He couldn't bring himself to finish the thought.

"I should break your neck." Gently, he peeled back her fingers and looked at the wound. "I can't tell how badly you're hurt." He had seen countless wounds. Why did this one affect him like this, as if his stomach were being ruthlessly slashed?

Jennifer couldn't bring herself to look at it. "If I was a bird, I wouldn't be flying right now. You were at point blank range, in case you didn't notice."

"I noticed," he bit off. He resisted the desire to carry her back to the car in his arms. "Let's get you to a doctor."

Kaminsky nodded, motioning for Rosalind to walk in front of him. "I'll radio for an ambulance."

Jennifer shook her head. "No. Not yet. I've got to know." She turned to the woman who had turned her life upside down. "Where is she?"

It was over. All she could do now was try to salvage her skin as best she could. Perhaps, she hoped, the judge had a grandmother he felt kindly toward. Rosalind looked at Jennifer.

"I sold her the day after I took her to a syndicate."

"Where?" There was no more patience to draw on. Kane growled out the word.

Suddenly looking very old, the light left Rosalind's eyes as she gave them the location.

Kane had been right. The organization was centered in Phoenix. They had another plane to catch.

Chapter 11

Overruling Jennifer's vehement protests, Kane brought her to a hotel near the hospital after she was treated and discharged. He turned a deaf ear to her words as he rented a room, then took her forcibly by the hand and walked her to her door.

She didn't want to waste time being treated like breakable fine china. They had to get to Phoenix. "But I'm fine, I tell you."

Firmly holding her uninjured arm, Kane unlocked the door and escorted her inside. Curbing his temper, he shoved the door closed. It slammed shut behind them, punctuating a statement he had yet to make.

"You are *not* fine. You are, at the very least, bordering on exhaustion. You haven't been sleeping well for the past three weeks and by my calculations, you haven't eaten in over twenty-four hours. Now I want you to lie down and get some rest."

Her fisted hands dug into her hips as she stood up to him. "And what are you going be doing while I'm resting? You haven't slept either, you know. Or eaten."

He gave her a hard glance meant to put her in her place. It didn't work.

"Stop trying to be me. The clothes wouldn't fit you." She opened her mouth, but he was quick to cut her off. "I'm going to make a few calls to get things started in Phoenix and let Newport Beach know what's happening. After that, I'm going to get us something to eat." He glared at her. "Does that meet with your approval?"

He was having trouble controlling his temper. He wanted to shout at her, to tell her that her actions at the apartment were exactly why he hadn't wanted to take her along in the first place. Ultimately, Kane held himself responsible. He knew better than to take her along. He had acquiesced to do so based on a logic that was nothing more than a flimsy rationalization. He had avoided analyzing his actions before, but he examined them now. There was only one conclusion to be drawn. He'd *wanted* to take her along, wanted an excuse for her to be with him.

Kane assessed the result of his momentary weakness. She looked awful. Her blouse was stained with blood and she had the dazed look that someone wore after being involved in a trauma. And it was all his fault.

"I could get the food," Jennifer volunteered.

Her shoulder ached and she had no doubt that it would hurt even more tomorrow. But it was a small price to pay, considering what the alternative might have been if she hadn't acted quickly.

Kane threw up his hands. "I have never met anyone as damn stubborn as you."

"Look in the mirror." She smiled as she pointed to the one hanging over the bureau.

Kane muttered something unintelligible under his breath as he tapped out the numbers of the Phoenix police department. With an economy of words, he informed Redhawk of the information they had received from Ward. The black market ring was centered in Phoenix, operating out of a florist, of all things. Though he would have wanted to be there when they closed in on the organization, time was of the essence in locating Katie. Captain Hernandez couldn't afford to wait until he and Jennifer arrived.

By the time they did it would all be over except for, hopefully, the reunion. Hanging up, Kane called his own captain next and let him know that Rosalind Ward had been found and arrested. Extradition papers were going to have to be filed.

When he finally got off the telephone twenty minutes later, Kane's ear ached. Jennifer had watched him the entire time, sitting tensely at his side on the bed. He saw a bit of the bandage peering out through the hole in her shirt.

God, that had been close. Too close. And now she looked a deathly white, despite the front she was trying to keep up. She had to be steeling off an enormous inner turmoil with that bravado. Kane was afraid that she would literally fall to pieces on him if she pushed herself too hard. This was too much for one person to handle. Maybe he should have bullied her into staying overnight.

He sighed, rising from the bed. "You should be in the hospital."

They would have had to strap her in to keep her there. There was no way she was going to stay in a hospital while he flew off to Phoenix to find her baby without her. They were so close now.

"The bullet just grazed me. It's nothing serious," she insisted. "The doctor at the hospital said so." She moved in front of him as he was about to leave the room. "You haven't thanked me yet, you know."

His expression clouded as he relived those horrible few seconds in his mind. "And I'm not going to. That was a stupid thing to do."

His flash of temper fueled her own. "I didn't have time to weigh the pros and cons. I saw the gun and I saw you and I pushed." He made her so angry she could scream. Didn't he realize that she had probably saved his life? "I like you better when the only gaping hole you have is your mouth."

She turned her back on him, afraid of what else she would say in the heat of the moment. She wasn't used to letting anger guide her tongue. That was Julia's role. She had always been the levelheaded one in the family. Up until now.

Kane spun her around to face him, wanting to shake her for the way she had made his heart stop. "Damn it, Jennifer, you could have been killed."

She realized that amid the fury, there was concern. Deep concern. The flame went out of her indignation. "But I wasn't. Get past it."

He held her arms bracketed between his hands, looking at her. "I can't. I keep seeing you lying on the floor with blood everywhere."

That had never happened. She realized now that in the one instant when the gun had gone off, Kane must have relived some other incident that had happened while he was on the force. Perhaps one where the person involved hadn't been able to walk away the way she did. It softened her heart toward Kane.

"I would have never given you any credit for an imagination," she told him with a smile.

It wasn't imagination he was dealing with. It was reality. During his first year on the force, he had seen his partner killed right in front of him. And he hadn't been able to do anything about it. If the same thing had happened to her—

"Don't you *ever* do anything that foolish again, do you hear me?" he thundered.

Jennifer looked up into his stormy eyes, suddenly wanting more than just warnings from him. She wanted reasons. Personal reasons. "Why?"

He was tempted just to walk out. It wasn't his style to explain himself to anyone. But she had saved his life and he supposed he owed her something. The truth as far as he was able to tell it.

He dropped his hands and shoved them into his pockets. "Because I don't know what I would have done if you *had* been killed, that's why."

She could see by the look in his eyes that he was backing away, shutting down the way he always did, she thought. Maybe she was hoping for too much.

Jennifer shrugged. "Traditionally, you notify the next of kin. In this case that would have been Julia and Nik—"

Damn it, what did she want from him? She knew that wasn't what he meant.

"I'm not talking about tradition. I'm not talking about anything that makes any sense to me, all right?" he shouted at her.

There were emotions within him, emotions he had no idea what to do with. Fears, feelings, desires. Everything that got in the way of his day-to-day life. He didn't have time for any of this, didn't have time to sort it all out. Not now, not ever.

He looked at Jennifer, ready to damn her for doing this to him, for awakening a beast that had been put to sleep so many years ago. He had come to terms with his life, was comfortable in his aloneness. Why was she rewriting the script?

But instead of damning her, he drew her into his arms and held her against him.

He closed his eyes as he heard her heart beat against his. Such a small sound. Such a comforting sound. "You scared the hell out of me." His voice was almost inaudible.

Jennifer pushed him just a little further, needing to hear more. "I guess there would have been a lot of paperwork to fill out if I was killed."

He framed her face in his hands and shook his head. The woman was impossible. "There's only one way to shut you up, isn't there?"

Before she could form an answer, Kane brought his mouth down on hers and kissed her, kissed her as if he would never have a second chance. All his fear, all his raging emotions, all the things he wasn't supposed to feel that were churning inside of him erupted, flowing over both of them as his lips slanted over hers.

He stole Jennifer's breath away from the very first moment.

Dazed, incensed and utterly confused, Kane only knew that he was too weak to resist the desire beating against his self-imposed cocoon any longer. As he molded Jennifer's body to his, his own heating to temperatures that would make an inferno seem cold by comparison, Kane deepened his kiss until it all but engulfed him as well as the woman who ignited his passion.

He couldn't help himself.

He hated being weak, hated being at the mercy of anything. Yet he was. He was at the mercy of this feeling. And at her mercy. If he couldn't kiss her, couldn't hold her like this, couldn't have her now the way he craved, then there was no point in his drawing another breath. Everything else would be senseless.

Kane knew it was all wrong. It was wrong to want her, wrong to take her. But his world was no longer black and white. A rainbow had intruded. A prism holding all the colors of the world had broken free, filling his soul. It had appeared, unannounced and unwanted, shattering his hard won peace, when Jennifer entered his life.

Greedy for the taste of her, Kane's mouth roamed over her fragrant skin, kissing her eyes, her cheeks, her chin. He couldn't get his fill. One taste led to a need for another. And another. He formed a hot necklace of kisses as he encircled her throat. As her pulse jumped in response, he felt his own excitement grow.

He ached to touch her, to press his starving body against hers. To take her. It was as if all control had been wrenched from him.

Damn, what was he thinking of? She had just been shot.

With effort, he drew his head away. His body implored him to stay. He rubbed his thumb along her lower lip and she kissed it. The foundation of his resolve developed more fissures and was on the verge of total structural failure, but he held on. "I'm sorry—"

No, not this time. She couldn't bear it if he pulled away again.

"That had better be an apology for not doing this sooner," she warned him, her voice thick with the desire he had brought to the surface.

If he did anymore, he felt that he'd be taking advantage of the situation. What kind of a monster would she think he was once it was over? "You've just been shot—"

"Grazed," she corrected, weaving her arms around his neck to show him just how insignificant the wound really was. "And I'm not dead." Anticipation hummed through her, reinforcing that fact for her. She raised her face toward his. "Make me feel like I'm alive again, Kane."

Didn't she know how difficult this was for him? How hard he was trying to walk away for both their sakes? "I'm not any good for you."

How could he say that? How could he believe that? "Let me be the judge of that."

He was already weakening as he felt her body against his once more. "You don't know what you're doing," he warned her.

She laughed softly. Was he really that noble? Or was he just afraid of consequences down the line? Whatever the reason, they'd sort it out later.

"It was my shoulder that was hit," Jennifer reminded him, smiling, "not my head, Kane. I know exactly what I'm doing."

He couldn't go on resisting both of them. Not her and himself. He tightened his hands around her waist, binding her to him. "Damn, but you're stubborn."

She grinned. "You noticed."

Jennifer tilted her head up and Kane's resistance broke into a million pieces, like a clay duck that had sustained a direct hit during target practice.

He knew he'd regret this later, perhaps even within the hour, but right now, he didn't care. That she would regret it was an even greater deterrent and might have stopped him, but she had stirred him too far, made him want too much to turn away on his own. With every movement, every gesture, she silently offered herself to him. It made him humble, needy, and so desirous of her that he couldn't even form a coherent thought and carry it to its conclusion.

He wanted to hold her, to love her, to touch her all over. But he felt clumsy, as if his hands had suddenly grown too large for him to use properly.

He was afraid of hurting her, afraid of what was happening inside of him. And most, of all, afraid that she would turn away at the last moment. Because Jennifer held the reins. She had all the cards and he none. If she would have told him to stop even at the last possible moment, he would have, despite everything within him that raged to burst free.

She saw the hesitation in his eyes, the war that threatened to claim him. "What's wrong?"

"I don't want to hurt you." And he would. One way or another, he would hurt her. He would shut her out. He knew himself well enough to know that he couldn't open up to her the way she needed.

He worried too much, Jennifer thought. His demons weren't hers and somehow they could vanquish the ones that haunted him, together. "You could only do that if you stopped," she murmured against his mouth.

This was insane. He tried to hold her away from him. "You've just been shot. You've just had a baby. How can you possibly—?"

Jennifer pressed a finger to his lips to silence the words, the protests. "Shh." Her hands over his, she guided them back around her waist. "I had a very easy birth almost a month ago and I'm a fast healer. Haven't I kept up with you so far?" She smiled at him, touched by the concern she saw in a man who claimed not to care about anything. "Everything else is in working order, Detective Madigan."

The words were sealed with a kiss as she lightly trailed her lips against his.

It was no use attempting to abstain. No use in telling himself that he could walk away from this at any moment. He couldn't. It would have been easier for him to walk across hot coals barefoot than to turn his back on her now.

He had never wanted anyone so much in his life. And God willing, he never would again, for the feeling was laced in exquisite agony.

"Maybe I should see for myself," he told her.

"Maybe you should."

Kane pressed her close to him as he absorbed the heat from her body into his own. The flame burning within her struck a match and he felt his body ignite like wood dried in the sun. He felt her soft moan echo in his mouth as he slipped his hands beneath her shirt and slowly cupped his fingers around her breasts, gently massaging them.

If this was all he was to have, it would have been enough and he would have been grateful. But he needed so much more from her. More than he thought anyone could ever possibly give.

His kiss deepened, searching, hungering. And she gave him everything. Each time a new demand rose, she met it, awing him. Humbling him.

Exciting him.

This was crazy, she thought, or attempted to think as his hands roamed her body, claiming each new place he touched, scattering her thoughts like dandelion seeds before the spring breeze. This should be happening somewhere else, at another point in time in her life, when she was completely free to dive into this swirling cauldron of sensations he was creating for her. Not now. Guilt rose up with spiky fingers, threatening to deprive her of this joy.

But you didn't get to choose your moments, she thought. You could only gratefully seize them when they happened, *if* they happened at all.

Jennifer felt his fingers fumble awkwardly as he began to work at the buttons on her blouse. "Wait," she murmured. She nudged his fingers away with her own, ready to help.

"I wasn't going to rip off your blouse." The look that entered his eyes was defensive. "I'm not an animal, Jennifer."

Oh God, she hadn't meant anything by it. Who had beaten him this way? Who had reduced him to this vision of himself?

"I know you're not, besides, this blouse is ruined. I just wanted to help," she whispered softly.

Her eyes on his, she undid the rest of the buttons on her blouse, then opened the front clasp on her bra. The loosened garments hung there, just barely resting against her skin, waiting for his touch.

Air lodged in his throat, unable to move as he watched her. He reached toward her, his eyes still meeting hers. He could see her desire burning there. Desire and something more, something far more precious, something far more gentle. It pulled at him even as he resisted its awesome power.

He couldn't let his emotions get tangled up in this. This was physical, purely physical.

It was a lie and he knew it.

Kane drew her blouse slowly, erotically from her shoulders. The unclasped bra slid down with it, leaving Jennifer nude from the waist up. Kane's breath quickened as he pressed a kiss to each bare shoulder. Without thinking, he shed his own shirt as he leaned forward, kissing her neck. He felt her sharp intake of breath as he slid a moist trail of kisses to her breasts. She moaned as his tongue encircled each budded area until they had risen to form hardened peaks. He caressed her stomach and she marveled at the care he was taking.

Jennifer arched against him, tangling her fingers in his hair, pressing his head closer to her burning skin. With each kiss, fresh arrows of desire were fired into her very core, making her throb. Making her want. She hadn't been touched by a man since the day Katie's father had discovered that she was pregnant and had walked out on her. Something vital had died then, something she was afraid was dead forever.

But Kane had resurrected it. With the way he had kissed her, with the way he had silently needed her, she felt her passion renew itself.

And all for him.

She found solace in his embrace, as much in her way as he in his. She needed him to hold her, to make love with her. To be her hero and slay all the dragons that loomed just beyond in the mists that lay upon the fringes of their world.

Kane opened the snap on her jeans. And then, his mouth still slanting over hers, seeking a point where he would be sated, knowing in his heart that it would never be reached, he slid the jeans from her hips. As they sank about her bare feet, he lifted her up in his arms and carried her to bed, carefully positioning her injured arm.

Jennifer knew that she would never feel safer than she did at this very moment. Safe, even though she was precariously perched on the summit of a precipice, waiting to go over.

She pulled him to her as he laid her on the bed, her mouth needy for his. Their bodies melded in a dance as old as time, in an exploration as new as the next sunrise.

This was all so fresh and different for them, as if it had never before happened to either one. Like two phoenixes rising from the ashes of their lives, they were reborn and redefined within one another.

His own jeans kicked off and abandoned at the foot of the bed, Kane looked at her. She was so beautiful that the ache within his loins and within his soul threatened to explode, taking him with it.

And yet he hesitated.

"Are you sure?" he asked Jennifer, his fingers trailing along the curves of her body, memorizing them one by one. She shivered beneath his touch. "You can still say no."

Sure, and then send in my application for saint of the month. Was he crazy? Didn't he feel her need? "This is no time to read me my rights, Detective."

Jennifer laced her fingers around his neck and gently coaxed his mouth to hers, leaving only a fraction of an inch between them.

"I'm sure." The words skimmed along Kane's lips, offering him a taste of her a moment before his mouth covered hers.

He restrained himself for as long as he could, wanting to pleasure her in return for the sweetness she sent sweeping through his soul. He brought her to a level above him, to wait and anticipate. He was fascinated by the way his touch excited her and awed by the way she gave without asking of him in return.

And in not asking, she ensnared him completely, even as he tried to resist. For this moment in time, he was hers, hopelessly hers, even though he had no place in her world, nor she in his. There were no worlds as he came to her, no him, no her, just them.

As he entered her, all he could see were her eyes. They had grown huge. But there was no hesitation in them, no withdrawal. No regret.

He heard his name whispered against his ear, wrapped in tissues of desire as she clung to him while they spiraled upward, faster and faster.

Explosions echoed in her head as her body was rocked by them, generating ecstasy so great, so pure, it brought tears to her eyes.

The tears were still there when the haze slowly drifted away. Still there as he let his body draw warmth from hers as he lay against her, momentarily contented.

Afraid he was too heavy for her, Kane raised himself on his elbow. He saw the sheen in her eyes. Tears. She was crying. Regret and guilt seized him with both hands. He should have stopped himself. Somehow, he should have found the strength to pull away.

A single tear slid down her cheek. He touched it with the tip of his finger. The teardrop broke apart as it dissolved and wet him.

He would have suffered anything rather than to make her cry because of him. "I'm sorry. I didn't mean to hurt you."

His expression was so solemn. What was he thinking? Had she done something wrong? "I'm not hurt," she said slowly, trying to guess what was on his mind.

Why was she trying to lie to him? "You're crying."

So that was it. She smiled as she touched his cheek. It was rough. Stubble was growing in. It made him look even more formidable. If that was possible. "Ever hear of tears of joy?"

He laughed at the idea. It was a hollow, lonely sound. People only cried for one reason. He knew, because once he had cried. Tears were for sadness. "Lines in a book."

He had so much to learn, she thought. So much to open up his heart to. And she wanted to be the one to help him do it.

"Reality, Detective Madigan," she corrected. "You remember, that commodity you hold so dear. This is the nice part of reality." She raised her head and brushed a kiss against his lips, then let her head drop back against the pillow. She was exhausted. "If this was meant to help relax me, you failed miserably."

He didn't feel like bantering. He had lost control and he didn't like it. Worse, he had dragged her in with him. "I had no intentions of doing that."

Oh, please, please don't be sorry. Something squeezed her heart, but she tried to keep her smile in place, hoping to tease him, to make him come around. She wanted to share this wonderful feeling she was experiencing, not be robbed of it.

She stroked his arm and watched a muscle tense. It made her feel isolated. "For a man with no intentions, you did very well."

"Jennifer, you can't—" At a loss for words, he tried again. "We can't—"

His voice strangled in his throat as she shifted beneath him. Her body, still warm from his, felt erotically inviting.

He was going to have to be helped across this chasm, she thought. "I could. We could. And we did." Her smile grew more serious. "Now please don't spoil it by saying something nobly stupid that neither one of us wants to hear and you don't really believe."

Kane rolled off her and pulled the sheet around him. His pensive, troubled expression hurt Jennifer more than she could possibly put into words. But she couldn't think of her own hurt feelings now. It was his that she had to keep foremost in her mind.

Gently, she placed a hand on his arm and made him look at her. When he did, she searched for the answer to her question in his eyes. "Didn't you want to make love with me?"

Couldn't she feel that he did? Didn't she know that it was all that had been on his mind since he first saw her? That was what kept getting in his way, tripping him up, like a kitten batting a ball of yarn around, chasing it to all corners.

"That's a stupid question."

She swallowed, trying to dislodge the huge lump that was stuck in her throat. It refused to leave. "Indulge me," she whispered, afraid her voice would crack if she spoke any louder.

"Yes." He almost spit the word out.

She blinked back tears. This time, they had nothing to do with joy. Had it just been nothing more than sex for him? She couldn't believe that. But then why wouldn't he grant her a shred of hope to hold on to?

"And you did," she said matter-of-factly, not knowing where she found the resolve to pretend that it didn't hurt. "We did." Sitting up, she dragged her hand through her hair and let it drop again, a damp, dark veil about her shoulders. "Let's not take it any further than that right now, all right?" She tried to see his face, but he kept it turned from her as he rose.

He nodded, not trusting himself to look at Jennifer. If he did, he was afraid that he would want to take her all over again. Nothing had been resolved or satisfied. It had only increased and held him prisoner of an emotion he neither wanted nor understood. The only thing he did understand was that it would be wrong to ruin her life and drag her into his.

He picked up his jeans from the floor where they had ultimately fallen and shrugged into them quickly, still avoiding looking at her.

Coward's way, his mind taunted. But he would be a coward, if that was the only way to protect her.

"I'm going to see about getting plane tickets to Phoenix and picking up something for us to eat." He drew on his shirt, fairly punching his arms through the sleeves as if they were the unseen enemy he wanted to defeat, rather than the emotions he couldn't see. "Maybe you can catch a few winks while I'm gone."

"Yeah, sure."

Jennifer was still staring at the door long after he had left the room. Knees drawn to her chest, arms wrapped tightly around herself, she had never felt so cold in her entire life. Or so alone.

Chapter 12

They were on the flight to Phoenix the next morning. The plane, like the others they had taken before it, was small. But somehow, this time it felt even smaller. A sticky awkwardness hung over them, surrounding them like an oppressively humid Louisiana summer night, leaving no part of them untouched.

Kane had hardly spoken to her since they had left the hotel room. When he did, his sentences were abrupt and short. It was himself he was annoyed with, but Jennifer had no way of knowing that. It was an instinctive, purely reflexive reaction on his part. Whenever someone showed signs of getting close to him, he withdrew within himself like a hermit crab seeking shelter from harm. His protective behavior blocked all attempts at communication.

But this time, it was different. It was more difficult. This time retreating was something he had to do knowingly rather than just mechanically react. And in doing so, it left him with a sense of bereavement he didn't understand.

Making love with her had been something pure, something wonderful. It was like being reinvented. For one brief shining moment, he had forgotten everything but the woman in his arms. It had been Kane's first real contact with another human being in more years than he could easily remember.

But he didn't want contact. He had done his best to avoid it over the years. Yet it had found him. And now, it wouldn't let him live in peace.

What had happened between Jennifer and him had left Kane utterly confused. Never having been touched by love, he was highly suspicious of anything remotely resembling it. Having been the victim of emotional bankruptcy, he didn't understand the nature, the reasoning behind selfless love. And most of all, he didn't understand Jennifer.

Why had she made love with him? A woman like Jennifer had everything going for her. Why did she risk constant rebuffing by seeking him out?

To complicate matters, Kane was unsure of himself. He was at a loss as to how to behave. Behavior had never been a question before. He never thought it through, never pondered as to what his next move was. He just acted and reacted. Black and white.

He had no frame of reference for rainbows. He had never felt like this about anyone. No one had ever mattered to him before, he hadn't let them. It was better that way, boring perhaps, but tranquil.

Now his peace was shattered.

He dragged a hand through his hair as he stole a glance at Jennifer's rigid profile.

He had come a long way from the small, lonely little boy who laid awake in his bed night after night, waiting for his mother to return. He had sealed those wounds, destroyed those feelings.

Or thought he had.

Wrong.

Kane drummed his fingers on the armrest, wishing he had a cigarette. Wishing he had his peace back.

The slight rhymthic tapping sound pulsed its way into Jennifer's consciousness. The drumming matched the beat of her heart. She couldn't go on like this, pretending nothing had happened in that small, airless hotel room. She couldn't just shrug her shoulders and say that's life. It wasn't life. At least, it wasn't like her life. She didn't make love with a man unless she cared. And she did. She cared deeply about Kane Madigan. Perhaps she even loved him.

The thought startled Jennifer as it crystalized in her mind. She loved him. She slanted a glance at him as the thought throbbed through her mind.

I love him.

She couldn't just let something like this go so easily, absorbed like a stone thrown into quicksand, sinking away without a trace to prove its existence. Within a few hours, if all went well, she would have her baby back and Kane would have no reason to be in her life. If it ended like this, she knew he would be gone permanently.

She couldn't allow that to happen.

She had to know where this could lead. If what existed between them could be nurtured to bloom or if it was just like a sunflower, destined to sprout and grow quickly, then die just as abruptly.

Jennifer searched for something to break the uneasy silence.

Kane looked at her shoulder and felt another twinge of guilt. She had been hurt because of him. Physically. He couldn't have her hurt emotionally as well.

"How's your shoulder?" he muttered more out of a sense of obligation than anything else.

Jennifer's head jerked in his direction as the sound of his voice scattered her thoughts. "What?"

He felt like an idiot repeating himslf. "I said, how's your shoulder?"

She moved it slightly. Her shoulder was the last thing on her mind, even though it ached now that she thought about it.

"All right, I guess. Mending." She looked at him pointedly, a smile playing with the corners of her mouth. She knew him well enough now to realize that this was his clumsy way of breaking the ice. "I'm sorry, I didn't mean to jump. It's just that it's been so long since you said anything, I'd forgotten what your voice sounded like."

He let out an impatient rush of air through his teeth as he sank further into his seat, his long legs crossed at the ankle. "I didn't know you could be sarcastic."

She kept her eyes on him, waiting for their gazes to lock. "There's a lot of things about me you don't know, Kane."

He shrugged, sorry he had said anything. "It's none of my business."

Damn him, why was he so stubborn? "It's only none of your business if I say so." She lifted her chin, ready for another argument. She could feel one brewing. "And I don't say so." She leaned over the armrest, her hand on his arm. "Ask me something."

The scent of her skin came to him in waves, intoxicating him like fine wine as he recalled the feel of it. The taste of it. Kane move his arm away and unconsciously clenched his hands in his lap. It was a struggle to maintain a disinterested pose. "There's nothing I want to know."

His words hurt, but Jennifer wouldn't retreat. She couldn't afford to. There was too much at risk to give up now.

"Well, there are things I want to know about you." Gray eyes the color of the sky before a winter storm slanted at her suspiciously beneath hooded lids. "I want to know what you were like as a small boy." She saw the scowl forming and knew he thought she was trespassing again. Words stuck to the roof of her mouth, like dried peanut butter, but she pushed on. "I want to know where you went to school. What your favorite food is." She took a breath. "And what you're hiding so fiercely."

His eyes were flat, unreadable, guarding a past he wasn't proud of. He had been unloved, abandoned. Not worth a mother's love or a father's care. Who could be proud of that? "I'm not hiding anything."

She whispered the words coaxingly to him. "Then talk to me."

He turned slowly to look at Jennifer. "All those questions you just asked—"

"Yes?" she asked hopefully.

"They're none of your business. There's nothing there, Jennifer," he insisted impatiently. "Nothing important. Nothing I want to talk about. Just forget it." A curtain went down, severing all communication.

Or so he thought. But he was wrong.

Jennifer was stung, but not defeated. "I have a right to know things like that about the man I made love with," she told him quietly.

An image of her, nude and loving, flashed through his mind and he ached just to think of it. But he couldn't let himself go like this, even if he wanted to. Instinctively, he acted in a given manner. To do otherwise would be like asking a dog to meow. He'd been years cocooning himself. He couldn't let it all unravel in a single afternoon. And unravel to what? He wasn't even sure anymore. He kept searching his mind for a clue as to where all this was going. It was like opening up a Christmas present only to find another box inside, and another inside that. Except that he had the distinct feeling that the last box held only tissue paper. No answers. Just the pain of nothing. Basically, if he had zero expectations of life and of people, then he would never be disappointed.

His voice was hard when he answered. "You should have thought of that before. I've opened myself up as far as I intend to, Jennifer. This is all there is. I'm sorry."

She wasn't going to cry, she told herself. She wasn't. It wouldn't solve anything. Only patience would, if she could scrape enough together. For the time being, she'd concentrate on the moment when she would be holding her baby again. That was all that truly mattered.

"All right, have it your way," she said quietly. "But I want you to know something."

He didn't want her offering him pieces of herself. He couldn't handle it. Yet he had to ask. "What?"

The soft cadence of her voice had him turning again to look at her. There was no malice within it. She was offering him something he wasn't worthy of touching.

"Despite what you might think, I don't take last night lightly." She licked her lips, her courage flagging. "Before Katie's father, there'd been no one."

Her words peppered through his system like buckshot, scattering, wounding him, arousing something that was fragile, something he needed to keep out of harm's way. With every fiber of his being, Kane was deliberately attempting to ignore the new, almost terrifying feelings that were surfacing within him.

He fought the desire to take her in his arms, to hold her, to lose himself within her. It was too dangerous and he knew the consequences.

He stared straight ahead. "With me, you still have no one."

"That's not how I see it," Jennifer answered.

She struggled to contain her hurt, struggled to refrain from lashing out at him. Maybe they both needed breathing space. This was an emotionally charged situation they were in, not just because of what was happening between them, but because of the drama that was unfolding around them. The drama that had brought them together in the first place. Maybe once that was resolved, she would be more equipped to handle the challenge before her.

Just as Jennifer fiercely believed that they would find Katie, she believed that the man who had made love with her last night cared about her more than he was apparently willing to admit for reasons she could only guess at. But she would unravel it eventually. One step at a time.

And one thing at a time. Right now, the most important thing was to find her baby.

She looked at Kane. He was staring out the window. They seemed to be almost drifting. She willed the plane to fly faster. "Do you think Graham has them by now?"

He looked away from the window. "Who?"

"Graham," she repeated. "Redhawk," she amended, remembering that he had only referred to the detective by his last name. "Do you think Redhawk has the kidnappers by now, or the syndicate or whatever they call themselves?" Whatever they were, *whoever* they were, she prayed that they had been kind to her baby, and to all the other babies they had so heartlessly taken.

Kane was grateful to return to a topic he had a vague amount of control over. "When I talked to him on the phone, Redhawk was going to take some men and check out the shop." He saw the boundless hope shining in her eyes, mingled with fear. Over the last few days, she'd been disappointed so many times. He hoped that this wasn't another one of those times.

"If Ward didn't lie to us and they're there, Redhawk will have brought them in by now."

He drummed his fingers on the armrest again, and then reached for her hand and squeezed it. "It'll be all right, Jennifer."

She looked at him in surprise. This was a breach of behavior for him. Maybe there was hope for him after all. "Thank you."

It occurred to Kane once again that she shouldn't have to be going through this. That she deserved better. And clearly she deserved better than he could offer. "Jennifer, about before—"

"Which before?" Was he apologizing for pulling back after the fact, or for making love to her to begin with? "In the hotel, or just now?"

It had never been easy for Kane to put his feelings into words and never so difficult as it was now. "Jennifer, you're a very special lady, and it just wouldn't work out between us."

He meant it, Jennifer thought sadly. He really believed in what he was saying. "How do you know without trying?"

The same way he knew that the sun would come up tomorrow. "I just know."

"Detective Madigan," she began formally, drawing herself up in her seat. The seat belt sign flashed on and she drew her belt around her, snapping it into place.

Kane followed suit automatically. The flight attendant was wandering down the middle of the aisle, checking to make certain that everyone had obeyed the sign.

"What?" he asked when Jennifer left his name just hanging in the air.

"You don't know everything."

With that Jennifer turned her attention to the most immediate reason for her existence. Finding Katie.

Unable to leave the precinct, Redhawk sent a patrolman to pick them up at the airport. Jennifer immediately began asking questions.

"They were using a florist shop as a front," the older man confirmed as he drove them in a squad car to the precinct. "Buds in the front, babies in the back," the policeman said with a shrug. "Takes all kinds, I guess. They had a whole sealed off operation in the back room. We didn't get the main guys," he added with a wistful note in his voice. "But we got two of them. Detective Redhawk should get something out of them."

Jennifer was holding her breath all through the narrative. "Did they find any children? Any babies?"

"Yeah, as a matter of fact, they did." He smiled faintly as he took another turn. "Two of them."

Jennifer closed her eyes and prayed.

The Phoenix precinct was bursting with activity by the time the patrolman pulled up to the front entrance. He let them out and drove off to park the car. Jennifer raced up the five stone steps to the front door ahead of Kane, her heart in her mouth.

"Slow down, Jennifer," he called after her.

She paid no attention as she opened the door and made her way to the squad room. Jennifer saw the grim-faced Native American almost as soon as she entered, despite the number of people in the room. She hurried to him just as he looked in her direction.

"Graham," she said, breathless, "did you find my daughter?"

Kane caught up to Jennifer within a few seconds. She felt his hand on her arm as they waited for the other detective to answer.

The grim expression dissipated as Redhawk smiled at them as if they were old friends. "Glad you got here." He waved the top of his pen toward two handcuffed men who were being brought forward. "We've just finished booking the two guys we got."

They looked like ordinary, harmless people, Jennifer thought. No different from countless others. Just like Rosalind did. How could they have caused so much havoc? How did they justify ruining so many people's lives?

"I think it's just the tip of the iceberg," Redhawk was saying to Kane, "but it's a good-size tip."

"My baby," Jennifer interrupted him. "Did you find her? Where are the babies you found?"

Redhawk grinned broadly. "We found two of them. The woman social services sent down has custody of them right now."

"And where is she?" Jennifer was having trouble containing her excitement. It was over. It was finally going to be over. She could hardly believe it.

Redhawk looked at the policeman herding the two men they had captured during their bust. "Take these guys into room twelve," he instructed. "I'll be by in a few minutes." He turned and indicated the hallway beyond the squad room. "This way," he told Jennifer.

They hurried down a pea green corridor that was overdue for a new coat of paint. The linoleum was checkered and smelled faintly of disinfectant. There were other smells in the hall that Jennifer couldn't place. Everything seemed almost surreal to her as she followed Redhawk to a small room at the end of the hall.

"Ms. Lincoln, I have one of the babies' mother here with me," Redhawk said by way of introduction as they entered the room that doubled as a kitchenette.

A woman in a smart buff tailored suit looked up from the two bassinets that were placed side by side on the conference table. She smiled benevolently at Jennifer. "Which one is yours?" she asked kindly.

Jennifer looked from one sleeping infant to the other. Her heart, so full a moment ago, felt as if it had dropped into her shoes. She didn't have to hold either one in her arms to know. She shook her head, tears stinging her eyes. "Neither."

Kane looked at her in surprise and saw the agony in her face. He placed his hand on her arm. "Jennifer, all babies tend to—"

She jerked away, her shredded patience at the frayed end. "Don't you tell me that they all look alike," she warned, turning on him. "Don't you dare tell me that. I *know* my baby. And she's not here."

One of the babies began to cry at the sound of her raised voice. Ms. Lincoln picked her up, cooing softly. Jennifer covered her mouth with her hands, trying to still the trembling within her. She regained a semblance of control.

"I'm sorry," she apologized to all of them, her eyes on Kane. "I didn't mean to snap." She felt tired, so very tired and drained. "It's just that after all this, neither one of them is Katie."

Redhawk poured her a glass of water from the small sink in the corner. "We're sending for copies of the footprints taken at each hospital—" he began.

Jennifer held the glass in both hands and she took a drink. The water cleared away some of the cobwebs in her throat. She shook her head at his words.

"I don't need to check footprints. Katie's not here," she insisted. Her voice felt as if it were getting caught in her throat. "Were there any others found?"

Redhawk shook his head sadly.

Damn, so near and yet so far, Kane thought, uttering an exasperated sound. The woman from social services looked at Jennifer with pity in her eyes as she continued soothing the crying baby in her arms.

"But records," Jennifer said suddenly. "They've got to have some sort of records." She turned to Kane, looking for support. "Don't they?"

Kane hated when she looked at him like that, looked at him as if he could leap over tall buildings in a single bound.

"Yes," he agreed slowly. "They had to keep some sort of records." Even if the records were only tallies they kept in

their heads, there had to be some sort of a record-keeping
system. And he intended to find it, no matter what it took.

Kane placed his arm around Jennifer's shoulders and
ushered her from the room. Looking at the two infants only
intensified her own grief, her own loss.

He turned to Redhawk. "Have you questioned those two
men yet?"

Redhawk was leading the way back to the squad room.
"Just about to when you came in."

Kane stopped before the room numbered twelve. The
room Redhawk had instructed the men to be brought to. He
glanced at the door. "Mind if I have first crack at it?"

The smile on Redhawk's face was grimly set. "That all
depends, Madigan. Just what do you mean by the word
crack?"

Kane knew what he wanted it to mean, but that had no
place existing side by side with his shield. "Just an expression. You can be present."

"I fully intend to. Don't forget whose bust this is." Redhawk placed his hand on the doorknob.

"I don't want the glory," Kane told him. "I just want the
answers." He began to follow Redhawk into the room when
he realized that Jennifer was coming with him. He turned,
blocking her access to the room. "Jennifer, you'll have to
wait outside."

How he could he do this to her? Didn't he realize what she
was going through? She felt as if she were an emotional
yo-yo. "The hell I will."

He moved her until her back was against the opposite
wall. "Now look, this one time you have to listen." His
voice was stern, but patient. "You're not allowed in there,
Jennifer." He saw the rebellion in her eyes and his voice became firmer. "I promise you, if either of them knows
where Katie is, I'll find out. We'll find your baby. I swear."
He saw that she was looking past his shoulder, into the
room. "Do you believe me?"

She felt numb as she nodded. "I believe you." If she
couldn't believe in him, she had nothing to hang on to. She
had no choice but to believe.

Redhawk had crossed into the hallway again. "You can wait in my office," he prompted gently, motioning to a room in the rear.

Jennifer shook her head. She planted herself just opposite the door of room twelve. "I'll wait out here, Graham."

Redhawk shook his head and smiled at Jennifer. "Have it your way. Hell of a stubborn woman you have there, Madigan." He reentered the room.

"She's not mine to have," Kane corrected quietly as he followed him in.

The door closed, shutting her out. Jennifer stood absolutely still, in direct contrast to the anxiety that was oscillating through her as she waited for the door to open again.

There was nothing within room twelve except for a table surrounded by four chairs. The window faced east and had already lost most of the direct sun for the day. A gloomy pall was over the room. The uniformed officer left as soon as the two detectives entered.

Kane circled the table slowly, his eyes on the two men who sat there. Both were visibly nervous.

The man closest to the bleak window watched Kane with wide, wary eyes. "We already told 'em," he blurted out in a high, squeaky voice that sounded like chalk scratching along a blackboard. He was sweating profusely. The sickly smell of fear permeated the room. "We're only messengers, nothing more than messengers." He twisted his head around as he watched Kane pace, a panther moving in for the kill. "We don't know anything."

Kane stopped. Pulling a chair out, he placed his foot on the seat. He stood opposite the man named Arnie. Kane leaned forward.

"Everybody knows something," he began slowly, his voice low, menacing. "And the more you know, the more it'll help you."

"Nothing. We know nothing," the other man, Fred, chimed in. He was scratching his bald head as he spoke, his breath growing short.

He was dealing with the second string, Kane thought. Just as well. They would be easier to break. He looked the two men over, judging how long it would take before he could make them cooperate. Not long, he guessed.

Redhawk stood back and gave him free rein. Kane hammered away, bit by bit, his voice even, almost peaceful. But no one could miss the barely veiled threat that existed just beneath the first layer.

Fred's eyes darted toward the door, where Redhawk stood, his arms crossed before him, a solemn, eternal sentry. It added to the fear that laced through the room.

"Don't even think it," Kane advised Fred, his voice a low growl.

It wasn't a version of good cop/bad cop that was being played out in the room. There was only one cop talking, one to be reckoned with. Kane knew just how to turn the blade slowly to evoke fear. Fear that ultimately grew so huge, it overshadowed the consequences generated by confessions.

The people who could punish them for breaking their silence were somewhere outside. The policeman they feared was here, holding them in tight rein.

"All right." Kane leaned across the table, his entire presence in Fred's face. Of the two, Fred was the one who was most manipulatable. "Where are the records for the sales being kept?"

"Adoptions," Fred corrected hoarsely. His fingers trembled around the cigarette Redhawk had given him. He brought it to his mouth, then had trouble placing it between his lips. He inhaled, holding it. The smoke seemed to do nothing to calm him. He glanced at the man next to him before saying, "In the wall behind where the fresh flowers are kept."

"Shut your damn mouth!" Arnie yelled at him, his voice screeching. He jumped up, knocking his chair over as he lunged for Fred.

Fred scraped his chair along the floor, dragging himself out of reach. Redhawk grabbed the other man before he did any harm.

"They're gonna find it anyway," Fred cried. "We might as well help." His deep-set black eyes darted toward Kane's face. "We are helping, right?" He licked his dry lips. "You'll remember we helped, right, Detective?"

His voice broke as he wiped the back of his hand along his mouth. Cigarette ashes scattered like gray dust on the table.

"I'll remember," Kane promised, his voice dark and dangerous. "Make no mistake, I'll remember."

Fred shrank back in his chair, as though he thought that if he pressed his body against the back of it hard enough, he would be out of Kane's reach.

Redhawk dropped Arnie back into his chair. The look the detective gave the man warned him to stay where he was.

Confident that the men wouldn't move, Redhawk turned toward Kane. "I'll have someone drive you over to the flower shop." Kane nodded.

"We have to go now. I'm not sure how much more of this Jennifer can take."

"You got it," Redhawk answered.

Kane stepped out into the hallway to tell Jennifer they had yet another lead.

Chapter 13

As Jennifer watched and two other policemen continued a thorough search of the rest of the premises, Kane stepped into the glass-enclosed refrigerated showcase where fresh-cut flowers were housed in appealing crystal containers. He handed several of the containers to Jennifer, clearing a path for himself to move around in. One by one, Jennifer placed them on a counter by the register.

Very carefully, inch by inch, Kane felt around the rear wall of the showcase. He was searching for the telltale uneven or raised white panel that might be hiding a wall safe behind it.

It had to be here somewhere, he thought. The man called Fred had been too frightened to risk telling him a lie. He wouldn't have sent Kane on a wild-goose chase, knowing he would return to the precinct empty-handed and angry.

The fragrance of carnations was everywhere within the small flower shop. Who would have ever thought that something so heinous as the stealing and selling of children was being conducted behind its closed doors? Jennifer shivered as she watched Kane search, impatience pricking at her.

After a minute, she peered inside the glass enclosure. "Room enough for two in here?" It would be cramped, but manageable as long as they didn't get in each other's way.

Kane was crouching in the extreme right corner, tapping on each panel and listening. "What, I'm not going fast enough for you?"

Jennifer was already stepping inside the narrow showcase. "Four hands are better than two." Her voice was falsely cheerful. She brushed against a container Kane had pushed to one side. It tipped, spilling yellow roses at her feet.

"But four feet tend to get in the way," Kane muttered, turning his attention to the panels.

Jennifer moved the flowers aside. Several thorns pricked her fingers but she hardly noticed. She began tapping panels at the opposite corner from where Kane had started. The second panel she tried sounded hollow. She knocked on it again.

"Kane?"

"Yeah?"

"I think I found it."

He was behind her before she finished her sentence. Gingerly using the tip of a pocket knife, he managed to lift the panel from the wall. Beneath it was what appeared to be a small wall safe. They exchanged glances. Jennifer looked immensely pleased with herself.

"Beginner's luck," Kane commented, but he was smiling at her. He sheathed the knife in his rear pocket and set the panel down.

"Open it," she urged eagerly.

"I think you overestimate my abilities." Kane stepped out of the showcase, then offered his hand to Jennifer. "Safe cracking is not my line."

She wrapped her fingers around his hand and followed him out. "But then how—?" she began, frustrated.

Kane held up a hand to silence her protests as he looked around. One step ahead of the game, Kane had asked Red-hawk for a man who knew his way around safes. "For that, we have Sergeant Albee."

Sergeant Alan Albee was a heavyset, clumsy-looking man with hands as big as shovels. He looked better suited to heavy construction work than something as delicate as opening a safe with or without a combination. But he had been employed in the family security business before joining the force, Redhawk had assured Kane, and had yet to find a lock or a safe he couldn't eventually master.

Jennifer looked at the sergeant dubiously as he filled out the showcase area with his bulky frame. She turned to Kane and lowered her voice. "He looks like he could open it just by smashing it with his fist."

The policeman overheard her and grinned over his shoulder, then crouched down and placed his ear against the safe as he worked the dial.

Kane stood back and watched. "Redhawk said he was the best."

"Couldn't you just blow it open?"

"We could," Kane agreed, "but it might damage whatever's inside. Besides—" he smiled his approval as he watched Albee "—I don't think that'll be necessary."

Jennifer looked. Albee was sitting back on his haunches, grinning. The small door of the safe was hanging invitingly open.

"All yours, Detective," Albee said.

With a grunt, he unfolded his large body and got out of the small enclosure. Jennifer thought it was a little like watching a circus act where a dozen clowns come tumbling out of one small car.

Kane pulled a crumpled handkerchief from his pocket and reached into the safe. Inside was a small box of data disks.

"Lucky thing we didn't use explosives. Whatever's on these disks would have been damaged, if not totally destroyed."

Jennifer stared at the box as he placed it on the counter by the register. She thought she was going to scream. They were inching along when she wanted to fly. "Now what?"

"Now we find a computer that can read what's on here," Kane murmured. He had been hoping for a ledger of some sort, not data disks. His computer expertise left a lot to be desired.

"There's one in the room where they found the babies," Albee volunteered, leading the way.

The back room was a small, sun-soaked, soundproof office. Against one wall were four bassinets. The oak desk against the opposite wall with its computer seemed out of place in the same area. The patrolmen had been all through the room and had found nothing amiss.

Kane looked at the computer as if it were an alien being descended from another planet for the sole purpose of plaguing him.

Jennifer expected Kane to turn on the machine and get started. When he made no move to do so, she looked at him. "What's the matter?"

Kane hated admitting to a shortcoming, no matter how justified he believed it to be.

"I have no idea how to operate one of those things." He waved a disparaging hand at the computer. He wasn't comfortable with a typewriter when he had to do his reports, much less a computer.

She looked at Kane in surprise. She had begun to believe that he was able to do anything, except bridge an emotional gap. Even Nik knew how to use a computer and he had dragged his feet about it all the way to the extension course she and Julia had enrolled him in.

"You're kidding."

Kane scowled at her expression. "I don't usually use a computer when going up against a criminal." He heard a defensive note in his voice and curbed it. "I'm better at thinking on my feet than staring at a keyboard, looking for the letter *t*."

Jennifer tapped the letter on the keyboard. "It's right there," she said with a smile. She nodded at the box of disks he held in his hand. "May I?"

"Go ahead." Still using the handkerchief, Kane took a disk out from the box and inserted it into the drive.

Jennifer turned the computer on, muttering a prayer that this was what they were looking for and that the data wasn't entered in code.

After an initial warm-up period, the hum coming from the computer took on an even rhythm and a blue screen with white letters appeared. It was a standard program Jennifer was familiar with. Tapping out a succession of keys, she was rewarded with a screen that contained a list of sales having taken place a year ago.

Jennifer sighed as she stared at it. There were cities listed beneath the word "nurseries" where purchases had obviously been made followed by the kind of flowers purchased and the names and addresses of the recipients.

Kane was looking over her shoulder as she scanned. He could feel the tension in her shoulders.

"Damn." He tugged a hand through his hair, frustrated. "That's just their sales records."

Jennifer blinked to hold back the tears she felt forming in the back of her eyes. She couldn't take much more of this, she thought, chasing after carrots that turned out to be only shadows on the wall. She scrolled from screen to screen, hoping to find something buried within the lists, some clue that might lead to the information they were really looking for.

They were all the same format. Nurseries, purchases, recipients.

She rubbed the heels of her hands against her eyes, clearing away the tears, and looked closer. That was odd, she thought. "Kane?"

He leaned over her shoulder, looking at the screen again. "What?"

She pointed to a line. "Look at the way this is set up." She indicated the flower arrangements. "All he sends out are carnations and roses." She turned to look at Kane. "Doesn't that strike you as being a little odd? What about other flowers? Daisies, orchids, violets, all the rest of them?"

Kane shrugged. "Maybe that's their specialty." There had certainly been enough of them in the store. He took another look, playing with a thought. "Or maybe—"

They looked at one another, the same thought occurring to both of them.

"—roses or carnations stand for boy or girl," Jennifer concluded eagerly. Oh please let that be it.

Kane was reading down the screen. "He's got cities listed under the nurseries. Nurseries could stand for—"

"Hospital nurseries," Jennifer cut in. "Oh Kane, this has to be it." She pointed to a line on the screen. "These are the cities where the babies were abducted."

He thought it over slowly. "There are a lot more here than just eleven babies."

"Eleven *known* abductions," Jennifer pressed. It all began to come together in her head at a dizzying speed. She *had* to be right. "Maybe there were more. Or maybe these are also babies whose mothers were convinced to give them up for private adoptions."

He nodded. It all made sense. He read another entry. "And the addresses belong to whoever 'bought' the goods. Adopted the babies," he clarified. "We have to get these printed up and faxed to L.A. and Nevada." He looked at the box and let out a low whistle as the magnitude struck him. There were six disks in all. "I think this is a lot bigger than we first thought."

She nodded, hardly able to contain herself. "Find me the disk with the most recent date on it."

Kane flipped through the box. The disks were all carefully labeled, separated by six-month increments. He pulled out one dated three months ago. "Here, try this one."

Jennifer hit the switch on the drive, popping out the disk they had just read. Kane removed it and inserted the one he had found for her. Holding her breath, Jennifer slowly flipped from screen to screen until she reached the very last entry.

Her heart pounding in her ears, Jennifer reread the words again. It was dated five days after Katie was born. The nursery was located in Newport Beach, California. "One dozen roses," she read aloud. "Sent to Mr. and Mrs. Bromley Culhane, Deerfield Lane, Lake Tahoe, Nevada." Jennifer's heart stopped as she went numb, then started again,

pounding wildly. She looked up at Kane. "Katie was kidnapped two days before. Oh, Kane." Covering her mouth,
she stifled a sob of both grief and joy. "We found her."

Kane's arms were around her before he even thought
about what he was doing, offering her comfort as best he
could. The end of the road was in sight. "We've hit the
mother lode, Jennifer. Can you print up a hard copy of
this?"

She clung to his arm for a minute, trying to steady herself. She nodded in reply.

He had always felt that the best way to treat a situation
like this was to be stern and prod the person into action, any
sort of action, until the shock had passed. He no longer
knew if this was the right way. He no longer knew anything
for certain anymore and it worried the hell out of him. Jennifer had blurred his parameters.

"Then do it," he said softly. "We need the information
on all these disks printed up. We might finally be reuniting
a lot of families before this is all over."

She sniffed a little and turned on the printer. It was silly
to fall apart now, when they were almost home free. The
stress she had gone through had been horrendous, but she
had not endured it alone. Kane had been there with her and
there *for* her, whether he knew it or not.

She pressed the command to print on the computer keyboard.

A few sharp, staccato sounds and the printer was off and
running, its rapid fire permeating the air like hundreds of
tiny firecrackers being shot off one after the other. Sheet
after sheet fanfolded onto the floor, holding dozens of tales
of untold anguish on each neatly printed page.

Jennifer was picking up the first stack from the floor
when Albee walked into the back room to inform them that
Redhawk had just called in over the squad car radio. The
patrolmen sent to the house of the man whose name was
listed as the owner of the flower shop had reported in. The
man had vanished without a trace. None of his neighbors
had seen him and they were concerned. It seemed that the

florist, an older man by the name of Victor Chambers, had
an excellent reputation in the neighborhood.

Kane held a corner of the first disk with the handkerchief and raised it in the air. "Tell the detective that we've
got something here that's going to make his day." He looked
at Jennifer and smiled. "As well as the day of an awful lot
of other people."

The printer was working on recreating the information on
the next disk. Jennifer had torn off the first sheet from the
stack. On it was the name and address of the man who had
her daughter.

"Lake Tahoe," Jennifer murmured in disbelief, looking
at the words on the bottom of the page. Her baby had been
flown to Lake Tahoe and placed in someone else's arms. It
seemed almost too incredible to believe.

"Next destination," Kane assured her, taking the list
from her.

"If this keeps up," she told Kane with a weary smile,
"we're going to qualify for a frequent flyer bonus before the
week is out."

"I'll use mine for a long vacation." He beckoned a policeman forward. "Take over for her, will you? I want all
these printed up in order." He indicated the box.

The man nodded and took the seat that Jennifer va-
cated, obviously at ease with the computer. Kane only shook
his head. Maybe he was the last of a dying breed, like the
dinosaur, holding out against progress. He didn't have the
time to think about it now. He glanced at Jennifer. He didn't
have the time to think about a lot of things now.

Jennifer followed Kane to the front of the store. Just beyond the wide plate glass window, she saw the police barri-
cade that forbade access into the cheerful little flower shop
where so many lives had been ruined. It was starting to rain.

Afraid to hope, or even think, Jennifer sought to divert
her thoughts in small talk. "Do you take them?"

Kane looked up from the list he was perusing. "Take
what?"

"Vacations." She couldn't see him doing it. She had a
feeling that he was defined by his work and had no life out-

side of his cases. It was as if, she thought, he really was hiding from something and that something was himself. Vacations forced one to be alone with themselves and perhaps he didn't really want to be.

Kane thought it was an odd question to ask at this point. "Why?"

He looked suddenly defensive, she thought. She had struck a nerve. Again. "I don't know, you don't seem the type."

With a sigh, he held open the front door and let her pass first. He waved her over toward the squad car. "Jennifer, you don't *know* my type."

She followed his lead and hurried toward the vehicle, running in the rain. "I know more than you think I do." *And more than you want me to.*

"Just get into the car," he ordered, exasperated.

They drove back to the precinct. The weather was positively nasty by the time they reached it. Redhawk was still in the squad room when they arrived. Kane presented him with the first lists that Jennifer had printed up, now slightly damp.

"And there's a lot more to come," Kane informed him. "Six full disks more. I left your patrolman printing up the rest of them."

Redhawk looked carefully at the names on the list, whistling low between his teeth. There were scores of entries.

"Wow." He dropped the list on his desk. "This is going to shake up a lot of lives," he murmured. "Six disks, eh?" Kane nodded in reply. "Looks like these people have been in business for a long time." He looked at Jennifer, his expression softening. "Your little girl on the list?"

Jennifer nodded, letting out a ragged sigh she had no idea she was holding. "The last entry."

Redhawk flipped to the page and looked at it. The words read so innocuously. "Lucky for you the guy was a nut about keeping records."

"Vanity, probably," Kane put in. "I've never met a criminal who didn't have it in one form or another. Any luck in finding the owner?"

Redhawk shook his head. But he didn't appear particularly worried about the fact. "No, but I figure between the two we've got locked up in holding and the Ward woman in Nevada, it's only a matter of time before we piece it all together. We've got a good description to go on."

He looked at Kane and Jennifer, then grinned. "Great work." A peal of thunder punctuated his words like giant cymbals crashing against one another. "Are you off to—" he glanced at the top sheet on his desk "—Tahoe?"

Jennifer rose from the seat she had taken next to his desk. "Just as soon as we can get a flight out."

Redhawk looked out the window. Sheets of rain were coating it one after another like a young girl trying on an endless parade of clothes. The storm had begun less than half an hour ago, but was now in full bloom. He listened as another crash of thunder ricocheted through the room. "That might be a problem."

"We could drive," Jennifer hazarded as she looked at Kane.

"It's over six hundred miles," Kane pointed out. "Even if we didn't wash away, we'd still be on the road by the time it cleared up and flights were available again."

"Besides, there's no sense in risking getting caught in a flash flood," Redhawk cautioned.

Kane knew how she felt, but there was nothing to be done. They had to wait out the weather. "If this is a private adoption, she'll still be there in the morning."

"By the looks of this—" Redhawk skimmed a finger down the page "—they're all private adoptions." He read some of the names on the right-hand side. People who had received the "bouquets."

"Just simple people wanting a baby." He shook his head at the grief represented here. "My son's adopted," he told them. "I don't know what I'd do if someone showed up on my doorstep, asking for him back."

That was something she hadn't thought about, Jennifer realized. It was another drama to be faced. God, she was so tired. When would it all be over? She looked over toward Kane and saw that he was busy tapping out a number on the telephone pad.

Kane was calling the airport for confirmation of something they already knew. After a few minutes, he hung up.

"You called it," he told Redhawk. "No flights out until after the storm clears." He looked at Jennifer. He knew if it was up to her, she'd be on the road, walking if she had to. He wondered if her capacity for love was always this endless. It was something he wouldn't be around to find out, he reminded himself.

"Hang in there, Jennifer," Kane told her. "We'll be in Tahoe before noon tomorrow."

"Say, how about dinner to celebrate breaking the case?" Redhawk suggested, tapping the list on his desk. "My treat. I'll even throw in an umbrella."

"Fine with me," Kane agreed, predominately for Jennifer's sake. He would be satisfied with grabbing a sandwich and sacking out. She needed to get out, to be around someone who could get her mind off all this. Redhawk seemed like the man for the job. He could talk, while all Kane could do was listen. "I've just got to check in with L.A. and fax them the sheets." He turned toward Jennifer, waiting. "Jennifer? Okay with you?"

She smiled, knowing what both men were trying to do. "Okay with me."

Dinner was at a little Italian restaurant not too far from the precinct. As Kane thought, Redhawk dominated most of the conversation. On the police force, first in Tucson, then in Phoenix, for twenty years, the man had a wealth of stories to tell, some sad, most amusing. As they worked their way from salad to main course to dessert, Jennifer felt her tension waning.

For his part, Kane sat back through most of the meal studying Jennifer. It still amazed him how such a delicate woman could wreak such havoc on his life. In less than a week's time, she had made him lose his edge. He was still a good cop, he thought, but not as good as he had been. He had gotten involved, deeply involved, and that had gotten in the way of his efficiency.

Maybe this was why, he mused, sipping his red wine slowly, surgeons didn't operate on their own. It got too complicated. Emotions got in the way of instincts, slowing the hand, slowing the brain. The heart, he had learned, was a hell of a roadblock.

And a damn pain in the neck to boot.

He knew he couldn't get involved anymore than he already was. What was happening between Jennifer and him wouldn't lead anywhere. It *couldn't* lead anywhere. For her sake. He listened to her laugh at something Redhawk said and felt a pang. Kane hadn't the slightest idea how to love someone and she deserved a man who could give of himself emotionally. A man who could make her laugh as well as feel. Whatever he might have had to give had long since been stripped away from him by the cruel realities of life.

He was dead inside.

Kane drained the last of his wine, then set his glass aside. For once, he would place someone's feelings above his own, he decided, because she was worth it. He wasn't running from his feelings, he was protecting hers.

The check arrived all too soon, signaling an end to the evening. It was getting late and Redhawk had a family to see to. Redhawk dug into his pocket for his wallet. "Well, I've talked long enough. I'd better let you two get some sleep."

"Let me at least split that with you," Kane offered, reaching for the tab.

Redhawk pulled it away. "Hey, don't you know better than to tread on an Indian's pride?" Redhawk flashed a perfect set of teeth in a wide grin. "I said my treat and I meant it." He took out two bills from his wallet, placed them on top of the check and rose.

"It was a lovely meal, Graham," Jennifer said as she got to her feet.

The dark eyes looked at her kindly. "My pleasure."

He accompanied them outside. The weather was still merciless, dueling with the ground, pounding angry fists along the pavement. They stood for a moment beneath the striped canopy and watched.

"Nothing's taking off tonight," Redhawk said with a shake of his head. "Better get a room for the night." The Phoenix detective shook hands with them both, his clasp genuine and warm. "If I don't see you before you take off, just leave the car at the airport and give me a call later. I'll have someone pick it up. Good luck to both of you." Turning up his collar, he began to leave.

"Wait. Your umbrella," Jennifer called after him, raising it in the air.

"You use it. Leave it in the car when you take off." He waved her back beneath the awning and hurried off to his bright pink Cadillac.

They stood in silence for a moment, watching the rain. Alone, neither seemed inclined to begin a conversation. Finally, Kane asked, "Do you want to go back to that place we stayed in last time?"

It took Jennifer a minute to realign the city she was in with the right hotel. He was referring to the Happy Inn, she realized. She recalled the stoop-shouldered man behind the counter. The rooms had been shabby, but clean. She nodded. "Sure."

With his hand placed lightly on the back of her neck to guide her, Kane held the umbrella above them and they made a dash for the squad car Redhawk had lent them.

It took them longer than it should have to maneuver through the rain-swept streets to the hotel. In the rain, the Happy Inn looked more forlorn than happy. They parked directly before the building and dashed inside.

The same man who waited on them the first night was behind the desk, his back to the door. He was busy watching a comedy on his ever-present television set and chuckling to himself. It was a soft, wheezy sound. He looked surprised when the door opened. The rain reached in, long fingers wetting the indoor/outdoor carpeting as Kane and Jennifer hurried inside.

The man sighed and turned from his set.

"Two rooms, please," Kane told him, closing the umbrella. He shook some of the rain from his jacket.

Jennifer met Kane's request with ambivalent feelings. Had she read too much into the other day? Had it been just a momentary aberration on both their parts? Or was there something there after all? Something that frightened this large man who instilled fear in the hearts of criminals, but shied away from her?

The little man behind the counter shook his head. "Only got the one room," the man told them. "Rain." He pointed to the window as if they hadn't noticed. "Nobody wants to be out in weather like this." Leaning over his counter, he squinted, trying to place them. "Weren't you two here the other night?"

Kane nodded curtly.

The man grinned, his moustache brushing the tops of his uneven teeth. "Always like return business." He turned to look at the single key hanging on a hook. He retrieved it and held it before Kane. "Got room number three," he told them, as if the number would make a difference. His small eyes darted from Kane to Jennifer and back again. "Okay with you?"

Kane hadn't wanted to share a room. He didn't want to be alone with Jennifer this last evening they had together. There were too many emotions smoldering within him, despite all his attempts at restraint. But he had no choice in the matter. It was too wet outside to go driving around, looking for another hotel.

He shrugged. "If that's all you have." His fingers encircled the key as he took it from the man. Kane quickly signed their names to the register. He caught the uneasy expression on Jennifer's face.

It stung, but he understood. He couldn't blame her, not after the last episode. He knew he shouldn't have left her like that, but he couldn't help it. It had been for her own good.

For his own good, he would have stayed and held her. And made love with her again, damning the consequences.

But the consequences involved Jennifer and he couldn't do that to her.

She almost wished that they had gone somewhere else. A single room, Jennifer thought. She knew she wouldn't have survived these last few days without him. How could she stand being so close to him tonight and not turn to him for comfort, for support? For love? He had become a very important part of her world. If it hadn't been for him, she wouldn't be planning to see her daughter tomorrow. Instead, she would have been going crazy, sitting by the telephone, waiting for it to ring. He embodied the only hope she had had.

And so much more.

Because it was so much more, Jennifer was afraid of how he would react to their being alone together. If he rebuffed her, she wasn't certain she would be able to handle it.

"Come on," he urged, opening the umbrella again. He held it over her. "Let's make a run for it."

Jennifer wondered, as she hunched next to him and dashed through the puddles and the rain, if he meant more than just making it to the room.

Chapter 14

The small hotel room was a carbon copy of the one they had stayed in before. It had the same threadbare brown rug, the same lifeless beige curtains hung at the window. The same double bed placed in the same position against the wall. Only the bedspread looked newer.

Jennifer looked at the bed, uneasily. Kane had made love with her in a room just like this. Would it happen again? Would he be as sweet and as loving as she needed him to be?

She glanced at the uncompromising set of his mouth. Or would he turn away from her? The room was warm, but a chill slid along her body, making her shiver.

Kane pushed the door closed behind him, locking out the rain. He dropped her overnight case on the floor and turned to see Jennifer looking at the bed. There was uncertainty in her eyes. He interpreted it the only way he could.

She was afraid, he thought. Afraid to be alone in the room with him. Afraid that since they had made love once, he was going to force himself on her. That she could feel that way slashed through his heart like the honed blade of a carving knife.

He shed his wet jacket and tossed it on the back of the rickety chair. It dangled, one sleeve brushing against the rug, slowly creating a darkening circle as the moisture slowly dripped to the floor.

"Don't worry." Kane's voice was gruff as it scraped along his throat, forcing the words out. "I don't intend to ravage you."

Jennifer's head jerked in his direction as his words burst on her brain. What had made him say that? She looked at him, confused. She had heard pain in his voice. Why? What was he thinking? She realized that beneath that go-to-hell exterior existed a vulnerable man who she had somehow unintentionally hurt.

There were walls between them, walls that she couldn't begin to understand, but she knew she never wanted to be the one to hurt him. She hated whoever had done this to him, whoever had wounded him so badly that he couldn't venture forth, couldn't just let himself feel and love like any other man.

She placed her hand on his arm. "I know that."

Kane moved his arm abruptly aside. He didn't want the slightest, most casual of contacts between them. She looked like a goddess that the rains had anointed, with her clothing outlining every sensuous curve of her body.

He curled his fingers into his hands, clenching them hard. He knew he could only exercise so much restraint before giving in to the raging desire that was feeding on him, consuming whole bits and pieces of him even as he stood there, attempting to deny its existence.

Jennifer tried not to let the fact that he pulled away from her hurt, but it did. Pressing her lips together, she looked down at her wet clothing. Her dress was plastered to her body, molding itself like a second, wrinkled skin. She looked awful. With a sigh, she dragged her hand through her damp hair.

"I'd better get out of these clothes," Jennifer murmured, more to herself than to him, "and give them a chance to dry."

Kane, his back to her, merely grunted something unintelligible.

"Easy for you to say," she muttered.

Tossing her overnight case on the bed, she flipped the locks and yanked her baseball jersey and robe out. Afraid that she might do something stupid, like cry, she hurried into the bathroom.

With the door shut, she let out a long sigh and attempted to collect herself. She was just edgy, she told herself. They were close to finding Katie and her nerves were just stretched to the limit, that was all.

Leaning over the cracked porcelain sink, Jennifer gave the tired, drawn woman in the mirror a silent pep talk. She was afraid that if she said the words aloud, her voice would carry through the paper-thin walls to Kane.

She splashed water in her face and got herself under control. Jennifer shed her wet clothes quickly, then arranged them along the thin silver rod that supported a drab salmon pink shower curtain. Slipping on the jersey, she toweled dry her hair. The dampness made it curl and wave about her face and shoulders like dark party streamers.

Party streamers. She smiled sadly at the thought, then stopped. Kane had taken down the party streamers in her house that first day, to spare her feelings. Maybe it was time to stop thinking and just start celebrating life and the moment. She was with a man she cared about deeply and she was going to find her daughter tomorrow. The moment looked very good.

Jennifer opened the bathroom door and left her robe where she had placed it. She wasn't going to need it tonight.

When she entered the room, she saw Kane tucking a blanket around the faded cushions of the herculean sofa. He worked methodically, preoccupied. He appeared so resigned, she thought, watching him, so rigid, like a robot programmed for the task. He didn't even seem to hear her come out.

"What are you doing?" Her voice was a soft whisper floating through the room until it reached him.

Kane felt his hands tighten around the edge of the blanket as he finished tucking it about the cushion. The sound of her voice had his stomach twisting into a knot. He turned, a steely answer on his tongue. It faded as his mouth suddenly dried. What she was wearing now was no better than the wet dress. The baseball jersey was short, brushing seductively along the tops of her thighs. His hands dampened.

Kane looked away, rubbing his hands on the back of his jeans. "You forgot your robe."

She felt a nervous quiver go through her, but stood her ground. He wasn't going to dismiss her so easily, not when she felt the way she did about him.

"It's warm. Why are you making up the sofa?" she pressed again.

He kept his back to her as he took a pillow from the bed. He tossed it at one end of the sofa. "I'm getting ready to go to bed."

She crossed to him. She stood so close to him, he could smell the scent of her skin, the clean, tantalizing scent of soap mixed with a hint of perfume and a trace of something that was hers alone.

Jennifer gestured toward the couch. "That's not a bed, that's a sofa. A lumpy, uncomfortable-looking sofa."

There was no arguing with her assessment. He shrugged indifferently. "I've slept on worse things."

He was so distant, so rigid. Jennifer felt a pang. Maybe she had made a mistake after all. Maybe her own needs had her reading things into his actions. "Like in a bed, with me?"

The small note of hurt in her voice had Kane turning around. He couldn't help the smile that lifted the corners of his mouth at the memory her words evoked. "No, that ranks as one of the best places."

Lord. He wanted to touch her. To hold her. Just to hold her.

"And as I recall," he added, the smile growing, "we didn't sleep."

She saw the flicker of desire in his eyes. So, she wasn't wrong. Her voice was thick with longing, with remembering. "No, we didn't."

He turned away again, unable to look at Jennifer without reaching for her. And it was best not to start anything.

"You're tired. We've got a flight in the morning." He glanced out the window. The rain was still beating down heavily. "Weather permitting."

He moved to lie down, but she placed her hand on his arm. That was all it took to stop him. "You don't have to do this, Kane." If he thought he was being noble for her sake, she didn't want it. She didn't want him being noble, she just wanted him.

He looked at her then, just her eyes. His own were flat, unreadable. "Yes. I do."

What was there inside of him that kept him from her? Why couldn't he let her in? "Do I frighten you that much, Kane?"

He nodded, wishing she'd get into bed and leave him alone. He wasn't made of iron. "Lady, you scare the hell out of me."

She searched his face, trying valiantly to understand. "Why?"

He blew out a breath and laughed, frustrated. Helpless. "Because you're under my skin. You've gotten in when all the doors and windows were locked and barred. Just like Houdini, somehow, you got in."

The revelation made her smile, but something in his manner kept her from threading her arms around his neck the way she wanted to. "Maybe I'm supposed to be in."

He shook his head firmly. He was meant to travel through life alone. He knew that, had come to terms with that. And then she had come along, knocking out the pins from beneath the very foundation of his life. She was making him care when he didn't even know how. He didn't understand any of it, except that he would hurt her in the end.

"No, you're not."

She heard the slight waver in his voice. It was enough. "What makes you so sure?"

He was losing ground and he knew it. "Because I am. Jennifer—" Kane framed her face with his hands, unable to resist just this slightest of touches "—I'm no good for you."

He wasn't going to talk his way out of this. Not when she felt he wanted her as much as she wanted him. "You have been, so far."

He dropped his hands to her shoulders, as if that would somehow make her accept the truth. His truth. "That's because I've been doing my job."

A smile played on her lips. "What happened in the hotel room in Vegas was part of your job?"

"No, damn it." He released her before he was tempted to shake her. "You're confusing things."

Jennifer slowly shook her head as she rose so that her mouth was inches from his, her hands braced on his arms. "No, I think you are. And it's so simple. Very, very simple."

The words floated along his lips, tempting him, making his desire boil over like a pot forgotten on the stove for too long.

"You've got a hell of a way of arguing."

She grinned. "Yeah, I know."

Kane buried his hands in her hair, pulling her toward him. He covered her mouth with his own, falling deep into the kiss that was waiting for him.

The thin fissures along the ramparts of his soul were widening into cracks and everything he had tried to keep in was seeping out.

He loved her.

Damn her soul for doing this to him, he thought, his mouth brushing along hers. He loved her. And it would be her undoing. He knew that. And yet, he couldn't help himself. He couldn't just walk away when she was offering this to him. He wasn't strong enough.

Having her in his arms now somehow made up for every single hurt he had ever experienced in his life. There had *been* no life before Jennifer, only an existence that had formed a man of granite, layer by layer. She had chipped away at those layers, until they were as thin as rice paper. Until they tore.

Her pure, undemanding gift was his salvation. And his undoing.

Kane kissed her over and over again, gently, reverently, humbly offering her something he had never known he had to give. His soul.

The way he kissed her, as if she were fragile, as if she would break from the slightest pressure, made her feel beautiful. And cherished. It instantly healed all the hurts she had inside.

He could feel his blood growing warmer, sizzling in his veins like a griddle heating too fast. He drew back and realized that the front of her jersey was damp. *Idiot*. "I'm all wet."

"A little water never hurt anyone." She entwined her arms around his neck.

"In this case, it might."

"Shut up and kiss me, Detective." Her lips touched his and his resistance disappeared as if it had never existed.

She was a glimmer of light he held in his hands and he was so afraid of snuffing it out, of losing it from his life. He proceeded slowly, cautiously, as if the slightest wrong move would wake him up to find that she had only been an elusive dream he could never have.

Though he knew how to pleasure a woman, how to gain pleasure from it himself, the feelings involved here were something he had never experienced before. There was a tenderness that had never been part of desire before, a concern that somehow, he would hurt her. For Kane it wasn't just a matter of two bodies meeting for an hour or a night. This was more. This *meant* something.

This meant everything.

He gently cupped her breast in his hand and thrilled to her soft moan as it vibrated along his throat a moment before her lips touched it. Nothing had ever aroused him more or filled him with such a fiery, sweet sensation as that single sound. It felt like flaming honey pouring through his veins, covering every part. He wanted to give her the moon, to lay jewels at her feet. To somehow let her know what she had done for him.

He could only kiss her and know it wasn't enough.

Kane felt her fingers, soft, fluttery, sure, move from one button to the next along his chest, working them free until his shirt hung open. Moving back, Jennifer pushed the shirt from his shoulders.

"I want to feel you against me, Kane," she murmured, her tongue skimming the outline of his lips.

Passion roared, demanding, pulsating, hot. But Kane struggled to contain its violent eruption. He wanted to give her all he could, to bring her prolonged physical pleasure. He wanted to worship at the temple of her body this one last time before she left his life without a trace.

No, that wasn't true. There would be more than a trace of her left, even when she was gone. It would be locked away permanently in his heart until the day he died. Even if it stopped right here, right now, the sensations she had aroused within him were forever burned into his soul. For one brief, shining moment, he had loved.

With hands that were annoyingly unsteady, his eyes on hers, Kane moved his palms along the bare skin beneath her jersey. He saw excitement and anticipation widen her eyes as he trailed his fingers along her thighs. Her breath quickened and her grip tightened on his arms.

He saw her reaction and reveled in it.

This he could do for her, this if nothing more. He could bring her to the highest peaks. He could pleasure her.

With a skilled touch, he found the center of her core and gently glided along the sensitive skin. His excitement fed on her soft exclamation as desire turned her sigh into a moan. Kane brought her to the edge swiftly, then took her over as his lips covered hers. Her cry echoed within his mouth.

She shuddered as she dug her nails into his shoulder. Dazed, Jennifer looked at him, her eyes filled with wonder. Her limbs were heavy, tired, yet she ached for more. Ached for him. How much pleasure could one body sustain?

He smiled at the surprise in her eyes. Last time, the earth had opened up beneath his feet and he had fallen in. This time, he intended to do it right. For this time would be the last time.

But he couldn't think about that now. The thought was too sad and sadness had no place here, in this room, with this woman.

His lips moving along hers, coaxing responses from Jennifer she had never known she possessed, Kane bracketed her thighs and gently, seductively moved her jersey up along her legs, lifting it to her waist, up higher until the only part of her that was covered were her breasts.

Her breath catching in her throat, Jennifer raised her arms up, her heart beating fast, her eyes a prisoner of the look within his. The air whispered along her body as he tugged off the material. She shivered, not from the cold, but from the anticipation.

Kane gently laid her back on the bed. Within a heartbeat, he had rid himself of his wet, cumbersome jeans and was next to her. His hands gently caressed her, worshipping every curve, every soft inch of skin. Then his mouth lay a hot, moist trail following the path his hands had taken, that had her twisting and arching against him.

Her body hummed with renewed desire, renewed needs.

She reached for him, wanting to feel him against her, wanting this golden sensation pouring through her to go on forever, yet needing to reach the summit again.

With him.

Jennifer locked her legs around his back, rocking against him, reveling in the feel of Kane's tough, hard body against her softness.

He was afraid of hurting her, afraid of being too rough. His needs dashed themselves against one another, like the pounding surf of an angry sea, vibrating within him. Yet he held back, bringing her up and over twice as his hands drew all the secrets of her body from her.

He wanted her to remember what he would never forget. He wanted her to remember one night of magic, when she was his. It was all he asked for. All he could hope for.

It wasn't fair, she thought. It wasn't fair, that she should want him so much that she could hardly stand it while he

could restrain himself to this level, as if he were just an ob-
server and nothing more. She wanted Kane to feel the way
she did, want the way she wanted. She wanted to share this
sensation with him.

But then as he entered her, she heard Kane's muffled
groan and realized that he wasn't as removed as she had
thought. That he was just as much bound to her as she was
to him.

The thought increased her excitement.

Together, joined as one, they drove each other up and
over the highest peak as passion urged them on faster and
faster. As the explosion wracked them both, Jennifer cried
out his name.

Kane buried his face in her neck to stop the words he
didn't want her to hear. She would feel bound by them and
it wouldn't be fair to her. He mouthed "I love you," along
the hollow of her throat.

The descent, as she lay in his arms, was slow and peaceful. He had been gentle with her, even at the end, when
passion was threatening to rip them both apart. The way he
had handled her, as if she were a fragile doll, told Jennifer
that this type of lovemaking, laced with tenderness, was
something new for Kane. She knew it couldn't have been for
lack of female attention. The man was far too good-looking
for that. It had to be because he chose it to be that way. That
made what they had shared all the more precious.

And there was something more. Something, just as that
glorious sensation was seizing her, holding her in the palm
of its hand, that she'd thought she heard. He had said
something to her. She could almost swear she had felt the
words, absorbed them through her skin as well as heard
them. But now, when she tried to recapture them, they were
just out of reach.

What had he said?

The steady sound of rain droned on outside their window. Shadows played with the light from the one lone lamp,
turning a shabby little room into a cozy haven. She nestled
against him, her hand laying along his chest. She felt the

comforting beat of his heart beneath her arm. "Who are you, Kane?"

He played with the ends of her hair, wrapping one strand around his finger. It felt incredibly silky, like her body. "A cop."

She thought she knew him well enough to feel that he didn't really believe he was defined by what he did. That was just his way of trying to put her off. "That's your *job*. Who are *you*?"

He opened his mouth, suddenly wanting to tell her. Wanting, by telling her about his past, to draw her completely into his world.

But she didn't belong there. She belonged where things were nice and refined and clean. He unwound the strand of hair from his finger and let it drop. "Nobody you should know."

She ached for him when he said that. There was an incredible sadness in his voice that he didn't seem aware of. "Oh, that's where you're wrong."

She didn't know him, he thought. "I'm not the kind of man to bring home to mother, Jennifer."

She propped herself up on one elbow, her hair trailing along his bare skin. She traced swirls of hair on Kane's chest lightly with her fingertips. He felt the muscles in his belly tightening as desire, full-blown, reborn, shooting hot, urgent darts through him, returned at the slight touch of her hand.

Jennifer inclined her head toward him. "Then isn't it fortunate for you that I don't have a mother to bring you home to?" Her mouth whispered softly along his as she touched it to his lips.

Kane's resolve broke into too many pieces to reconstruct as he pulled her to him. With a laugh, Jennifer straddled his body.

Kane could only shake his head as he fit his hands along her hips. She was playing with fire. "You're going to regret this, you know."

She smiled, lightly caressing his cheek. He turned his face into her palm and kissed the sensitive skin he found there. Jennifer felt shivers of silvery anticipation beginning.

"I don't think so." She saw the doubt in his gray eyes. "We'll talk about it then," she promised.

He was stroking her body and felt her begin to move against him, ever so slowly, fueling his arousal. "You don't take no for an answer, do you?"

She smiled, mischief in her eyes. She leaned forward, just out of reach of his mouth. "I would..." The words trailed off.

"When?"

Jennifer nipped at his lower lip, then pulled back as Kane moved to deepen the kiss. "If I thought you meant it."

He had to struggle to stifle the groan as she moved along him with a steady, quiet rhythm. "And if I said I did?"

She only had to look into his eyes. "I'd know you were lying."

He laughed against her throat as he pulled her to him. "You're incorrigible."

Her eyes grew serious as the laughter left them. "I'm a lot more than that."

"Oh?"

Her body was completely over his as she lowered her face so that it almost touched his. "I'm your destiny."

He couldn't argue with her. He knew she was wrong, but all he wanted to do at this one moment in time was to kiss her and to make it last forever.

This time, the lovemaking that erupted between them was almost explosive as Kane tried to bury his memories and the demons that haunted him within the soft sweetness of Jennifer's willing flesh.

Most of all, he tried to hide from the knowledge that tomorrow would come.

But now, there was only now. There was only this moment in time and this magnificent, beautiful woman, giving him more than he thought possibly existed, evoking from him more than he knew he possessed.

Tomorrow would take care of itself and be here all too soon. He fought to keep it at bay as long as he could. And soon, it was. This time, when they plummeted over the edge together, they fell asleep in each other's arms, for once at peace.

Just before he drifted off, his arm around her tightly, listening to the even rhythm of her breathing, Kane was aware that he had never known such contentment.

And most likely, would never know it again.

Chapter 15

There was no awkwardness this time. Jennifer could feel its absence as soon as she woke up. Instead, there was the feeling of contentment purring through her like a kitten stretched out before a warm fire on a winter's evening. It felt right.

In sleep, Kane had draped his arm over her chest and gathered her close to him. She was pinned beneath its weight.

Jennifer smiled and let out a slow breath as she curled against his body, absorbing the warmth he generated. Absorbing the moment. She took the opportunity to study his features. Asleep, the troubled, brooding look that was so characteristic of his face even in repose, was missing. He looked almost peaceful.

And heart-stoppingly handsome, she thought.

Slowly, taking care not to rouse him, Jennifer lifted a hand to his face and ever so lightly brushed away the hair that had fallen over his eyes.

He had secrets, problems, but she had time and eventually, somehow, it would all work itself out. She knew it. She couldn't feel this strongly about him and just have it abruptly end. She'd only been in love once before in her life. Looking back, she realized how that emotion paled in comparison to what she was experiencing now. It was a candle compared to a fire. A drop of water compared to a flood.

What she had felt for Brad had been entirely different. A summarized version of what was really a huge classical novel. She hadn't felt then as if love consumed all her heart, all her soul. When she was in love with Brad, she hadn't felt as if she would go through life miserably incomplete if she wasn't part of him and he wasn't part of her. The thought of her parting from Kane left Jennifer bereft.

Kane murmured softly under his breath, still apparently asleep, and turned his face away from her, burying it in the pillow. The early morning sunlight streaming in through the faded beige curtains had turned his skin golden.

Like a god, she thought. A strong, silent, sullen god.

"I love you, Detective Kane Madigan, with all your warts and all your demons," she whispered softly. "I love you. Big time."

Unable to resist, Jennifer raised her neck and pressed a kiss to his shoulder.

Kane opened his eyes. He had been awake for several minutes now, but had been content just to lie here, savoring this island of peace he found himself on in a world he knew was constructed of quicksand. Content just to hear her breathing softly, feeling the gentle rise and fall of her breasts beneath his arm. This was more than he had ever dreamed of.

He had heard her when she had innocently whispered her love and his pulse quickened. For a second, just the smallest measurement of time, he let himself drift and believe.

But he was a realist. And the drifting ended.

It would never work between them, he knew that as well as he knew his name, his past. His future. He could give her only moments. She deserved forever.

Stretching, Kane pretended to wake up. He rolled over and looked at her, then stopped. He hadn't been prepared. Something lurched in his stomach to find her so close to him, her hair tumbling about her bare shoulders, the dewy kiss of sleep still fresh on her skin. Desire bloomed, full-blooded and wanting through his body, knowing that beneath the thin sheet she was nude.

And his.

Torture, Kane thought, was made up of moments just like this.

"Hi," she murmured. To his ear, it sounded more like a seductive sigh. "Sleep well?"

Kane lightly combed his fingers through her hair, then watched, fascinated as it rained through his fingers. "Like a rock."

It had probably been his first peaceful night in years, he thought. Usually, he slept very lightly, attuned to every noise. She was definitely blunting his edge. But not his appetite.

"That's a perfect way to describe your arm," Jennifer laughed.

He realized he had draped it over her again. "Oh, sorry." He moved to lift it.

"No," she protested, wrapping her arms around his to stop him. He looked at her quizzically. "Don't be sorry," her voice was soft, melodic. Coaxing. "I like the way it feels to have you so close."

Damn if she wasn't doing it to him again. Making him want her more than he wanted to breathe. Would he never be free of this? Never be free of the all-consuming desire to have her, over and over again? He'd never felt like this before, never wanted like this. Once should have been enough to satisfy him. But all it had done was whet his appetite for more.

Kane sighed, then looked around. It was daylight, he suddenly realized. "What time is it?"

She had already checked the time when she woke up. She glanced at her watch again to reassure him. "We're due at the airport in two hours." There was mischief in her eyes when she raised them to his.

Kane felt a smile taking hold, though he knew it had absolutely no business being there. Last night, when he had made love with her, he had promised himself that it would be the last time.

He had lied.

It was as if his mind had completely abdicated control to his body. He slipped his hand beneath the sheet and found her waist. Spanning his fingers so that they cupped her derriere, Kane cradled Jennifer against him.

"The airport's only fifteen minutes away."

She grinned, settling in comfortably, her body heating from the slightest movement of skin against skin. "I know."

Slowly, he began to knead her soft buttocks as urges pounded through him, growing, seeking an outlet. "It'll take us fifteen minutes to get dressed and ready." Was he ever going to be able to look at the sky on a cloudless day and not think of her eyes?

Her breath was already beginning to back up in her lungs. Jennifer leaned forward and lightly traced his lips with the tip of her tongue. She felt him shiver slightly and gloried in her own power. It excited her, exciting him. "Maybe even less."

He wanted to take her now, this instant. To drive himself into her and feel her hot, moist flesh surrounding his. He managed to maintain control, but it wasn't easy. "That gives us, what—?"

Fluids, molten hot and furious, were pouring through her veins. "An hour and a half," she whispered.

With ease, Kane shifted so that she was suddenly beneath him on the bed, his elbows bracketing her body. "What do you think we should do to occupy ourselves with the rest of the time?"

She moved beneath him, her breasts sliding against his chest, igniting a fire water could never put out. "I'm open to suggestions," she breathed, her smile softening as she watched his eyes.

He groaned as demands slammed through his body, crying for release. Gently, he had to go gently. She had to remember this with only tender memories.

"You *are* a suggestion." He framed Jennifer's face with his hands, his fingers caressing her skin as if it were the most delicate treasure he had ever perceived. "The most seductive, suggestive suggestion I've ever had the fortune to encounter."

Jennifer wrapped her arms around his neck, arching against him. "More. I want to hear more."

He laughed and shook his head. "Too bad. I don't feel like talking anymore."

She drew a deep breath as his mouth lowered to hers, anticipating the exhilarating ride ahead. "Funny, suddenly neither do I."

Somehow, though he didn't quite understand it, Jennifer had made him feel like someone else. Someone light, buoyant. Alive. She had made him feel as if there were no shackles holding him down. Kane knew that it was only an illusion, built of vapors and air, but it was one that he would always treasure. There, in that shabby hotel room, paradise had been created for him, a paradise that he would carry with him until the day he died.

He was still basking in the aftereffects of making love with Jennifer as he sat on the plane that was taking them to Reno Cannon International Airport. Taking them to Jennifer's daughter.

Taking them to the end of the line.

There were things he still didn't know, things that had nothing to do with the case. Things that had only to do with her. The more he knew, the harder it was to distance himself and walk away. But he had to know. And one thing in particular.

"Tell me about him," he said quietly.

"Him?" Jennifer echoed Kane's last word, but she instinctively knew who he was referring to. A man who had ceased to matter.

He had no right to ask and part of Kane resisted knowing anything about the man who had held her and made love with her. Who had made her moan and twist and whisper his name in the dark. But another part wanted to absorb every last shred, every last detail.

He seemed, Kane thought, bent on creating his own private hell.

"Katie's father." Trying to strip his voice of emotion, Kane still fairly growled out the words. He had had his story checked out and Brad was clean. But that didn't fill in the gaps.

Was it a good sign? Was he trying to get closer, or was he using the shadow of Brad as a sword to drive a wedge between them? Whatever the reason, whatever the cost, Jennifer knew she wouldn't lie to Kane. *Couldn't* lie to Kane.

She resigned herself to the conversation. "What do you want to know?"

He shrugged, almost a helpless victim of his own curiosity. Questions were easy enough for him to word when they related to a case. He could hone in on the exact angle, the exact focus. Here he felt as lost as a honeybee circling a field of wildflowers, not knowing where to start first.

"Why?" The single word encompassed everything. The question had been vibrating in his brain ever since he had met her. Why hadn't he met her before? Why hadn't he met her while there had still been a prayer of resurrecting more tender feelings? Why had she come into his life at this point in time and not at any other?

Jennifer laughed softly, at a loss. "Why what? Why did I fall for him?"

"Did you?" He knew he would have rather heard that what she and the baby's father had had was a meaningless affair. That it had been "just one of those things" that happened between consenting adults. He didn't want to hear that she had actually loved the man.

But Kane knew Jennifer wasn't like that. She wasn't given to the casual melding of bodies. If she made love with someone, it was because she loved. And that hurt all the more.

"Yes," she said slowly. "Yes, I did." Jennifer settled back, knowing this had to be aired out, even if the telling hurt. It couldn't just be shoved aside like clothing that she had outgrown and forgotten. "He was handsome and bright and witty. And he made me laugh."

And he would only make her cry, Kane thought, hating the faceless man who had been there before him. His expression grew stony. ''That's no reason to make love with someone.''

He was jealous, she thought, clutching the realization to her. He wouldn't be jealous if he didn't care. ''Maybe it was the way he read poetry.''

''Poetry?'' Kane spat the word out as if it left a bad taste in his mouth.

She almost laughed, but didn't. ''You know, the funny stuff that usually rhymes.''

For a moment, she remembered a more innocent time. She half waited for something to react within her, but there was nothing. It was all gone, as if it had never really existed.

''He could read Byron beautifully. Unfortunately,'' she shrugged, ''he was more suited to a part in Milton's *Paradise Lost* than to Byron's *Don Juan in Hell*.''

Kane raised a brow, waiting for Jennifer to refer to something he could understand. Poetry was part of English classes buried deep in the past.

''The snake,'' she clarified. Her expression sobered. ''He was married.''

Kane pinned her with a look, a quirk of one brow being the only indication of his surprise. ''You made love to a married man?'' That didn't fit the picture of the woman he knew.

''I didn't know it at the time.'' There was no bitterness in her voice. There was absolutely no feeling whatsoever. That part of her life was over. And it had yielded something incredibly precious to her. Katie.

''That was a little detail he forgot to mention while he was reciting.'' Jennifer knotted her hands in her lap as she remembered. ''He mentioned it fast enough when I told him I was pregnant, though. Suddenly, he was very much the family man. And the family didn't include me or our baby.''

''The bastard should have been shot,'' Kane said vehemently, surprising himself as well as Jennifer with his verbal reaction.

Jennifer grinned. "That's what Nik said. Nik was all set to make good on it, too, until Julie and I stopped him. Nik was always very protective of me."

There was a fondness in her voice when she spoke of her family. A fondness Kane knew he envied.

She let out a long sigh. It was good to get this out. And bury it once and for all.

"I haven't seen him since he walked out on me. Ran, actually," she recalled, "to his bright red Ferrari. I hope he got a speeding ticket that day."

"And you haven't tried to get in contact with him since then?" Kane knew the answer to that before she said it, but he wanted to hear it from her.

Jennifer shook her head. She never wanted to see Brad again, not even by accident. She was grateful that Katie appeared to have her features, not Brad's. The only fear she had had while carrying Katie was that each time she looked into her child's face, she would see Brad.

"No."

"Not even to tell him about Katie?" Kane prodded. With her sense of honor, perhaps she thought the man deserved to know. After all, he was Katie's father.

Brad would have been the last person she would have turned to. "No, especially not then. When I gave you his name and telephone number I told you that I didn't want to have any contact with him and I meant it. As far as he was concerned, Katie didn't exist. When I told him I was pregnant, he informed me that I was going to get an abortion. It was when I refused that he left. Katie is mine," she said fiercely, "not his."

"Did you love him?" Kane watched her eyes as he asked. She might try to spare him, but her eyes would give her away.

She thought about it for a moment, as if to be sure of her answer. "I thought I did." Then she smiled and shook her head. "But no, I didn't really love him. I loved the idea of being in love, I think. It had never happened to me before and I wanted something magical and romantic with a handsome, caring man who said all the right things." She shrugged. "I guess I got carried away."

Jennifer paused as she looked at Kane pointedly. "It wasn't the way it was with you."

He shifted uncomfortably in his seat, as if it were suddenly alive and moving beneath him. "I wasn't fishing for that."

Was he so terribly afraid of commitment? she wondered. "I know you weren't, but I wanted you to know that. I only *thought* I was in love with him." She remembered last night and all the passion that had existed in that one small room, making time stand still. "I had no idea what the real thing felt like."

"And now you do." Kane couldn't help the cynical twist to his lips. It was almost reflexive, a holdover from the past when he held everything suspect. He now knew she didn't fit into that category.

If he was trying to push her away, it wasn't going to work. She'd never been one to give up easily. "Yes, now I do."

"Jennifer—" he began, not knowing what to say next, only that it couldn't go on like this.

"Care for any complimentary nuts?" They looked up, startled, to see the flight attendant standing in the aisle, bending over them, a small tray of plastic-wrapped nuts in her hand. She raised it slightly, as if to coax them into making a selection.

"No, thank you." Jennifer took a breath, grateful for the momentary respite. Kane just shook his head.

She waited until the woman left before turning to Kane. "All right, you've heard my story, now what about yours?"

Kane stiffened slightly. "What about mine?"

He was going to make this like pulling teeth, she thought. After what had happened between them, she had hoped that he would finally open up to her, at least a little. "What is it?"

He looked off through the window. A huge layer of clouds covered the sky like a single wavy roll of unfurled cotton. "I don't have any."

Why did he have to be so stubborn? Especially after she had just answered his questions. "If that was true, then why are you so withdrawn? Why do you shrink away every time I ask you a question that doesn't have to do with your work?"

He shrugged carelessly. "Just your ordinary shrinking violet, I guess."

"That would be absolutely the last way I would describe you." She tried again. "Does it have anything to do with your childhood?"

She was the most persistent woman he had ever known. "Look, you don't want to know," he told her curtly. He didn't want her pity and that was all that was to be gained by telling her about his past.

"Yes, I do." Didn't he understand? She needed him to share this with her. "I *have* to know.

The urgency of her voice had him looking away from the window and at her. There was something in her eyes he couldn't read. "Why?"

She hadn't wanted her feelings for him to be declared this way, but maybe it was for the best after all. "Like it or not, I'm in love with you. I need to know details about the man I've fallen in love with."

Love. What an overwhelming four-letter word. He didn't believe her.

Love wasn't for men like him. Besides, she only thought she was in love with him because she was grateful for what he had done, nothing more. He wasn't fooling himself. "If you've fallen in love with me, I'd say you've got a hell of a poor track record, Jennifer."

His words were like a cruel slap in the face, but somehow, she held on. Pride had her lifting her chin. "Maybe you'd say that, but I wouldn't."

He was doing this for her own good, she suddenly realized. He was capable of something selfless like that. Something stupid like that.

Why couldn't he see the man she did? "Kane, I don't know anything about you, but I know enough to love you."

Her words made no sense to him. "Like with Katie's father?"

She was right. He was trying to distance himself from her for some noble reason that made no earthly sense to her. "If you're trying to make me doubt myself, it's not working. That was different."

He narrowed his eyes and looked at her. "How do you know?"

"I just know, that's all," she insisted. She had a feeling he knew as well and was just trying to deny it. "There are no magic formulas to tell me that I'm on the right path with you. Just instinct." She thought back. "There were signs with Brad that it was all wrong."

"Brad?"

"That was his name," she reminded him. "Brad Kingsley."

He frowned. "Sounds like a name belonging to someone who'd be self-centered." An image of a self-absorbed man in a five-hundred-dollar suit came to him.

That would be the way to describe Brad, Jennifer thought. Narcissistic. "He was. More than a little."

She realized that Kane was trying to divert her from the subject. *Nice try.*

"But the point I'm trying to make was that there were signs that Brad was all wrong for me and I ignored them. Maybe I was enjoying the flowers and the attention a little too much to—"

"And the poetry," he interjected.

"And the poetry," she agreed with a smile. "A little too much and it got in the way of my seeing things clearly. The way things were. If I had taken a good hard look at Brad, I would have realized that for him it was a game and I came in second, a far second to Brad himself." She placed her hand on his to reinforce her point. "I don't see that with you."

He didn't like being mentioned in the same breath as the other man. "I don't play games—"

"No, you don't." That was one of the things she respected about him. "And you don't let me cling to illusions, either. You've tried everything you can to push me away.''

He looked down at the hand that was still on his, realizing how much he liked it there. "So why isn't it working?"

"Because you really don't want me to go," she told him quietly, believing it with all her heart.

Why was she making this so difficult for him to break free? Didn't she know it was for her own good? That he would only drag her down?

"That's just the sex talking." His words were purposely hurtful.

She didn't believe that. She knew what he was doing. "No, not the sex. That's you talking." She lowered her voice so that only he would hear. "The sex is beautiful, gentle, wonderful. But it's not the sex that's keeping me. It's what's in your eyes. It's the way you hold me." She remembered and a sigh escaped. "As if you're trying very hard not to."

"There might be a reason for that."

She wasn't going to let him play with the words. "Whatever the reason, I'll wait it out."

"You might have a long wait."

She shrugged. It would be worth it. "I have time. I'm not going anywhere."

And neither, he thought, was this relationship.

No matter what she *thought* she felt, he couldn't let it go any further. She had given him far more than he had ever dreamed he'd experience in his life and the best thing he could do for her was just to leave.

They rented a car at the airport and drove the fifty-eight miles to Lake Tahoe. Redhawk had promised to get in touch with the police chief ahead of time and let him know the circumstances behind their visit.

The police chief, Ed Sawyer, looked genuinely concerned when they arrived. For more than one reason.

"It's a terrible ordeal you've gone through," he said, taking Jennifer's hand. "And a terrible ordeal yet to be faced."

"I don't understand," Jennifer said, looking at Kane.

"I know the man who's adopted your daughter." The chief smiled sadly. "I just about dropped my teeth when it came over the fax machine this morning.

Kane felt Jennifer's hand tighten on his. "Will he be any trouble?" Kane wanted to know.

The chief shook his head. "No, there won't be trouble," he assured them. "At least, not the kind of trouble you mean."

Jennifer thought she knew what the man was referring to. She recalled what Redhawk had said to her last night about the way he would have felt if someone had turned up on his doorstep to reclaim his son.

But in this case, it was only a matter of days, she thought and then felt a pang. She had had Katie only three days herself and the bond had been instantaneous. What if—?

She didn't pursue her thought.

"If you don't mind," the chief was saying, "I'd like to come along with you myself."

Jennifer and Kane exchanged looks. If he wasn't anticipating any trouble, why wasn't he just sending a regular uniformed policeman along? It wasn't as if the man who had adopted Katie was a desperate criminal or anything. Was he?

"Any particular reason?" Kane asked.

The florid-faced man looked up at Kane as he ran a hand through hair the color of newly harvested cotton.

"A damn good particular reason. I've known Brom Culhane all his life. His father and I served in the army together. Brom's my godson and a decent human being who doesn't need this kind of trouble heaped onto what's already happened."

Jennifer didn't understand why the man seemed to be yelling at them. It was her child they were trying to rescue. Culhane might be an innocent party, but he had no right to Katie. Why was the chief acting as if they were the guilty parties in this case?

The chief jammed his hat on his head as he led the way out of the precinct and into the back parking lot. He stopped at his car.

"You'll get your daughter back, all right," he promised Jennifer. "I guarantee it. But Brom's going to need a friend when it happens." He sighed, opening the rear car door for Jennifer. He frowned. "Not that it'll really help much."

Jennifer fought against a sinking feeling as she sat down in the car.

Silently, she reached for Kane's hand.

Chapter 16

"Oh, Mr. Culhane, doesn't she look as if she's always belonged here?"

Ida Kelly whispered the words to the tall, dark haired man standing on the other side of the crib. They were both looking at the tiny infant who slept between them. Sentimentality was not something that Ida bore comfortably, but it seemed to overwhelm her at the moment. She wiped a tear away with the corner of her apron.

"It's hard to believe she's only been with us a few weeks." Gently, she raised the thin cotton blanket over the scrunched little form. "But she's already got my heart in that tight little fist of hers."

Which was saying a lot, Bromley Culhane thought, glancing at the woman. Ida let very few people into that crusty, heavily guarded area she called a heart. His wife had been one of them, as well as he. And now this tiny human being who had entered his life at precisely the right moment, just when he needed her most.

Brom looked down at the baby and smiled. Even now, at this unformed stage, she was a beauty. Dark lashes formed half crescent moons sweeping along cheeks the color of fresh peaches in the summer.

Ida sighed as another tear threatened to betray her. "She looks just like the Mrs. did." The old woman shook her head as she gripped the shiny bar of the crib. "I wish she could have seen her. It would have done her heart such good just to have held the wee one once."

He could almost see Alexis holding the baby in her arms. Thoughts of his wife had sharp, pointed daggers raking through him, cutting him like so many tiny blades.

It was going to be a long time before he could think of Alexis without the pain, without the anger setting in. Anger against a fate he couldn't see, couldn't fight. Lord, it had all been such a horrible waste. A beautiful, gentle life, snuffed out practically before it had had a chance to bloom. Just like that, in a blink of an eye.

He shut his heart to the grief, unable to deal with it.

Brom refrained from skimming a fingertip over the small cheek before him. He didn't want to wake the baby. It was still hard to believe she was here, like a tiny miracle.

"Alex would have loved her," he agreed softly.

It had been Alexis's fondest dream to have a child with him. But after five years of trying, she had finally resigned herself to the fact that she was barren. They had turned to adoption as their next hope. But adoption through the normal channels had promised to be a long, drawn out process without an immediate end in sight, only frustration. His Alexis, normally so full of hope, had grown despondent before his eyes as he watched, helplessly.

That was when he had run into Jack MacKenzie. He and Jack had shared a boyhood playing in the Lake Tahoe area. They had grown up, aspiring to make their mark on the world when childish ambitions made such things possible. Brom had gone on to become part owner and manager of a casino while Jack had graduated law school and clerked at a prestigious law firm in San Francisco. Eventually, they had lost touch with one another until literally bumping into each other outside Casino Camelot, Brom's casino.

As they talked over lunch, Brom was surprised and then pleased to discover that Jack worked for an organization that handled private adoptions.

"You'd be surprised how many babies are being abandoned every day by girls who are hardly more than children themselves. Baby Blooms gives them an alternative. It gives them some place to stay while they're having their babies and then helps them place the infants in a good home." Jack, ever flamboyant, had leaned over the table and smiled confidently. "I'm sure we could help you and your wife adopt a child. You just tell me what you want and I can make your fondest wish come true."

"Just like that." Brom had meant it as a joke.

But Jack had been serious. "Just like that."

"Like a fairy godfather," Alexis had laughed, delighted, when Brom told her about his chance meeting with Jack and its result. "Oh, Brom, it's serendipity."

Brom had been slightly more skeptical about the matter, but Jack had given him brochures about the organization, plus his personal assurances. And he had grown up with Jack. It had seemed like an answer to a prayer.

The paperwork he and Alexis needed to fill out was nominal compared to what a regular adoption required. All that seemed necessary was a willingness to love a child. And the ability to pay for birthing costs and a little to help the natural mother along her way. It had seemed reasonably little to ask in exchange for a miracle.

Brom looked down at his daughter and thought how excited Alexis had been, anticipating her. They were going to have a child to love and nurture. A child to watch as she grew into an adult. It seemed to be too good to be finally true.

It was then, amid all this hope and promise, that the first signs began to manifest themselves. Brom felt his heart squeeze tightly just from the thought of it.

Alexis, with her almost pathological fear of doctors, had at first refused to consult a physician about the pain that kept slicing through her. Wincing, she had practically denied its existence until Brom had all but forcibly carried her to see Dr. Blackstone. And then sat holding her hand as they heard the diagnosis that was to be her ultimate death notice: cancer of the ovaries. An advanced case. It was what her mother had died of.

He'd been too grief-stricken to function at first, too numbed to even think about going through with the adoption. But Alexis had begged, pointing out that life went on and that perhaps, just perhaps, they could beat this. Wouldn't it be awful to let this opportunity finally to have a child of their own slip through their fingers because they were so immersed in her problems?

Alexis, his laughing golden girl, had been the strong one. There had been no wailing, no cries to the heavens of "Why me?" She said simply, "It was me," and accepted the diagnosis.

But not the death sentence.

That she fought, fought like a tigress with every last breath of strength within her. And because she wanted a baby more than anything else in the world, Brom had agreed to go through with the process. His only specification to Jack was that he wanted a girl, a daughter they could raise to grow up exactly like her mother. Alexis had laughed and said if she had a choice, she would have wanted the baby to look like him.

Now the baby was here.

And Alexis wasn't.

Alexis had died suddenly, her life leaving in almost a whisper, six weeks ago. She had died in his arms less than two months after the initial diagnosis, peacefully leaving him to try to carry on in a world that no longer contained her. Grief had draped over him like a huge shroud, cutting off his air supply, cutting him off from everything. It had taken him two weeks just to learn how to function again, to come to terms with the fact that he was alive and she was not. He had forgotten all about the adoption application, all about the fees he had given to Jack, until Jack had called him three weeks ago, to tell him that he had his daughter.

Dazed, disoriented, completely lost without the woman who had been by his side for the last eight years, the best eight years of his life, Brom had almost told Jack that he had changed his mind. He couldn't bring himself to tell him that Alexis was dead and with her, the essence of his very soul. That had been too private a revelation to make.

But Alexis's voice had whispered in his ear as he stood, talking on the telephone, telling him that this was right. That he should go through with it. That this was the child they had wanted and he was to raise the baby in her memory.

So he had agreed and the next day Jack had arrived on his doorstep, delivering this beautiful baby girl into his arms. As soon as he held her, Brom knew he hadn't made a mistake. This was meant to be.

A peace had seeped into his soul. Still holding her, with Ida fussing around him, Brom had brought the baby into the nursery that Alexis had taken such joy in decorating for her.

It was going to work out, Brom thought, looking at his daughter now. God help him, it was going to work out. The infant slept, arms and legs tucked in against her tummy, a living link to the future. A future he and Alexis were to have shared.

Now it was all up to him.

He had named the baby Alexis, after his wife. Jack had told him that the mother, a seventeen-year-old girl from a well-to-do family in Beverly Hills, hadn't named the baby yet. Her reason, he explained, was that she was afraid of getting too attached to the baby if she gave her a name. So Brom had given her Alexis's name and hoped that his wife's spirit would somehow infuse itself into this tiny being and live on in her.

Ida looked at Brom now, concern in her clear blue eyes. "And when is it that are you planning on going back to work, sir?" she asked gently.

A premonition had Brom taking a leave of absence a week before Alexis's death. When she died, he had stayed away, attempting to get his bearings, attempting to find his place in this world that didn't have her in it. He'd been gone for seven weeks now.

"Another week, Ida. The Casino can get along without me for that much longer. Adam's taken over until I get back," he said, naming his partner. Brom needed this time now to forge the beginnings of a new life. "I want to get to know my daughter a little better."

Ida gave a short laugh. "There's not much to know at this age." She had raised three children and helped with five grandchildren. "They sleep a lot, wet and cry. And eat." A fond smile lifted the thin lips as she looked at Alexis again. "They don't really get to know you until they're a little older than this."

Alexis stirred and yawned. The lush lashes swept away from her cheeks as she opened her eyes. Now that she was awake, Brom couldn't resist picking her up. He needed to feel this tiny weight in his arms and know that she was real. She had the ability to heal his wounds the way he knew nothing else could.

He grinned at the dour, gray-haired woman. "Oh, I think she knows me already."

Brom had made an all-out effort to immediately bond with Alexis. He had stayed up each night, insisting on handling each of her feedings even though Ida had been more than willing to do it herself. In three weeks he had become an expert in preparing formulas and had become skilled in the dubious art of changing diapers. His only problem, thus far, was burping Alexis. He was afraid that his large hands would somehow hurt her tiny back. But he was getting better at it all the time.

Brom placed his finger within the tight fist, coaxing her digits apart. Alexis's elegant little fingers wrapped themselves around it as her expression shifted slightly, the corners of her mouth lifting.

"See?" Brom looked at the old woman. "She knows who Daddy is already, don't you, darling? That's a smile."

Ida sniffed as she looked closer. "That, sir, is nothing more than gas."

"My daughter wouldn't have gas." He grinned, patting the tiny bottom.

The doorbell chimed, bringing an immediate frown to his face. He didn't feel like talking to anyone yet. When Alexis had died, the house had been filled with people offering their condolences. Kind words from people who had loved her. He knew they all meant well, but he wanted to be alone with that part of his grief. At this point, he could only tolerate Ida and the baby.

He glanced at Ida. "I'm not expecting anyone. Are you?"

Ida was already shuffling toward the door, her beige, orthopedic shoes rubbing along the rug. "You want me to tell them to go away?"

He grinned at her words. Always to the point, that was Ida. "Tactfully."

She shrugged as she made her way into the hall. "Amounts to the same thing."

Brom shook his head. Ida Kelly had a good heart, even though her manner tended to be a little crusty. She had been with him since he had bought into Casino Camelot and moved into the house. That had been two years before he had married Alexis.

The baby began to fuss a little and he patted her bottom gently as he moved toward the window. It faced the back, with a magnificent view of the lake. Sunlight was streaming in, its warmth settling on the baby.

Alexis became quiet and watched him with huge blue eyes as if he were the focal point of her world. Brom felt his heart melting.

"Just you and me, Alexis. And Ida to cook for us. I'm not much good at that. But I'll come through for you in everything else, I promise, Alexis." She would never be Alex to him, the way his wife had been. No, this was Alexis. She would always be Alexis, a little bit of heaven to have and to cherish.

"You're going to be a heartbreaker, you are," he said to the round face. He watched a pin-size dimple dance just beneath her right eye as she gurgled. "I can see you going out in fifteen years. No," he amended, pretending to be stern, "make that eighteen. I'm not letting you go out on a date until you've earned a black belt in karate." He chucked her under her chubby little chin. "And nobody's going to be good enough for you, you know that, don't you?"

Alexis gurgled again, as if in complete agreement with what he said.

Brom nodded in approval. "See, we've reached an understanding already. This has the makings of a great relationship." He heard a noise behind him and turned to see Ida standing in the doorway. The woman looked as pale as the snow that covered the mountains during Tahoe's peak season. He moved forward, concerned. "Ida, what's the matter?"

"Mr. Culhane—" Ida's voice cracked and she had to begin again. "Mr. Culhane, there's someone here about the baby."

He didn't understand. He only knew that the look on Ida's face brought a chill to his heart. "What do you mean, about the baby?"

As he stepped into the hall, holding Alexis against him, he saw the others. What was the police chief doing here and who were these two people? His voice became formal as protective instincts rose within him. "Ed, what's this all about?"

Jennifer didn't wait for any further explanations to be exchanged. The chief had given the housekeeper a cursory explanation at the door. All Jennifer saw was the baby in Brom's arms. Her heart skipped a beat, then thudded against her chest.

"Katie." The name floated from her lips in a whisper that was a prayer of thanksgiving.

Brom's arms tightened around the child. "Who?" he demanded.

Jennifer looked up at Brom, as if seeing him for the first time. "My baby." She reached beside her for Kane's arm, refusing to take her eyes from the infant. A sob caught in her throat, threatening to break free. "Oh Kane, it's Katie." She saw the dimple wink and dance beneath the baby's eye, as if to verify what she already knew. "It's really her."

Brom looked at the man who had been his father's best friend, who had taught him how to fly-fish and who had once locked him in jail for a few hours to knock some sense into his head about running away when he was twelve.

"Ed, I don't understand what's going on here. Who are these people?" He didn't like the look on Ed's face. There was sorrow etched into the fine, spidery lines along the man's eyes.

"Brom," the chief began, uttering his words slowly, as if each weighed more than he could bear, "we need to go somewhere where we can talk."

He wasn't going to like this, Brom thought, but he nodded. "Ida—" He turned toward the woman to hand her the baby.

"No," Jennifer protested, placing her hand on his arm. After all this time, she had to hold her daughter, to press her to her breast and know that it was finally over. She was terrified that if she looked away for a moment, Katie would be gone again. It was going to take time to get over that feeling. "Let me hold her."

Brom, his expression stony, handed the baby to Ida.

Kane tried to ease the tension. What if it turned out to be wrong? What if the entry on the disk was incorrect? "Jennifer, you can't be sure yet," he began. He couldn't bear for her to be hurt again.

But Jennifer wouldn't be deterred. "I'm sure."

She had a copy of Katie's footprint in her purse, had carried it with her since the beginning. But she didn't have to compare it to one taken from this child before her. She didn't need an expert to tell her what she already knew. This was her baby.

"Sure of what?" Brom demanded. "Who is Katie and who are you?"

Kane began to explain, but the police chief cut in. "Brom, this is the baby's mother."

It took a moment for the chief's words to register. Brom looked at Jennifer, confused. "There has to be some mistake, Ed. Alexis's mother is a seventeen-year-old girl who lives in Beverly Hills."

Jennifer's heart went out to him. There were only victims in this mess, she thought. "Is that what they told you?"

Brom looked into the woman's eyes and saw the baby's reflected there. But his need to deny was strong. "There's some mistake," Brom insisted, praying that it was true. "I adopted Alexis privately. The papers are all legal. They've been filed. Jack MacKenzie is a friend of mine. He works for an organization called Baby Blooms. It's a stupid name, but—"

He knew he was rambling. Brom reined himself in, braced like a soldier expecting to go against insurmountable odds. And lose. "Ed, are you telling me—" He couldn't bring himself to finish.

Kane felt pity for the tall man in front of him. He fervently hoped that they would apprehend the bastard who was responsible for all this heartache. And that he would be given five minutes alone with him, his shield tossed aside.

"She was stolen," Kane told Brom quietly. There was no arguing with his tone. No room for doubt. "Three weeks ago from Harris Memorial Hospital in Newport Beach, California."

It felt as if the bottom of his world had just fallen out. Again. Brom heard Ida give a little gasp behind him.

"It's all right, Ida," he said mechanically. His eyes locked with Kane's. "I don't believe you." The words were a last, desperate challenge.

The chief placed a fatherly hand on Brom's shoulder. "I checked out their story, Brom. That little girl was part of a huge black market operation. The people responsible are going to be behind bars for this."

Brom was stunned. He couldn't understand why someone he had known for a greater part of his life would actually lie to him like that. Would do this to him. "I've known Jack for most of my life."

Kane had never been close to anyone in his adult life. But he could understand the sting of betrayal. "Apparently there are aspects of his life that you didn't know. This is turning out to be a pretty extensive operation. We're just beginning to piece it together. Babies have been stolen from hospitals in California, Nevada and Arizona. Eleven in the last eleven months as far as we know and a lot more than that according to records we found."

"Damn him, how could he?" Brom cried. There was no answer to his question.

"May I?" Jennifer held out her arms to Ida, her eyes on the baby the woman held.

The housekeeper set her mouth grimly and looked to Brom for direction.

He had no choice. Brom nodded his consent.

Jennifer took her baby into her arms for the first time in three weeks. "Oh, God." Tears filed her throat as she lay her face against the baby's. The last time she had held her came flooding back to Jennifer as her tears began to fall. "Mommy's here, Katie," Jennifer said quietly, vainly attempting not to sob. "Mommy's finally here."

Brom could hardly bear to watch the reunion. He felt sorry for the ordeal this woman had been put through, but he wasn't about to give up Alexis so easily. "You will forgive me, Mrs.—"

Jennifer realized that he was addressing her. She wiped her eyes. "Sinclair. Jennifer. And it's Miss."

Solomon had it easy, Brom thought bitterly. He hadn't loved the baby in the case that had been brought before him. "Your daughter was how old when she was abducted?"

With Katie in her arms again and Kane beside her, Jennifer felt strong, whole. Her voice didn't waver as she answered. "Three days old."

"How can you be sure that this is your daughter?" He was clutching at straws, but maybe one would float him to safety.

Jennifer looked over her shoulder at Kane. He had voiced the same observation when she had declared that neither of the two babies they had found in Phoenix were Katie.

"I just know, that's all." Brom looked at her with the eyes of a lawyer about to destroy a witness's case. Jennifer touched the area just below Katie's right eye. "She has a tiny dimple right about here. It only comes out when she grimaces."

"Or smiles," Brom added sadly.

Jennifer looked at Brom, elated. Then he had seen it, too.

Brom had noticed the dimple almost immediately after he had brought the baby to her room. It was unusual, but it didn't mean that there weren't other babies with this physical feature. He wasn't giving Alexis up on a technicality.

He turned to the police chief. "I want a print made of her foot."

The chief called for the prints man at the precinct. While they waited for the man to arrive, Kane had taken over filling in Brom on all the details surrounding both Katie's abduction and the trail that they had followed.

Half an hour later, they had their results. Brom held the print that had just been taken and looked at the one Jennifer had produced. Both had been taken of the left foot. It was a perfect match. With the confirmation, there was no use in denying it any longer. The baby he had taken into his heart was Jennifer's.

And no longer his.

He vaguely remembered saying goodbye to the chief as the man left. An invitation to join the older man and his wife for dinner at his house vaguely buzzed in his head. There were other things crowding it out.

The three people looked at one another in an uneasy truce. Ida had left the room, unable to bear the situation. There was nothing that could be said to ease the heartache that pulsed in the room.

It wasn't meant to be, Brom thought. Life had given him something precious, twice, and then taken it that many times away. But it wasn't the woman's fault. He imagined what it must have been like for her, discovering that her baby had been stolen. She had been through enough without him adding to it.

"Listen," Brom began slowly, "my wife bought a lot of things in preparation for the baby." The nursery was filled with clothes and toys. He had no use for any of it now. "Maybe you'd like to have them."

"Oh, no," Jennifer protested, touched by the offer. "I couldn't."

On the way up to Brom's house, the chief had filled them in on Brom's immediate situation. She felt perfectly awful about adding to his grief. It wasn't his fault that her daughter had been stolen. All he had wanted was the same thing she had. A baby to hold and love.

Brom shrugged, trying to remain gracious, though it was difficult. "I certainly won't have any use for them. It's a shame to let them go to waste."

She thought of how empty her life had felt when she'd lost Katie. Now this man was experiencing the same thing. And there wasn't anything she could do for him.

"Maybe you could try adopting another baby," Kane suggested. "There are plenty of legitimate organizations that could help you—"

Brom met Kane's suggestion with a firm shake of his head. "No, without my wife, there's no use. I realize that now." He was just going to have to accept his fate. He looked at the baby and felt the loss eating away at him already. "I know you want to get going, but would you mind if I held her one last time?"

Jennifer's heart went out to him. "Of course."

Gently, she transferred the little girl to him. Brom tenderly took Katie into his arms. Jennifer saw the pain in his eyes. Her own filled with tears for him. Damn, this shouldn't be happening like this, she thought. She didn't want to hurt anyone. She just wanted her baby. It seemed a tragedy that he couldn't share in the joy of seeing Katie grow up.

"I live in Bedford, California," Jennifer began hesitantly. Brom looked at her quizzically. "It's just above Newport Beach," she explained. "If you're ever there, you're more than welcome to come and visit Katie."

No, that would only prolong the torture. And remind him of what he didn't have in his life. She meant well, he thought, but that didn't matter. Brom began to demur. "No, I don't think—"

"You know," she went on hurriedly, convinced by the way he held Katie that she was doing the right thing, "it's kind of rough growing up these days. Katie already has an uncle, but she could use another." Jennifer's eyes held Brom's. "If you're up to the part."

Brom began to protest again, to say that he didn't want charity. But the baby wiggled in his arms and he looked at her, his emotions spilling over. There was no question that the baby, regardless of her parentage, regardless of her name, had won his heart. It was firmly wrapped around that tiny finger, as firmly wrapped as her fingers had been around his such a short while ago.

Brom smiled at Jennifer. "I think I'd like that." He studied her intently. "You're sure?"

Jennifer grinned. "I wouldn't say it if I didn't mean it."

Kane placed a hand on Jennifer's shoulder, unaware of the image that helped convey. "The lady never says anything she doesn't mean," he assured Brom. "Trust me."

Kane had already sized Brom up and decided that what he saw before him was a decent human being. One who had gotten the short end of the stick more than once. He could relate to that better than most.

Brom took Jennifer's hand in his. "It's a deal. I'm Alexis's—sorry, Katie's," he amended, "uncle from now on." He kissed the baby's tiny head before relinquishing her. "Hello, Katie," he whispered, holding her close one last time.

Goodbye, Alexis.

Brom handed the baby to Jennifer and stepped back. He cleared his throat. He needed the healing salve that only work could provide him with now. Work, and time.

"Now if you'll both excuse me, I'm sure you want to be on your way and I have to go to work." A sigh escaped him before he could stop it. "I've been away much too long."

Chapter 17

It was over.

He had done what he had vowed to do. Jennifer was reunited with her daughter. He'd kept his word to her and to himself. When they arrived at Reno Cannon International Airport, Jennifer had called her sister with the latest news. Both Julia and Nik were going to be waiting for her at John Wayne Airport when their plane landed. All the ends were tied neatly in a bow.

There was no reason for him to linger in her life. His function was over. He knew that.

He had seen how happy she was with her daughter and heard her on the phone with her family each time she had called them. She belonged to a unit, while he was a loner and could never fit in. It would always be that way with him. These last few days they had shared something together, but it was out of the normal parameters of her life.

Now things would go back to normal for her. What they had experienced because of the charged situation they were in would start to fade. He would be the odd wheel. Kane decided to make things easy for her. She wouldn't have to feel the discomfort of trying to explain to him why it was over. He'd leave now.

They had taken off fifteen minutes ago. In less than forty-five minutes, they would be landing. If a break was to be made, he thought, it had to be now and it had to be clean.

For her own good.

The words echoed in his head, magnifying themselves with each pass.

He wouldn't have to see her again, except at the trial. She'd undoubtedly be called as a witness. But, knowing how slowly the wheels of justice turned, that could be more than a year from now. More than enough time to erase the image of her face from his mind, erase the impression of her body from his soul.

Who the hell did he think he was kidding? There wasn't enough time left in eternity for that to happen.

He fumbled at his pocket and realized that he was searching for a cigarette, something he hadn't done in over a day. Trading one hopeless habit for another, he thought cynically.

She was sitting beside him, cradling her baby to her. The little girl was awake and cooing. And drooling a lot, he thought. Something twisted inside him when he thought that this was the last time he would see them.

Can't be helped.

"You look natural that way." When Jennifer looked at him, a question forming in her eyes, he added, "Holding a baby."

"Do you want to hold her?" She realized that he hadn't held the baby, not even once.

"No," he protested, even as she passed Katie to him "That's all right." He didn't *want* to touch her. It made it so much harder on him.

"She won't break." Jennifer smiled at the tiny face. "She's tougher than she looks, I think."

Katie felt as if she weighed next to nothing as she wiggled and cooed at him. This was not a good idea. He was trying to separate himself from Jennifer and the baby, not bond even more than he already had. He looked down at the infant and felt something strong, something paternal instantly stir within him. How could someone so small have such immense power?

"Here." He handed the baby to Jennifer abruptly. "I'm not any good at this."

She sighed. Her arms ached, but it was a welcome ache as she took her child back. Kane looked at her quizzically.

"It feels wonderful." Her eyes softened as she looked at him. "Thank you."

He didn't want her gratitude. He didn't want any of her sweetness getting in the way and interfering with what he knew had to be done.

"Hey." He shrugged carelessly. "I was just doing my job."

Who did he think he was fooling, she thought, a fond smile taking hold. She wasn't buying the tough-as-steel exterior any longer.

"No, no you weren't. Your job included making inquiries and following up leads. It didn't include letting me come along. That went beyond the boundaries of your job and you know it."

If he had a cigarette, he'd have something to do with his hands. Then he remembered where he was. Short flights were strictly nonsmoking. Out of luck, no matter which way he turned, he thought.

"You argued a good case," he answered, pointedly making his voice sound disinterested. His eyes strayed to Katie and he remembered the look on Jennifer's face when she first saw her baby in Brom's arms. It had seized his heart. "Besides, it was interesting to see that the myth has some basis in fact."

She had no idea what he was referring to. "Myth? What myth?"

His lips twisted in a half smile that held no humor in it. "The one about a mother's love knowing no bounds." He hadn't meant to say that. The words seemed to have slipped out on their own.

As she rocked Katie in her arms, she searched Kane's face, trying to see things he wouldn't tell her. "What makes you say it's a myth?"

He shifted uncomfortably in his seat, wishing the plane had landed five minutes ago, before he had opened his big mouth. "Firsthand experience, I suppose."

She had surmised as much from the bits and pieces he had let fall. And from what she could read in his eyes when he wasn't zealously guarding his own small turf.

"Kane." Her voice was coaxing, persuasive. "Please tell me."

He was about to rebuff her again, then stopped. After all, what did it really matter? He'd never see her again once they landed. At least, not in close proximity where they could talk. Where they could touch. Perhaps saying the words would be good, just this once. Maybe forming them, giving them verbal shape, would somehow draw them from his mind, like the poisonous sting of a rattlesnake bite being sucked out to save a life. Maybe telling her would draw them from his heart, where they had hidden all these years, he now realized. Festering. Being around her, seeing all this love, all this caring embodied within one person, had forced him to look at his childhood again and see that it had been the cause of all the emptiness in his life. Emptiness had always been preferable to pain.

He spoke as if it had happened to someone else, light-years away. To a little boy who had cried alone in his room at night. Kane never cried. He didn't know how.

"I was born in a coal mining town in West Virginia. My mother walked out on us when I was eight. She just left a note held down on the kitchen table by a carton of milk. The milk had turned sour by the time I came home from school. In it she said she couldn't take being trapped any more."

His throat grew tight as he spoke, but his tone remained matter-of-fact. "My father liked to take a drink now and again. And again and again." How many times had he woken up in the morning to find his father sprawled on the floor? Kane drove the dark image from his mind. "When he wasn't in the mines, my father was in his bottle. She put up with it as long as she could."

Jennifer couldn't fathom that as an excuse. "And she left you behind?"

He heard the accusation in Jennifer's voice and was warmed by it, though he tried not to be.

"I was part of the trap, I guess." Even now, though he denied it, it hurt to think that. "I used to hum to myself at night, the song she would sing while she worked around the house. Some tuneless thing—I don't even remember the name. She never could sing, my mother. I'd lie awake in my bed and watch the shadows and hum. Waiting for her to come back. One night, I stopped humming. I knew she wasn't coming back."

It had taken him a year to realize that. A long, agonizing year. A year had been a long time for an eight-year-old.

"And your father?" Her voice was hardly above a whisper.

There were times he had wondered if his father had even noticed his wife's absence. "Went on drinking. Maybe a little more than before. Somehow, I don't exactly know how, he kept on going to work." Kane shook his head, still mystified. "He could still work, no matter how drunk he had gotten the night before. Drunk or sober, he could always work. And always hit."

Her hand covered his on the armrest. His fingers, she realized, were rigid as he spoke. "He beat you?"

He tried to smile, for her benefit, not his own. "Only when he could catch me."

"Oh, Kane." A world of sympathy and love were in her cry. No wonder he didn't trust love. No wonder he couldn't open up or understand so many things. She wanted to hold him in her arms, to kiss him and make the past disappear as if it never existed. "I'm so sorry."

She could see him pull back, his eyes growing flat, his expression hardening. Oh God, not again.

"I didn't tell you so you could be sorry. I'm telling you so that you'd have your answer."

He had lost her again, but there was something in his tone that made her heart fearful. "Answer?"

"Yes, as to why this thing between us isn't going to go any further than it has." He saw the fear entering her eyes and forced himself to block it out. To block out his response to it. "When this plane lands," he continued stonily, "your family's going to be waiting for you."

"So?" She didn't see the problem. "That doesn't mean that—"

That they couldn't be together? Was that going to be her protest? "It means *exactly* that." He turned so that he was looking directly into her eyes. "Can't you understand that this is no good? That you have no idea what kind of a man I am, or the kind of man I'm not?" He wasn't a man who could give her the warmth, the loving support she needed. He didn't have that in him to give.

Jennifer hung on with both hands. "I think I know better than you."

He scowled. She was incorrigible. "Woman's logic."

She wasn't going to let him push her away, no matter what he said. "Works for me, Kane." The cheerful edge left her voice. "I know that you're kind and caring and sensitive."

"No, I'm not and I can't change. I'll always be an outsider, a loner. I don't belong in a family. There's too much closeness in your family and I'm never going to be a part of that. It would only lead to hurt feelings in the end and ultimately, I'll wind up alone again. I might as well stay that way now and save you the trouble of having to go through it with me." He forced himself to sound cruel. If possible, it hurt him more than her. "You've just gotten carried away with the situation. You think I rescued your baby for you. It was my job, nothing more, do you hear? My job."

No it wasn't, damn you. "If you mean do I think of you as a hero, yes, I do. A damn reluctant one. I've been holding out for a hero all my life. And you're him, no matter how much you deny it. And I haven't gotten carried away with the situation. I've gotten carried away with the man." She realized her voice was raised. Katie was whimpering. Jennifer lowered her tone. "With you. And you can be part

of the family. A family isn't a rigid statistic. It isn't just two
point five children and a mother and father. A family in-
cludes anyone you care about, anyone you love. Otherwise, we're all like strangers working in an office building.
Love makes the difference, Kane,'' she said fiercely.
''Love.''

Why was she making this so difficult? Did she have to be
beaten over the head? ''You don't know what you're saying.''

She could feel her tears rising. She was losing him because of his own stupidity, because of some chivalrous no-
tion he had that he was bad for her. ''I'm saying I love you
and you're worth it.''

This was ripping him up inside. The feelings he swore he
didn't have were piercing him through in a thousand different places. Suddenly, he was that little boy again, standing
in the kitchen, clutching the note. He wasn't going to go
through things like that again.

''Jennifer,'' he told her sternly, ''don't make this any
harder than it is.''

She could taste defeat, but she refused to swallow it.

''Hard? You think this is hard? I'll make it *damn* hard for
you, Kane. I'll make it impossible for you to forget me.'' To
keep from touching him, she laced her hands together beneath the baby. ''I intend to be the first thought you have
each morning and the last thought you have each night. I
intend to prey on your mind and fill the corners of your life
until you're ready to come around and admit that you love
me.''

That was just the problem. ''Jennifer, I don't know how
to love.''

She wasn't accepting that. It was too pat, too flimsy. ''No,
I think you don't *know* that you know how to love. I think
your problem is that you're afraid of loving. Afraid of being hurt.'' She forced her tears back, though they burned
and stung her eyes. ''But I won't walk out on you. I'm never
going to leave any note under a carton of milk telling you
I'm gone.'' She took a breath, trying to steady the ache she

felt. "You're just going to have to learn to believe that. Look me up when you do."

The plane was touching down. Kane set his mouth grimly and she knew she'd lost the battle. But maybe, just maybe, not the war.

When he unbuckled his seat belt, Kane rose and helped Jennifer up. With silence painfully hanging between them, he accompanied her into the terminal.

A moment later, Julia and Nik were there, engulfing them. Julia was quick to ask Jennifer if she could hold her niece. It seemed as if all life was centered around this tiny being as Julia took Katie into her arms.

Seeing them like this only reinforced Kane's feeling that he had no place in the scenario. He began to edge away.

Julia looked up, her dark eyes bright with tears. "Oh God, I don't know how to thank you, Kane."

"She'll find a way," Nik assured him. "Julia's never at a loss for words."

Kane shrugged, avoiding Jennifer's eyes. "Just doing my job," he repeated.

Nik, elated at the turn of events, placed his hand on Kane's shoulder. "Listen, do you have a few minutes to spare?" He subtly directed him toward the terminal exit. "I've closed the restaurant for the afternoon. We can have a private celebration and—"

But Kane was shaking his head, cutting off the rest of Nik's proposal. "I'll have to take a rain check."

He began backing away. He was running, behaving, he now realized, in his old reflexive, defensive way. He reached for a cigarette. Old habits died hard, he mused.

"I've got to get in and start on the paperwork." Kane laughed ruefully, though the sound was empty. "The way I type, it might take me all year."

Knowing he had to do this one last time, he turned to Jennifer and began to say something. The look in her eyes froze any false excuses he might have given her. His facade slipped a little.

"Have a nice life, Jennifer."

Damn you, how can you leave? "You too, Kane." She continued to look steadily into his eyes.

She didn't believe that he could actually walk away. Until he did.

Julia and Nik exchanged looks, then Julia turned to her younger sister. Katie was trying to swallow her gold chain and Julia extracted it gently.

"What was all that about?" Julia asked.

Jennifer let out the long sigh she had been holding, swearing to herself that she wasn't going to cry. "That was about a pigheaded man not coming around," she said quietly. She looked at the two people who made up the remainder of her family. "Let's go home, okay?" she urged. "Suddenly, I'm very tired."

"Jen, maybe if I talked to him—" Nik offered.

Jennifer shook her head. "No, talking to Kane isn't going to do any good. This is something he's going to have to work out for himself if it's going to be any good for either of us." She smiled at Nik, then brushed a kiss on his cheek. "Thanks for the offer, though."

Nik placed his arm around Jennifer's shoulder and, picking up her overnight case, guided her toward the exit as Julia walked beside them with Katie.

It was a curse. Nothing short of a curse.

Damn her, she had placed a curse on him and it was coming true. In spades.

Two weeks. He had spent two damn weeks with her memory humming through his brain like some post-hypnotic suggestion. Like a melody that refused to leave no matter how hard he tried to block it. Night and day, day and night, there it was, interfering with every damn thing he did, every damn thought he had.

He'd always known that his life was empty, but he had chosen that path for himself. Now it wasn't empty, it was hollow and the hollowness vibrated within him like a scourge, taunting him. It seemed completely bent on destroying his peace of mind. No, scratch that, he thought. Not his peace of mind, his very mind.

Whenever he closed his eyes, she was there. He relived every moment they had shared together, every word, every taste, every scent. It was as if he had been indelibly branded. And doomed to relive it all over and over again, like a tape stuck in automatic reverse playing on and on and on. And to his surprise and dismay he'd also relived the moment when he'd looked into Katie's eyes and felt his heart stir. Both mother and daughter had some sort of weird hold on him and he didn't like it. No, not one bit.

"Hey, Madigan."

Valdez's words broke into Kane's self-imposed fog. He looked up from the report he had been typing for the last hour and a half.

"What?" he snapped.

Valdez stood, looking over Kane's shoulder, an amused expression on his face. "You realize that you've been pressing the *e* key for two and a half lines now."

Kane looked and saw that Valdez was right. The single letter repeated itself over the length of almost three lines. It looked like a scream running down the page.

Valdez crossed his arms before him, leaning a hip against Kane's desk. "This report being written in code?"

With the black market scam uncovered, the special task force had been been revamped to help reunite families with abducted children as well as look into the adoptions that had been conducted via coercion where the birth mother had been "convinced" to give up her child.

"No, it's not being written in code." Kane ripped the offending page out of the typewriter. Over an hour's worth of work, completely shot, he thought, crumpling the page. His concentration had been shredded down to nothing.

Valdez studied his superior silently for a moment. In the last two weeks, Kane had become totally impossible to be around. "Want some advice?"

Kane took another sheet from the desk and fed it into the typewriter. It jammed. Cursing, he pulled it free and tried again. "No."

Valdez had expected as much. "Well, you're going to get it, anyway. I'd go see her if I were you."

"Well, you're not me." Kane's head jerked up as he realized what he was admitting to. "And see who?"

"Yeah, right." Valdez laughed. He gave a knowing wink. "The woman who's eating at you so much. That classy lady you took with you to Phoenix and Vegas. Jennifer—" he snapped his fingers, searching for her last name "—Sinclair."

"I'll be all right," Kane growled. As he moved the platen, the paper jammed again.

Valdez carefully removed the paper for him and rolled in another sheet. He grinned. "You were never anyone's concept of a pussycat, but you've gotten to be hell to live with."

"I said I'd be all right," Kane insisted angrily. "I'll survive, okay?"

Valdez shrugged his narrow shoulders philosophically. "Well, you might survive, but I'm not sure if we will. Or the equipment, for that matter." He nodded at the typewriter. "It's getting kind of old to be taking this sort of abuse."

"*I* don't need to be taking this sort of abuse," Kane corrected. Rising, he slammed his chair against the desk and stormed out of the squad room. He kept on going until he had left the precinct.

The day was unseasonably warm and sticky. It was hot, he thought irritably.

Doesn't it ever cool off in this place?

Jennifer's voice floated to him, clear as a bell, filling out the recesses of his mind. He shut his eyes, struggling with his newly resurrected emotions. And losing.

He'd been losing for the past two weeks.

Jennifer had been right, he thought suddenly. She was his destiny and he was running from it. Running from her.

Kane fumbled at his breast pocket. There was a pack of cigarettes there, a pack he had purchased just that morning. He took it out and began to shake free a cigarette. The pack was already half gone.

Henderson passed Kane on the front steps on his way into the building. He stopped, staring.

"Starting again?" He shook his head, obviously disappointed. "I thought you said you didn't need those things any more."

Kane looked at the pack in his hand. What the hell was he doing to himself? Very deliberately, Kane crushed the pack.

"I don't." He tossed the crumpled pack to Henderson. "There's only one thing I do need."

He could have sworn he heard Henderson mutter hallelujah behind him as he hurried to his car.

It was time, Jennifer thought, to stop keeping a light burning in the window, both figuratively and otherwise. Kane wasn't coming. He was a stubborn man and he had vowed not to let her into his life. She had honestly thought she made a difference in it, but obviously she had thought wrong. He could do very well without her.

She moved restlessly about the living room. Katie had just fallen asleep and Jennifer knew she should really attempt to get a little sleep herself. But she couldn't. She kept waiting for Kane to call.

She was going to drive herself crazy if she kept this up.

Time to realize that all dreams didn't come true. She had been very lucky and had found her baby. That, she reminded herself, meant everything in the world to her.

The next order of business was getting her life into a routine and then going on with it.

Without Kane.

Jennifer bent down to gather up the newspaper where it had fallen this morning. Nik had stopped by to see how she was doing and had wound up reading the sports section. It was baseball season and he was following his favorite team.

She tossed the paper on the coffee table without even glancing at it. Nothing except Katie held her attention lately.

Damn you, Kane. She'd been so sure, she thought. So very sure.

She brushed away a tear with the heel of her hand and cursed his soul to hell for not loving her the way she loved him.

When the doorbell rang, she started. It was too late for Julia or Nik. She hoped it wasn't another reporter. She'd given interviews to two leading magazines and one news program, then had drawn the line and said no more. She wasn't up to rehashing her ordeal another time. It only brought back vivid memories of Kane.

Jennifer's eyes widened as she tightly held on to the door knob and stared at the man on her front step.

Kane frowned. "You're supposed to ask who is it before throwing it open like that." He walked in, almost as if he were being propelled by some unseen hand. "Didn't anyone ever teach you that?"

What was he doing here? She was afraid to hope. She'd done too much of that and her supply was exhausted. "I'm sorry, I was too preoccupied to stop and think." She closed the door behind him.

He didn't want to be here. He didn't want to be anywhere else.

"A robber isn't going to be too preoccupied to rob you if you give him half a chance," he snapped at her.

Well, nothing had changed. "Did you come by to give me a lecture on safety?"

His nerves frayed, Kane almost snapped out an answer, then reined himself in. "No, I came by to ask you a question."

He was here because of the case, she thought dully, nothing more. She might have known. Her heart felt like a piece of lead inside her chest. "What?"

He looked around. She appeared to be alone. That made it a little easier. But not much. "Is it Byron or Shelley or some other guy?"

She stared at him as if he had lapsed into a foreign language. "What?"

"Poetry," he said impatiently, feeling like a linebacker standing in the middle of a ballet recital. "Was it Byron you said you liked?"

It was only then that she realized he was holding a thin book in his hand. She had just assumed it had something to do with his work.

She wasn't answering. He felt like an idiot. "Or Shelley or some other guy?"

She was afraid to hope where this was heading. "I didn't say. But it's Byron." She spared a glance at the book before looking back at his face. "Why?"

He glanced toward the door. Maybe he should just turn around and go out again. No, he had come too far. He had to see it through.

"Well, I thought I should read it." She was still looking at him as if he had two heads. Maybe he did, he thought. "If we're to have things in common, I mean."

Jennifer could feel them coming. Tears. Fresh and hot and overflowing from her soul. She took the book out of his hand. It *was* Byron. She let the book drop on the sofa as she threaded her arms around his neck. This man was not going anywhere ever again.

"We already have things in common."

He thought of both their lives and didn't see a single common thread. But he liked the way her arms felt around him. As if they belonged there. And he belonged here, with her. "What?"

"Love." She smiled into his eyes. "It's a great starting point."

He let his hands drift to her waist. God, he had missed holding her. It seemed like two years, not two weeks. "I also want you to take the curse off me."

"The curse?" she echoed. "What curse?"

Subtly, he drew her closer until her body fit completely into his. "The one you placed on me at the airport." She still looked perplexed. He elaborated. "It's been two weeks and I can't get you out of my mind. Everywhere I look, you're there—or I want you to be there. Take it off, Jennifer. Take the curse off."

A grin spread over her lips. "Not a chance, Detective."

She smelled good. In the middle of the afternoon, barefoot and slightly disheveled, she smelled good. All he wanted to do was make love with her until he died. "Then you leave me no alternative."

She cocked her head, waiting. "You're going to arrest me?"

"In a way." His smile faded as he grew serious. "Look, Jennifer, I know I haven't the right—"

She wasn't going to let him talk himself out of this again. "Detective, when will you get it through that thick head of yours that you have every right? That I don't want my rights read to me? The only right I care about is the right to remain with you." She brushed her lips against his. "Forever."

He glanced at the book on the sofa. "Does that mean you're going to explain this stuff to me?"

She laughed. "Every day for the rest of our lives if you want."

He smiled into her eyes as he hugged her to him. "Well, not all the time."

She could feel him wanting her and her heart thrilled. "No," she agreed, "not all the time."

He took a deep breath, as if he were about to jump off a bridge. "I love you."

Jennifer caressed his cheek, blinking back tears. "I know that."

Kane shook his head. "You're supposed to let me say it."

"You already did." Kane looked at her. What was she talking about? "That night at the hotel. You whispered 'I love you' against my neck."

He felt too content to even pretend to be annoyed that she had stolen his thunder. She could steal anything she wanted, as long as she married him. "You weren't supposed to hear that."

She almost hadn't until she had replayed the sound in her head. "Too late." She slid her body along his as she rose up on her toes until their mouths were level. "Now kiss me before you have to arrest me for assaulting an officer."

"In a minute. I want to tell you something."

"As long as it ends in 'I love you' again, you can tell me anything."

"I *do* love you and it's a scary thing because I've never loved anyone before," he admitted. "I've never *let* myself love anyone before. I wouldn't let myself love you, but I didn't seem to have any say in the matter. Now I can't seem to do without you."

She felt her heart overflowing. "I have a solution."

This time she wasn't going to beat him to the punch. "So do I. Marry me, Jennifer. Marry me and I promise I'll try to love you the way you deserve to be loved." Kane kissed her and felt as if he had finally found a home for his heart.

"You big idiot," she whispered against his mouth just before he kissed her again, "you already have."

"Then it's yes?"

"What do you think?"

"I think," he told her, "that I have a lot of lost time to make up for. Starting now."

* * * * *

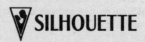

▼ SILHOUETTE

Sensation

COMING NEXT MONTH

PROMISES IN THE NIGHT Barbara Bretton

Larkin Walker had been looking for Mr Right and then Dr Alex Jakobs walked into her life! It was only then that she realised that the real challenge lay not in finding love, but in holding on to it...

TARGET OF OPPORTUNITY Justine Davis

Kyra Austin was *not* his usual type of woman, Cash Riordan realised. But then his usual type of women weren't tall, intuitive, *dangerous* bodyguards, determined to protect him at all costs. Cash didn't need protection: what he *needed* was Kyra!

HEROES GREAT AND SMALL Marie Ferrarella

The second in a delightful trilogy featuring the Sinclair family.

Bromley Culhane had fallen utterly in love with his new-born adopted daughter, Katie, and was devastated when he learnt that the baby had actually been kidnapped. Brom was determined to return her to her real mother. But just what was Katie's pretty aunt, Julia Sinclair, trying to hide?

A WALK ON THE WILD SIDE Kathleen Korbel

He Who Dares

J.P. O'Neill had been forced to kill his partner in self-defence, but no one—least of all Lauren Taylor—was buying that. To prove his innocence, he'd have to track down whoever had framed him. But to survive, he'd have to trust an innocent lady lawyer who was convinced he was as guilty as sin...

COMING NEXT MONTH FROM

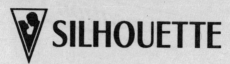 SILHOUETTE

Intrigue

*Danger, deception and desire—
new from Silhouette...*

Special Edition

Satisfying romances packed with emotion

Desire

*Provocative, sensual love stories for the
woman of today*